Other books in this series
FLASH: Dogleg Island Mystery Book One

THE SOUND OF
RUNNING HORSES

Copyright 2016 by Donna Ball, Inc.

ISBN-10: 0996561021
ISBN-13: 9780996561020

Published by Blue Merle Publishing
Drawer H
Mountain City Georgia 30562
www.bluemerlepublishing.com

This is a work of fiction. All characters, events, organizations and places in this book are either a product of the author's imagination or used fictitiously and no effort should be made to construe them as real. Any resemblance to any actual people, events or locations is purely coincidental.

Cover art www.bigstock.com

THE SOUND OF RUNNING HORSES

A DOGLEG ISLAND MYSTERY
BOOK TWO

Donna Ball

CHAPTER ONE

At two o'clock in the morning in a little town like Killian, Maine, nothing was moving on the streets except the occasional patrol car, and Tracy took care to avoid those. Still, as she waited alone in the park, concealed by the shadows of the concrete block building that held the restrooms, she worried. She worried that someone might drive by and spot her, crouched there in the dark where no one ought to be. Conversely, she worried that she was so well concealed that Steve might drive by without seeing her. She worried that her little sister might wake up and notice she was gone. She worried that Steve would change his mind and leave without her. There was a streetlight near the picnic tables. Maybe she should go sit there. Maybe she should text him again. But if she turned on her phone the light would be like a flashlight in the dark, and if someone did happen to drive by, and if that someone happened to be a policeman…

Tracy wasn't usually a worrier. In fact, there wasn't much in this world that she found worth worrying about. But she had this one little superstition, and that was that when everything was going just right something was bound to go wrong. But if you thought about all the things that could go wrong, and listed them in your head, they wouldn't happen. And so far, they never had.

She had met Steve online four months ago, and since then everything, absolutely everything, had gone right. She'd fudged a little about her age and posted a picture with a glamour filter that made her look twenty-one at least, and sexy as hell. Steve was twenty-eight. She'd met him after school at a pizza place a month after they'd started chatting online, even though her best friend Sylvie said she was crazy, that he'd turn out to be a serial killer or a pedophile or acne-scarred. He hadn't been any of those things. In fact, he was even cuter than his picture, with dreamy green eyes and a scruffy goatee that made him look a little wild. He had a tattoo of a dolphin on his arm and said he was studying to be a marine biologist. Okay, that part turned out not to be true, but he *had* worked on a boat. And the important thing was that he hadn't even noticed her age, or if he had he hadn't cared. Later, she'd admitted she was still in high school, but he'd been cool with that too—probably because she'd let him think she was eighteen and only a few months from graduation. He was, quite simply, the most amazing person she'd ever met, which only went to show what Sylvie knew, and Tracy loved him madly. He loved her too, and told her so all the time. All Tracy wanted to do was spend the rest of her life with him. She could hardly believe he felt the same way about her.

Of course, her parents would freak if they found out she was seeing a guy that much older than she was. They didn't even allow her to date seniors. So she ended up sneaking out of the house to see him, and not once had she gotten caught, not even close. Everything was going just perfect. Better than perfect.

But then her grades had started to slip, and she'd been reported for skipping school the day Steve and she had driven to the beach, and she'd gotten into a big fight with her parents. They'd grounded her, which meant no more pretending to go to the movies with Sylvie while she was really out with Steve. They'd even threatened to take her phone if she didn't pull up her grades by the end of the month. That's when she knew she had to run away.

Tracy heard the sound of a car engine rounding the corner at the intersection of Pine and Park, and in another moment she saw the flash of headlights. Her heart slammed and she shrank back against the building, but as the car turned into the park near the streetlight, she noticed the distinctive primer-gray passenger door and heard the familiar thrum of the stereo's subwoofers. She snatched up her backpack and ran into the light.

Steve leaned over to push open the passenger door for her and she climbed in, tossing her backpack into the backseat. The car smelled like stale cigarette smoke and spilled beer, the best smells in the world to her. Steve wrapped an arm around her neck and kissed her hard. Then he grinned at her. "Ready for an adventure, baby?"

She replied breathlessly, "Ready!"

Tracy Ann Sullivan was fifteen years old. A year ago she had never smoked a cigarette, or shoplifted condoms from a drugstore, or even made out with a boy for longer than a few minutes. Until now, the furthest she had ever been from home was summer camp. She was basically a good girl. If anyone had told her that within a week she'd be wanted for grand theft auto, armed robbery, and murder, she would have laughed.

But that was exactly what was going to happen.

CHAPTER TWO

Places, like people, can be deceptive. They are multilayered, complex, formed of richly textured histories that are all too often born of conflicting ideals and, more likely than not, far from what they were originally intended to be. Murphy County, Florida, was just such a place. It was part of the meandering Gulf Coast that was referred to by tourism officials as "The Forgotten Coast" and by Florida purists as "Southern Alabama." Steeped in swampy wildlife and lined with sugar white beaches, home to verdant green pine forests and barren wind-swept dunes, it was, much like the people who were drawn there, a study in contradiction.

The casual tourist, wandering off the beaten path onto the narrow highway that meandered in and out of the lazy sun-drenched towns along the Gulf Coast, would notice sparkling waters and rust-stained shrimp boats, ramshackle warehouses and neat concrete block houses. He might remark upon the quaint two-story brick public library or the charming white clapboard B&B. It would not occur to him that the sun-sparked harbor that stretched so peacefully from the shore had once been the scene of one of the bloodiest naval battles of the Civil War, or that in 1814 a brutal storm had pounded the coast for forty-eight hours and resulted in more fatalities than Hurricane Katrina and Superstorm Sandy combined, or that in 1749 one of the world's most successful serial killers had disposed of the bodies of thirty-one teenage victims in the sandy soil beneath his house. The average person, upon coming here, would think it must surely be one of the most peaceful places on earth. And so, for the most part, it was.

Most of the world had forgotten, after two and a half years, the brutal murder that had made national headlines, the young deputy who had almost died, the scandal that had all but ripped the county apart. The news was old, the reporters had drifted away, new and more virulent headlines jostled for position in the twenty-four-hour news cycle. The average person, casually meeting two of the major players in that drama—at the beach, for example, or cruising the calm Gulf waters off the Florida shore—would not even make the association. Aggie Malone and Ryan Grady looked like any other young couple enjoying an afternoon with the family dog on their boat. And that, today, was exactly what they were trying to be.

But appearances could be deceptive, and no one onboard the boat that day understood this better than Flash.

Flash was a black and white border collie with striking blue eyes and a lightning-bolt shaped blaze on his forehead. Those were courtesy of genetics and Mother Nature. The distinguished notch in his left ear had been earned in the line of duty, when he confronted a bad man with a gun. He was, by virtue of his nature and his environment, innately curious and deeply thoughtful, and he understood a good deal more than most people gave him credit for. Most people, of course, did not include Aggie, who was in charge of Dogleg Island, or Grady, who was in charge of everything else.

Flash understood, for example, that the events of the past few months, which had ended with Aggie looking sick and weak in the hospital and with Flash being stitched up by a veterinarian, had "taken their toll," as Aggie said, and put them all "under a lot of stress," in Grady's words. Words were one of Flash's best things, with numbers coming in not far behind, and he understood what most of them meant. But what was easiest for him to understand were the things that weren't said, and there had been a lot of unsaid things in their household lately. That was why he was glad that today was their day off, and they were spending it doing nothing. Nothing, Aggie had told him only that morning, was sometimes the most important thing you could do. As someone who had spent many a fine afternoon doing exactly that, Flash wholeheartedly agreed.

They were onboard the *Agatha Lorraine*, a twenty-four-foot cruiser that Grady owned with his brother Pete, and which was named after Aggie, and Pete's wife Lorraine. There had been a christening ceremony last summer at which Aggie and Lorraine had broken a bottle of champagne against the hull—it had taken them two tries—and then they'd all gotten on the boat and taken it out to sea, where they had a picnic and fished for flounder and laughed a lot. Today Flash, Aggie and Grady were headed to Wild Horse Island, which Grady said was about eight nautical miles up the coast from Dogleg Island where they lived, for another picnic, and to do nothing.

It was a perfect day for it. A brassy sun softened the edges of a steel blue sky, and the ocean was just bouncy enough to make it interesting. Aggie, whose skin smelled like coconuts and glistened in the sun, relaxed in a deck chair, wearing shorts over her swimsuit and a big-brimmed hat. Flash stretched out on the hot boards beside her, lapping up the salty air while the wind combed through his sun-baked fur, listening to Aggie read aloud from a small book she'd found in the cabin.

"It says here that Wild Horse Island used to be pretty popular with pirates. They'd stop for fresh water and pineapples—they grew wild there—and maybe even bury a treasure chest or two."

Flash perked up his ears at that. Pirates were something he knew a little about, and about which he was eager to learn more. Once he, Aggie and Grady had watched a movie about pirates, and Aggie and Grady had laughed a lot. There was a place in town where Aggie and he went sometimes that had pirates, and that seemed to impress Aggie. "Just think," she had said once, peering into a glass case that contained something old and rusty and completely incomprehensible to Flash, "three hundred years ago a real-life pirate probably stole this from somebody. Better than the movies, huh, Flash?"

He was still putting together in his mind what, exactly, a pirate was; he was still putting a lot of things together in his mind. So far he had decided they were somewhere between bad guys, because they stole things, and good guys, because they made Aggie smile. This fascinated him, the whole concept of in-between, so he paid special close attention when Aggie and Grady talked about pirates. You never knew what you might learn when you paid attention.

Grady tossed her a grin over his shoulder from his place at the wheel. There were squint lines around the edges of his sunglasses, and his open shirt billowed in the wind. He had sun-colored hair that was shaved closed in the back but thick and wavy on top, and over the past few months, while he'd been out of work taking care of Aggie, he had developed a light, neatly groomed shadow of facial hair that followed the shape of his jawline. He called it his "protest beard," and Aggie teased him about it because he never could decide what he was protesting. He guided the boat casually, leaning against the captain's chair with one hand on the wheel. "Where have I heard that story before? What I'd like to find is a barrier island on the coast of Florida that doesn't have a treasure chest buried on it."

"A bunch of French pirates and a bunch of Spanish pirates even had a battle over the rights to it one time."

"I think I saw that in *Pirates of the Caribbean.*"

"They found a skeleton there in 1876."

"Only one?"

"It says here," Aggie went on, undeterred, "that the Wild Horse Island Nature Preserve is one of the most diverse of all the Gulf Coast barrier islands, with an inland prairie surrounded by wetlands, dunes and hammocks, nesting grounds for over two hundred forty kinds of birds, loggerhead turtles, etcetera, etcetera. Oh, this is interesting. Wild Horse Island supposedly got its name from the herd of wild horses that are supposed to live in the prairie there. They're descendants of the horses that swam ashore from a Spanish shipwreck in 1742. Imagine that."

Flash pricked up his ears at that. He'd only seen horses once, but he'd never forgotten it. There was a place that rented out horses for people to ride on the beach on Dogleg Island, and he and Aggie had gone there once on a call. It was their job to go wherever there was trouble on Dogleg Island, and this time there'd been an argument with a man who wanted his money back because his horse ride had ended early. Flash actually hadn't paid much attention to how Aggie resolved the dispute, because he couldn't take his eyes off the magnificent creatures that ambled around on the other side of the fence. He'd never seen anything like them. He could tell by the length of their legs that they would run like the wind, and suddenly all he wanted in the world was to see them run; maybe even to run with them. He was perhaps two seconds away from launching himself over the fence when Aggie gave him a stern look that let him know that would not be a good idea. He'd backed off, of course, but a part of him had never gotten over the disappointment.

Now was it possible he might get a second chance?

"Hate to tell you, sweetheart," Grady said, "but the only way you're going to see a horse on that island today *is* to imagine it. There might have been horses there once, but they died out long ago. Nobody's seen a trace in at least a century."

Flash couldn't prevent a sigh as he rested his head on his paws again.

Aggie gave Grady a sour look from behind her sunglasses. "You sure know how to take the romance out of a situation."

"Aw, now you've gone and hurt my feelings." The engine changed timbre, thrumming more slowly as Grady throttled down and turned the wheel toward a long dock that jutted out from a blue water cove. "I've always thought I was the most romantic guy I know. People tell me that all the time. Why, only the other day, as I was cuffing a suspect, the dude turned to me and he said, 'Captain Grady,' he said, 'I just want you to know you're the most romantic guy I ever met.' Now, there's a good chance he was only trying to get on my good side, seeing as how I was about to haul his sorry ass to jail for a strike-three misdemeanor, but…"

Aggie, laughing, threw the little book at him. The wind caught it and snapped its pages open like wings. It might have gone overboard, but Flash was too fast even for the wind. He snatched the little book out of the air with barely a leap, and brought it back to Aggie. She ruffled his fur and kissed the top of his head as she took it from him, still laughing. Flash sat close to her, grinning with the satisfaction of a job well done.

Ryan Grady was a deputy with the Murphy County, Florida, Sheriff's Department, but by mutual consent between himself, the incoming sheriff, and the Florida Department of Law Enforcement officer who'd been investigating him, Grady had been relieved of his caseload for the past three months. Grady's infractions, which amounted to little more than exceeding his authority during a breakdown of command, disobeying orders and subsequently giving orders that endangered the life of a sitting sheriff, had been the least of the department's problems during that high-profile investigation, and everyone had been happy to have Grady simply fade into the background for a while. The fact that his actions had resulted in the apprehension of a sociopathic killer and had saved Aggie's life—and Flash's—was why Grady had spent most of those three months taking training courses and doing paperwork instead of looking for another job. That, and the fact that Grady was, for a number of reasons, one of the most valuable deputies in the department.

There wasn't much about this part of the Gulf Coast Ryan Grady didn't know. He had grown up there, as had his father, his grandfather, and countless generations before, on the most central of the county's barrier islands, Dogleg. Aggie was a relative newcomer, even though she'd been chief of police on Dogleg Island for almost two years and a Murphy County deputy for two years before that. She loved the place with a fierce passion that was second only to her love for Ryan and Flash, and she was proud to call it home. But if Grady said there were no horses on Wild Horse Island, she wasn't about to argue with him. Chances were, someone in his family had written the book she'd been reading from, anyway.

"So what about pirate treasure?" she said, getting up to return the book to the little cabin where she'd found it. "Think we might find some of that?"

"Baby, what do you need treasure for when you've got me?" He managed to tap her nose with a kiss as she edged past him. "But if you were looking for treasure, you'd be more likely to find it a little farther out." He gestured toward the west, where nothing but brilliant glittering blue sea stretched to the horizon. "Over there about six miles is the wreck of the *Santa Carmelita*, a galleon that broke up during the Spanish-American War. Pete and I used to dive over there as kids, looking for the gold it was supposed to be carrying."

"Oh, yeah?" She looked at him with amused interest. "Did you find anything?"

"Not so much as a cannonball. Didn't keep us from trying, though. The closest thing to treasure I ever found around here was four hundred grand in heroin I helped the DEA confiscate from a drug boat that was breaking up on the reef when I was in the Coast Guard."

"Hmm," she said. "Pirates, drug runners...Looks like the bad guys would catch on and find another route."

"Not just the bad guys," he pointed out. "Remember that billionaire's yacht that went down out here about ten years ago?"

"Before my time," she reminded him.

"Well, it was a big deal when it happened. These waters definitely aren't safe for vessels over thirty feet."

She looked at him uneasily. "And how big is this one again?"

Grady grinned as he powered back the engine for their approach to the dock. "Twenty-four feet." He touched her waist lightly. "Here, take the wheel. I'll tie up."

"I've got it."

Aggie wasn't much of a sailor—or a swimmer either, for that matter—and those who had grown up around the water greeted her ignorance with everything from tolerant amusement to outraged disbelief. But she had lived with Grady long enough to learn the basics, and was almost proficient enough to call herself "crew" when they went boating. However, her record for tying-off without actually falling in was about fifty-fifty. That was where Flash came in.

She unlooped the rope from the front cleat and tilted her head backwards to Flash. He was by her side in an instant. The bow drifted to within a few feet of the dock, and Flash took the end of the rope in his mouth. Grady gave a shout of laughter as Flash jumped onto the dock with the rope in his mouth, made a half circle around one of the pilings, and waited until Aggie was close enough to grab the end of the rope he held for her, spring lightly up onto the dock beside him, and tie the knot.

"How did you teach him that?" Grady demanded, still laughing.

She shrugged, but her pretense of nonchalance was betrayed by her grin of pride. "You know Flash. He pretty much teaches himself."

The truth was that she'd had very little else to do besides learn to tie knots and teach Flash tricks in the six weeks she'd been out of work, recovering from surgery that had left her weak and disoriented and too easily frustrated. It had also left her with two ugly scars on the right side of her head and nothing but a cap of white fuzz and pink skull where her hair once had been. When she referred to the surgery, which was rarely, she didn't mention that it had been to remove a bullet from her brain. Those who knew her knew the story, and those who didn't know it didn't need to know. She wore a short platinum wig in public to avoid explanations, and also because she didn't like to be reminded of the whole thing. She had been an invalid long enough. It was time to get on with her life.

Grady handed her the cooler, then shrugged into a backpack that held the rest of their supplies and joined her on the dock. He paused to give Flash a hearty pat on the shoulder. "We're raising a prodigy, Malone, that's all there is to it."

"Genius runs in my family," Aggie agreed. Then, as Grady turned to retie the knot she'd already tied, she rolled her eyes in exasperation. "Seriously, Ryan?"

He dropped a companionable arm around her shoulders, unapologetic. "I love you."

They walked down the dock leaning into each other, with Flash trotting alertly beside Aggie. The day was hot and still, with no sound but the lap of the water and the occasional shriek of a gull. A lizard darted across the sun-bleached boards and Flash gave a quick chase, but returned to Aggie when the creature disappeared beneath the dock. He could have caught it if he'd wanted to.

Wild Horse Island was accessible only by boat and considered a primitive nature preserve. The Florida Department of Environmental Protection maintained the dock and the trails, and a park ranger patrolled the area on a semi-regular basis, but for the most part it was unspoiled wilderness and known mostly to locals. Consisting mostly of marshes and prairie, it wasn't a particularly popular destination even for those who knew how to find it. There were no good beaches and it was too rocky for water sports. In October the mosquitoes and gnats were so thick you couldn't take a breath without inhaling one; in December and January the marshes flooded out the trails, and in June the green bottle flies took over. For a few months in the summer the island was a nice enough spot for hiking and nature-watching, but most people didn't bother. Today it appeared Aggie, Grady and Flash had the place to themselves.

There was a sign at the end of the dock that read:

Welcome to Wild Horse Island State Park
Nature Preserve
Day Use Fee: $5.00
No Facilities
No Open Fires
No Overnight Camping
No Firearms
No Alcohol
No Ranger on Duty

An arrow pointed left to the picnic shelters, and right to the hiking trails. Grady tucked a five-dollar bill into an envelope he took from the stand and stuffed it into the green box below it. They turned right along the sandy path. "Are you up to hiking half a mile?" he asked.

"I can outwalk you any day of the week, Ryan Grady."

"We can go another couple of miles if you want."

"Well," she admitted, lifting the brim of her hat to wipe away a ring of sweat, "maybe when the heat index gets below one twenty."

He reached into his pack and handed her a bottle of water, keeping one for himself. They hiked a while in easy silence, sipping from their water bottles, squinting in the blazing sun even behind their sunglasses.

Grady said, "So, I had an e-mail from the folks."

"I know. They copied me."

Aggie and Grady were newly married enough that she still looked over her shoulder whenever he introduced her as "my wife," and he had not yet gotten over the thrill of doing so. She had never met her parents-in-law, who had retired to Ecuador some years previously, but she already adored them—partly because they had produced Ryan, and partly because whenever they sent out a family e-mail, Aggie's name was always included as a recipient, and they signed it, "Love, Mom and Dad."

"So?" Grady prompted.

"So what?"

"The date, Malone, the date. They're flying 2500 miles to attend a wedding reception, they have a right to know."

Aggie and Grady had been married by a chaplain in Aggie's hospital room before she was even strong enough to get out of bed, with only Ryan's brother Pete, his wife Lorraine, and their former boss in attendance—as well as Flash, of course. Ryan's mother had cried over the phone when she welcomed Aggie into the family, and so, to Aggie's great surprise, had his dad.

Aggie had never known her father and had no memories of her mother, who'd died of a heroin overdose when Aggie was a child. She had been raised by a firm but loving grandmother in an unpainted house outside of Macon, Georgia, and had no real sense of what a traditional family was like. Part of her was thrilled to be so warmly embraced by Ryan's family; another part was utterly baffled by them. Among the things that she simply couldn't understand was why it seemed so important to everyone to mark the occasion of Ryan's marriage with a celebration of some kind. They wanted dancing, decorations, photos, and a wedding cake. Aggie didn't see the point.

But part of being married, she supposed, was occasionally agreeing to things that didn't necessarily make sense.

She said, "I told you, not until my hair grows back."

He grinned and tugged at the brim of her hat. "And I told you, I'm into the look. Very Sinead O'Conner. I'm thinking of shaving my head in solidarity. How cool would we look in our wedding photos?"

She jabbed him in the arm with her elbow. "You try it and there won't *be* any photos."

He said, "Pick a date."

"Maybe next spring."

"I'll check my calendar."

She grinned and bumped his shoulder lightly with her own, and Flash, who was trotting beside her, grinned too.

Grady gestured to a sandy cove up ahead. "How about here?"

The beach was narrow but the water was clear, and calm enough for Flash to play in. There was a nice breeze and a little shade from the grassy dunes that surrounded it. Flash went over to inspect the place and Aggie and Grady followed.

Grady bent to drop the pack on the ground and suddenly stiffened, his eyes alert. His hand dipped into the pack and came up with his gun.

"What?" Aggie's eyes searched their surroundings, alarmed. "Snake?"

"I heard something." His voice was low, his expression intense. "Look at Flash. He did too."

Aggie glanced at Flash, whose ears were up but who, otherwise, did not appear particularly concerned. She said, "Ryan, it's public park. People are allowed to—"

He held up his hand for silence. She listened, and heard nothing.

"Ryan…"

He took a holster out of the pack and snapped it onto the belt loop of his shorts.

Aggie said, "Oh, for Pete's sake."

"I'm not going to shoot anything," he told her, "just have a look around."

It was at that moment that Flash, with his nose to the ground, suddenly turned and scrambled up the dune. Grady was only one stride behind. Aggie followed more carefully, avoiding sandspurs and tangled vines. She didn't call out or try to discourage either one of them. She knew that would be pointless.

Flash dug his way up the dune, the slippery sand and tangled roots no match for his agile paws, and turned east. There were many exciting things to explore, of course, but Flash was interested only in things that were new. The man hiding in the bushes behind the dunes wasn't new, and didn't interest him. The wild things did.

He was off the trail now, on the scent of what might have been, what *could* have been, four-footed, long-legged, and hoofed. And why shouldn't he think so? He caught a whiff of something wild and exciting on the ocean breeze; of course he would follow it. Of course he would explore. But as he crested the dune and swiveled his head to reorient himself to the scent, something else caught his attention. It was his duty to investigate.

That's where Grady found him a few minutes later, pawing at the black plastic bag that was half-covered by sand and sea grass, tossed off in the weeds where no one would likely find it.

"Son of a…" Grady, his voice tight with disgust, let the epitaph drop as he sank to one knee and holstered his gun. He dragged the bag out of the sand.

"Well, what do you know about that?" Aggie came up behind them, her voice full of forced cheer. "Pirate treasure."

Grady scowled as he jerked the bag open.

There wasn't much of interest inside: a couple of old life jackets, battered and torn and smeared with oil, some pieces of broken planks, painted blue, and what might have been part of an oar handle. There were some empty plastic water bottles, and a once-white baseball cap, now all smudged and dirty, with a blue anchor on it. Flash spent some time investigating the cap, but he didn't learn much from it he didn't already know. Certainly nothing worth losing the scent of horses for.

"What the hell is the matter with people?" Grady muttered, looking at the detritus that spilled out of the bag. "They can't find a better place to toss their trash than a wildlife preserve?"

Aggie turned over one of the life jackets and noticed someone had written something—it might have been SP or SB—in permanent marker on the collar. She picked up a piece of painted wood and glanced at it, then let it drop again. Another day, she might have teased Grady about pulling his gun on litterbugs, but she said instead, "I don't know. This looks like the kind of stuff that might've washed ashore. Maybe it was just a good Samaritan, cleaning up the shoreline."

Grady's scowl only deepened as he stuffed the garbage back into the bag. "There's a trash can at the dock. Lazy SOBs couldn't walk a few hundred yards to dump their crap?"

"We'll take it with us," Aggie suggested.

"Whatever." He straightened up, taking out his phone. "I'm going to give Roger a call and tell him to keep an eye out. We might have some illegal campers or homesteaders on our hands."

"Homesteaders" was a polite term for squatters, the homeless or otherwise independently inclined who could be a real problem in state parks and campgrounds, particularly in the warm climates of

Florida where it was possible to live outside virtually year-round. For the most part, law enforcement adopted a live-and-let-live attitude toward the disenfranchised, but in a protected area like Wild Horse Island, the risk of wildfires and environmental disruption was too great to ignore.

Aggie listened while Ryan left a message on the voice mail of the local Park Service office, which was too small to maintain a full-time staff. Roger Darby, their neighbor on Dogleg Island, was the park ranger assigned to Wild Horse, along with the other, smaller state-run parks on the barrier islands that dotted the coast of Murphy County. Technically, he was in charge of both litterbugs and squatters in the state parks, but Aggie didn't think he would take the infraction as seriously as Ryan did.

When Grady put his phone away, she said, as casually as possible, "You know, Ryan, not everybody would think to bring his service weapon to a picnic on a deserted island. Something I should know about?"

He turned to her, regarding her intently from behind the dark lenses. "You really didn't hear anything?"

She shook her head. "Really."

It was a moment before he could make his lips tighten in the semblance of a smile. "My bad, then. Come on, let's unpack that cooler."

But as he turned to go back down the dune, Aggie's phone buzzed. She fished it out of the pocket of her shorts and held up a hand for patience as

Grady looked back at her. "Hold on, cowboy." Her brows knit when she read the text.

Grady said, "Don't tell me."

"It's a water rescue." She started typing a return text on her phone.

"Ah, come on. You get half a dozen of those a week."

"They're talking shark."

Now he was interested. "Injuries?"

"Don't know yet."

She started down the dune and slid the last few feet. Grady caught her elbow to steady her.

"Are they closing the beach?"

Aggie replied, "Not until I get there."

"We'd better hoof it, then."

Flash's spirits brightened at the word "hoof" and he stretched out his legs, racing to the beach. Maybe he'd get his chance at those horses after all.

Sometimes, of course, he misunderstood.

CHAPTER THREE

The primary duties of the Dogleg Island Police Department were public safety, traffic regulation, law enforcement, and emergency management. Dangerous beach conditions, including riptides, aggressive marine life, and environmental hazards, fell into the categories of both public safety and emergency management, which was how the chief of police came to be the only person on the island with the authority to close or open the public beaches. Since Aggie had been on the job, she had closed the beaches twice: once because of an offshore oil spill, and once for a hurricane. The chances of her having to do so again today were extremely remote, but her job was to investigate and make a decision. Aggie always did her job.

It was a half-hour journey, and by the time they got there the excitement was over. The EMTs had transported a woman with minor injuries, including a cut on her leg that in no way resembled a shark bite, to the emergency room on the mainland. Word on the beach was that she had been struck by a piece of floating debris—possibly a tree trunk or driftwood—and panicked. Several people claimed to have seen a dorsal fin near the site of the accident, but the consensus was it had been a dolphin.

Maureen Wilson—Officer Mo to most people—was the second person in the island's two-person police force, a powerfully built black woman with twenty years in law enforcement and a scowl that was rumored to be able to make a pit bull roll over and show its belly. She looked overheated and annoyed as she brought Aggie up to speed, complaining bitterly all the while about the stupid ordinance that would bring the police chief in on her day off just because some fool from Indiana who'd never seen a shark that wasn't swimming on her TV screen decided to make a fuss. Aggie told her to call the hospital and speak directly with the doctor who was treating the victim, then Aggie pulled on a tee shirt over her swimsuit top, hung her badge around her neck, and went to interview witnesses.

Grady looked amused while Maureen stomped off to the shade of the pavilion to make her phone call, and then casually wandered off to interview a few witnesses himself. Flash sniffed around for evidence. Flash wasn't entirely sure what a shark was, but he was always glad to help Aggie do her job. They talked to some people on the beach on their way to the lifeguard stand, all of whom were either sweaty and impatient or sweaty and anxious. Some people, tired of waiting, were already splashing in the waves, and when asked whether it was safe, Aggie replied, "Swimming along the beaches of Dogleg Island is always at your own risk. Some days are riskier than others." Then she added, "But if it were me, I'd wait until the warning flags were down."

Brian McElroy was waiting at the bottom of his lifeguard stand, and lifted his hand in greeting as they approached. "Hey, Chief Malone. Hey, Flash."

Aggie liked Brian, and so did Flash. He always took time to give Flash's ears a good rub, and he smelled like the same coconuts that Aggie did. There was something different about Brian today, but before Flash could figure out what it was, he remembered that the best thing about Brian was his lifeguard stand, which Flash loved to scramble up and take in the view. Aggie had a photograph of him framed on her desk, sitting in the lifeguard stand surveying the water.

Brian chuckled as Flash bounded up the ladder, watching him go. "That dog is going to put me out of a job, Chief."

Brian was a good-looking kid with sun-bleached curls and a quick smile. He and his brother Mark were fraternal twins who looked nothing alike and, as far as Aggie could tell, had nothing in common except their love of the water. Mark, who waited tables at Pete's place when he wasn't on the water, was actually the more handsome of the two, dark where Brian was light, and muscular where Brian was lean. Mark had captained the high school football team; Brian had captained the swim team. People liked to say that Brian was the brains of the team and Mark the brawn, which wasn't very fair, although probably accurate. Both boys had been volunteering as life-guards every summer since they turned sixteen, and now, ten years later, were among the most reliable lifeguards in the corps. Since Dogleg Island's life-guard program was completely voluntary, that was important.

The boys' father had been a big-time lawyer before he retired on Dogleg, and now served on the city council, dispensing pro-bono legal advice now and then. Aggie supposed his sons could afford to be part-time professional students and summer life-guards for a while longer, but sooner or later they would have to get real jobs, and she would miss them when they were gone.

Aggie said, "So tell me what happened."

Brian shook his head, blue light bouncing off his reflective sunglasses. "Sorry you had to come out on your day off, Chief. Like I told Officer Mo, there was a pod of dolphins not far offshore this morning, so I was keeping a close eye on that section of water. I didn't see it happen, but I couldn't have turned my glasses away for more than a second before I heard the woman scream. I never saw anything in the water that looked like a shark, but after we got her out, I saw what looked like part of a coconut tree on the tide. You know those things can do some damage, and we've had a good bit of debris wash up since the last storm."

Aggie interrupted, "You mean the hurricane? But that was four months ago."

"Yes, ma'am, but the currents change over time, and a lot of the debris that had settled to the bottom—asphalt, siding, trees and chunks of concrete—they're just now starting to wash ashore on some of the barrier islands. It'll probably go on for a couple of months."

"No kidding?" Aggie looked at him with new respect, but also a measure of skepticism. "How do you know all this?"

"Masters in oceanography," he said. "I was hoping to get a job with one of the science ships when I graduated, but…" He shrugged one shoulder. "So far no luck. I'm working on my PhD, but it's slow going."

"Wow." Now Aggie was really impressed. "Good for you."

"Anyway," he went on, "the lady—the victim—had a pretty bad cut on her leg and kept saying something had hit her in the water, and that's when folks started crying 'shark.'" He gave another short, disgusted shake of his head. "We haven't had a shark attack in these waters in five years. But you know people. Anyway, I guess you talked to the EMTs. They didn't think it looked like a shark bite either. Lot of noise about nothing, if you ask me."

"We definitely need a better system," Aggie agreed. She glanced around. "Are you the only guard on the beach today?"

"Well, it's the first of the week, and we always run a short schedule in August," he explained. "A lot of the guys are getting ready to go back to school."

She nodded. The trouble with part-time volunteers was that there was very little to keep them from setting their own schedule.

Brian nodded his head toward the warning flag that was flying from his stand just above Flash's head. "What do you want me to do?"

Grady came up behind them. "Nobody's noticed any particular increase in seabird activity this afternoon, which means there probably aren't any schools of fish nearby. No fish, no shark food, and probably no sharks. How's it going, Brian?"

"Pretty good up until about an hour ago." Brian brushed his hair back from his forehead, turning his gaze back toward the waves. "You're right about the birds. I was thinking right before it happened that it's too hot even for the pelicans to dive."

Aggie waited for Maureen, who was tromping across the sand with her notebook in hand, looking even more disgruntled than when she'd left. "Doc says she's fine. Six stitches. Said he pulled some splinters out of the wound. Wood, not shark teeth."

Aggie looked up thoughtfully at Flash. "What about it, Flash? Any sign of sharks?"

Flash glanced down at her, then turned and descended the stairs, his tail waving an all-clear. Aggie turned back to Brian. "According to my team of experts, the waters are safe. Take down the flag, sound the all clear. I'm going for a swim."

At the word "swim," Flash spun toward the water fast enough to leave a divot in the sand, and Aggie laughed as he raced to the surf. Brian climbed lightly back up the lifeguard stand to remove the flag, and Aggie tilted her head toward Grady ruefully. "Well, it was a good idea, but looks like our day off is going to be spent right where it was last time—at home." Then she shrugged philosophically. "Just as well, I suppose. We've still got to finish painting the deck."

He dropped his arm around her shoulder. "Well now, let me see," he mused. "Paint the deck, go on a picnic with a beautiful girl. Choices, choices. Come on." He squeezed her shoulders. "We've got half a tank of fuel, a cooler full of sandwiches and beer, and the day's not even half over. Let's go back out."

She looked at him uncertainly. "Oh, I don't know, Ryan. We're home, already. Why don't we just go back to the house and crack open that cooler in the air-conditioning?"

"That doesn't sound very romantic. And as you know, I'm all about the romance. Come on." He put on his most persuasive smile. "Sunset on the water? And I brought champagne."

Her brows went up. "You did? What for?"

"To share with my wife while we watch the sun set over the ocean from a deserted island. And," he added, "I think I left the cooler on the dock at Wild Horse."

A stifled laugh escaped her. "You're a nut," she said, but she called for Flash and slipped her arm around Grady's waist as they walked back to the boat because, for the first time in weeks, he sounded like himself again.

CHAPTER FOUR

They were well out to sea before Aggie uncovered the cooler, neatly tucked between the live well and the storage bench, half-covered by Grady's shirt. She gave him a dour look and he returned a grin. "Sorry," he called over the sound of the engine and the slap of the waves. "Guess I was wrong. Want to turn back?"

Grady had a way of getting what he wanted. But then, so did Aggie. And all she really wanted out of that day was to see Grady relax.

When they approached the dock this time, there was another boat, smaller and sleeker and with the State of Florida's green logo stenciled on its hull, already tied up there, bobbing in the wake of the *Agatha Lorraine* as Grady brought her in close. "That's a Park Service boat," he observed. "Roger must've gotten my message."

Flash helped Aggie tie off again and waited until they unloaded their picnic supplies to race back down the trail toward the cove where they'd been before. Nose to the ground, tail flying, he was out of sight in seconds.

Aggie said, "Do you think we'll have time to explore the island a little before dark? I'd like to see the prairie."

"Not much to see but a bunch of high grass," he said, hoisting the strap of the insulated cooler over one shoulder and his backpack over the other. "But sure." He glanced at her. "You holding up okay?"

She gave him an annoyed look and took the backpack from him. "Like I said, I can—"

"Outwalk me any day of the week, I know. But there are no wild horses in that prairie."

"Spoilsport."

"You might see a rattlesnake or two," he offered helpfully.

"Thanks a lot."

That was when Flash started to bark.

Flash's policy on barking was very simple. He did not bark at people he knew, or sounds he knew, or things that smelled familiar. Sometimes he barked at squirrels, just because he liked to see them run, but mostly he barked when he thought Aggie needed to know something. Midway down the trail, Flash found something that Aggie needed to know about very badly.

When Flash started barking and didn't stop, Aggie and Grady did not need to debate what to do. Grady pushed the cooler into her arms and said, "I'll check it out." He started down the trail at a jog. Aggie was delayed by just the amount of time it took her to drop both the cooler and the backpack on the ground, and she was right behind him.

The sandy path curved around a tall dune just before forking to the left, toward the cove where they had originally set up their picnic, and toward the right, where it led to an elevated boardwalk that wound through the marsh. As Aggie came around that curve, breathless and a little light-headed from running, she saw Grady, six or eight feet off the path, kneeling beside the prone form of a man in a park ranger uniform. Flash stood beside him anxiously.

"Call dispatch," Grady said, casting her a quick glance over his shoulder. "We need medics. He's unconscious, but breathing, pulse is slow but steady."

She was already dialing. "What does it look like? Heart attack? Heat exhaustion?"

But as she moved forward, Grady leaned back from the unconscious man, his expression grim, and she could see that it was, in all likelihood, neither of those things. The back of Roger Darby's head was thick with blood.

Grady said, "Better tell them to get a couple of deputies out here too. This was no accident."

The Murphy County Sheriff's Department maintained a speedboat for emergencies such as this, and both it and the EMS water rescue boat were on site within fifteen minutes. By that time Roger Darby had regained consciousness but was too weak and disoriented to answer questions, despite Grady's insistence on asking them.

The deputies who arrived were John Evers, who had worked with Grady for almost five years, and a rookie Aggie had never met. As soon as Roger was on the stretcher, Grady and Evers spread out to search the area, leaving the rookie to take statements. He looked nervous and uncomfortable as he took out his notebook. "Um," he said, following with his eyes the direction in which Evers had gone. "I'm not supposed to be out of sight of my FTO. Maybe I should…"

Aggie smiled reassuringly. "I'm Aggie Malone, police chief of Dogleg Island. Maybe I could act as your field training officer while John is gone. We all kind of share the duties in Murphy County."

He looked moderately relieved. "Yeah, okay. I guess so."

"You know how to take a statement," she reminded him.

"Sure, it's just that…well, this is my first real crime."

Aggie prompted, "I'm a witness."

"Oh." He colored slightly and fumbled to get his pen out of his shirt pocket. "Right. So how did you find the victim?"

Aggie held up a staying hand, giving a slight, reproving shake of her head. "I happen to know the man you're going to be working for, and the first thing he taught me was how important good manners are when it comes to getting along with the public. In fact, he's a real stickler for it. What's your name?"

He said, "It's Sam. Sam Brown."

"And who do you work for?"

He caught on quickly. He said, "Chief Malone, I'm Sam Brown with the Murphy County Sheriff's Department. Do you mind if I ask you a few questions?"

She smiled at him. "You're going to do fine." She gestured the way down the trail, saying, "Actually, it was Flash who found him."

Sam Brown took down her statement as they walked back to the dock, Flash trotting proudly beside her.

He'd been wondering when someone would remember that he had done the finding.

Roger Darby was being loaded onto the rescue boat when Grady returned to the dock. Darby had a bandage around his head and an IV in his arm, but he lifted his hand weakly to Grady when he saw him. Grady turned to Aggie. "How is he?"

"They think he'll be okay. The cut on his head looks worse than it is. What about you? Find anything?"

He shook his head. "Evers is walking the shoreline, but damned if I could see anything at the scene that looked like a weapon."

Then Grady looked at the rookie deputy, his eyes narrowing. "You're new, aren't you?"

Sam straightened his shoulders. "Yes, sir, Captain. Sam Brown. I start training with you tomorrow. But we were shorthanded, so…"

He trailed off as Grady continued to stare at him. Grady said, "Where's your Taser?"

The young man's hand went to his utility belt even as a red flush crept up his neck. "I just came on shift when we got the call. We were in a hurry and I didn't think I'd need it."

Grady drew in a sharp breath, then caught the way Aggie lowered her sunglasses to look at him. The effort he made to keep his tone neutral was obvious as he said, "Next time, full uniform." Then, "What's the time line?"

Sam glanced quickly at his notebook, still flushing. "We got the call at 1:43. Mr. Darby clocked his arrival at the dock at 12:45. He estimates he walked fifteen minutes from the dock before the attack happened."

Grady tightened his lips with regret. The call from Dogleg had come in at twelve thirty. They'd missed being here when Roger Darby arrived by only a matter of minutes.

Which also meant that whoever had attacked Darby had most likely already been here before they left.

Grady said, "What's the regular patrol schedule for the park?"

"Um…" Brown turned a page of his notebook, and another, his color mounting.

Aggie gave her spouse a dry look. "Roger picks up the fees every Monday and checks the trails and out-buildings every other week. Something you can easily find out from the park service's website, by the way."

"Did Darby remember anything about the attack?"

Brown looked relieved to know the answer. "No, sir. He was pretty groggy. But he did say he didn't notice anything unusual when he got here."

Grady frowned. "Well, whoever attacked him didn't fly in. Go see if you can help Evers find some sign of a boat. Somebody might have been able to pull a small boat onshore and hide it in the weeds. And watch yourself. Whoever did it might still be here."

Brown hurried off, and Aggie turned with Grady back toward the hiking trails as the rescue boat left the dock. "You know you're not supposed to be working cases, hotshot," she said. "You're on limited duty."

"I'm not working anything," he replied. "It's my day off."

She thrust her fingers into the pockets of her shorts, squinting a little in the bright sun even behind the sunglasses and big hat. "I guess I owe you an apology."

He gave her a puzzled look.

"When you said you heard something in the woods," she explained. "I thought you were imagining things. I didn't see any other boats so I assumed there weren't any other people. I didn't think about a small boat that could hide in the weeds."

For a moment he looked preoccupied, almost as though he still didn't know what she was talking about. Then he put on an expression of exaggerated superiority and dropped a companionable arm around her shoulder. "Don't let it get to you, Malone," he said. "Just because you lack my keen detective skills and years of expertise doesn't make you a bad cop. You'll get there."

She rolled her eyes behind the dark glasses and shrugged out of his embrace, moving ahead of him on the trail.

"I saw that," he called after her.

She lifted her hand in a dismissing wave over her shoulder and called back, "I love you."

Flash had come to understand at an early age that there were some things he did better than anyone else. That was not to take anything away from those he loved and admired: Grady, for example, was much better at driving a boat than Flash could ever be, and Aggie was far superior when it came to negotiating disputes—which, as she had told Flash repeatedly, was what their job was really all about. And of course no one could beat Pete when it came to making hamburgers. But what Flash excelled at—one of them, anyway—was finding things.

To be fair, one of the deputies who worked for Grady probably would have found the stick eventually, because they worked hard and did their jobs, which was something Flash had heard Grady say on more than one occasion. But they never would have found the other thing, the bad thing, the thing

Flash very much did not want to find. There were some things Flash was just better at.

Grady joined the other two deputies walking the shoreline until they found a spot on the weedy shoreline where it seemed likely a small boat had tied up, with skid marks in the sand and broken palm branches. Flash and Aggie remained at the scene of the attack, looking for evidence. Flash knew they wouldn't find it there, so he left the trail where blood had already begun to soak into the sand and began to sniff in thinner sand. Grady returned to tell Aggie what they'd found just as Flash began to push his way through the undergrowth back toward the marsh.

"Evers is documenting the scene," Grady said, "hoping maybe the perp dropped the weapon or tried to dispose of it in the weeds, but I don't think he'll have much luck."

"What kind of boat do you think it was?"

He shrugged and sipped from his water bottle. "Bigger than a canoe, smaller than the *Agatha Lorraine.* Maybe a two-man sailboat? Of course, there're only a couple of thousand of those along the coast. I'm hoping Roger will be able to help us with the ID when he's up to it."

Aggie watched Flash's waving tail disappear down a narrow sandy game trail that was thick with low palms and tangled vines. "We're pretty far from civilization," she said. "Wouldn't it have to be a fairly substantial boat to cross that much open water?"

"Not if you're a good sailor. I could probably make it in a kayak on a calm day."

"Then again, you're Superman."

He grinned at her. Then he added, glancing around thoughtfully, "You know, we're not that far from the place we stopped the first time."

She blotted sweat from her forehead with the back of her arm, pushing back her hat. "Got it, Sherlock. You were right, I was wrong. Somebody was watching us, hiding back in the bushes. You probably scared him off when you pulled your gun."

"Maybe." He still looked thoughtful. "I wonder why Flash didn't bark, though."

Aggie wondered the same thing.

Grady said, "I'm going to walk back there, see if I can spot anything."

She said, "I'll stay and keep an eye on Flash. You know," she added, as casually as she could, "technically this isn't our case."

"Yeah, well, technically it's our day off." He started back toward the trail. "Stay hydrated."

She lifted the water bottle she'd brought from the boat in a small salute as she turned to follow Flash's path through the undergrowth.

No one ever questioned how Aggie always knew where Flash was, not even Aggie herself. It was just something she did, in the same way that Flash, on the rare occasions they were separated, always knew where to find her. She wound her way around sticky shrubs and thorny vines along the narrow game trail that paralleled the official marsh boardwalks, watching for snakes and alligator slides as she skirted the marsh, swatting at gnats that buzzed around her face and landed on her sweaty arms and legs. A tall white heron regarded her apathetically from across the moss-green water, and a few minutes later an ibis took flight. There was no sound except the buzz of the insects and the distant whoosh of surf. She had never been to Wild Horse before but could understand, from just the small amount she'd seen of it, why its diversity had earned it protected status as a state park. She wished she'd had more time to explore it with Grady and Flash—and that they'd done their exploring from the safety of the hiking trails and boardwalks.

Aggie spotted Flash several hundred yards away in a stand of high sea grass, investigating something on the ground. She called out to him and he looked up, waiting for her to arrive. Aggie picked up the pace.

Flash was standing over a long thick stick that was clearly out of place in this environment. If someone had tried to throw it into the marsh, he had missed by a good ten feet, which meant he either had a terrible throwing arm, or had been in a big hurry. Aggie squatted down beside Flash, rubbing his shoulder with one hand and using the water bottle to nudge the object over. The jagged end of the club was stained dark and wet, smeared with bits of sand and dried grass. She said, "Good job, Flash."

He leaned into her caress, agreeing with her, and then took off again, nose to the ground, as Aggie took out her phone and dialed Grady.

"Hey, babe," he answered on the other end. "Something interesting here. You know that bag of garbage we found? It's gone."

Aggie said, "Well, I know where part of it went, or at least I think I do. Flash found what looks like one of the pieces of wood—you know, the one that looked like a broken oar?—in the grass by the marsh. It's got blood on it."

He said, "Okay, I'm on my way. I'll tell Evers to meet you with an evidence bag. Where are you?"

Aggie looked around for landmarks. "I'm maybe a quarter of a mile away from the attack site, on the marsh side. I can see the boardwalk due west."

"Yeah, well that narrows it down." She could hear him breathing as he climbed down the dune back toward the trail.

"There's a heron in the water about a hundred yards away," she added helpfully.

"See, sweetie, this is why it's a good idea to take your service weapon on a picnic. If you fired a shot we could locate you."

"If I fired a shot out here in the middle of a state park, one of you kick-ass deputies would probably take me down," she replied, watching Flash. "Here's a thought. Turn on the GPS on your phone."

"Ah, what's the fun in that?"

"Yeah, I know." Aggie drained her water bottle, found a twig to stick in the ground beside the evidence, and upended her water bottle over it. She walked toward Flash, who was interested in something else at the edge of the marsh a few dozen yards away. "Totally takes away the John-Wayne quality of the whole thing."

He said, "John who?"

Aggie said, increasing her pace, "Hold on, will you? Flash has got something. It might be a snake."

"Baby, you've got snakes on the brain today."

She started to trot. "I'm in the middle of a Florida swamp. What else should be on my brain?"

Grady cautioned, "Don't run. You know you're not supposed to run."

Aggie ran.

Finding things, for Flash, was not difficult. Sometimes the things he found were useful to Aggie, like car keys or missing socks or a stick with blood on it. Sometimes they were not so useful, like broken beer bottles in the sand or bad-smelling toads in the backyard. But for the most part he liked finding things—except for the things that were buried. The bad things were almost always buried. And finding them never made anyone happy.

He pawed at the wet, loose sand until he found what he knew was there, then stepped back, waiting for Aggie, feeling unhappy. When she got there she looked down, and he heard her catch her breath with a choked, wet sound. The weight of the unhappiness was so heavy then that Flash sank to the ground, his head between his paws. Aggie knelt beside him, resting a hand on his fur, her breath coming fast and shallow.

"Oh, Flash," she whispered.

Grady demanded from the telephone, "What? Is Flash okay? What happened?"

Flash had uncovered a scrap of fabric, too dirty now to determine its original color or purpose. And attached to the fabric, also black with dirt and the beginning of deterioration, was a human hand.

CHAPTER FIVE

Although Wild Horse Island was served by Murphy County, it was a state park and technically out of their law-enforcement jurisdiction. No one in the Murphy County Sheriff's Department complained about that, and John Evers lost no time calling the Florida Department of Law Enforcement and informing them that they had a suspicious death on their hands. While they waited for the authorities to arrive, Aggie and Grady shared sandwiches from their picnic lunch with the other deputies, and Flash dozed in the shady cabin of Grady's boat. Finding buried things always made Flash tired, as well as sad, but everything usually looked better after a nap.

Jim Clark, known as JC by his colleagues both because of his initials and his tendency to quote scriptures at unexpected moments, was the crime scene investigator out of the Regional Operation Center of FDLE twenty miles away. It took his team two hours to get to Wild Horse, and JC, who was not a particularly good sailor, arrived pale and sweaty but in good spirits. He was a skinny man in a straw hat, Hawaiian shirt and khakis, wearing square-framed reflective sunglasses and a green canvas shoulder bag on a strap across his body. If Grady had not assured Aggie that JC was one of the best investigators in this part of the state, Aggie could have easily mistaken him for a geeky tourist.

"The Lord hath delivered me from my travail," he declared, shaking Grady's hand with the enthusiasm of someone grabbing a lifeline in a stormy sea. "How the hell have you been, Ryan Grady, and what did you touch?"

Grady grinned and said, "JC, my wife, Aggie."

Aggie extended her hand. "Also known as Chief Malone, Dogleg Island. And we didn't touch anything."

JC shook her hand. 'I do admire a woman who understands crime scene procedure. Is that your dog?" He glanced around as Flash sprang onto the dock and trotted toward them.

"That's Flash," Aggie said. "He understands crime scene procedure too."

JC offered a hand for Flash to sniff while Grady added, "I've got two deputies securing the site, but I didn't see any point in trying to seal it off, seeing as how bears and deer aren't known for respecting crime scene tape."

JC straightened up from petting Flash, pulled out a plaid handkerchief from his bag and mopped his face with it. It was hard to tell whether or not he found Grady's comment amusing. "You do any wild hog hunting lately?"

"No, not lately."

"We sure had some times, back in the day."

"We sure did."

"Well, let's get this show on the road. How deep do you say the body is?"

Aggie spoke up. "Not deep. Two feet, if that."

JC looked at her thoughtfully. "'My breath is corrupt, my days are extinct, the graves are ready for me,'" he said with a sigh. "Job 17:1."

Aggie murmured, "Oh." And Flash looked at him with interest, one ear cocked. Grady smothered a grin.

JC glanced around the area. "No cameras on the dock, I guess."

Grady shook his head. "This place gets maybe a hundred visitors a year. I'm guessing the park service figured their money was better spent on maintenance, and I'm not sure I disagree."

JC nodded. "Shame, though. Sure would make my job a lot easier if we had pictures of all the comings and goings the last couple of months. Oh well, that's why they call it work, I guess."

JC called instructions to the men who were unloading equipment on the dock behind them, then said to Grady, "All right, lead the way. You say your dog found the remains? What were you all doing way out here on the east side of Eden, anyhow?"

Grady told what he knew while they hiked back down the trail toward the scene, with Flash trotting along beside them and JC interrupting now and then to ask a pertinent question. "So what was it you heard that made you go looking the first time?" he wanted to know.

Grady frowned a little, hesitating. "That's the thing. I've been trying to figure it out, but I can't quite put my finger on it. I just remember thinking it didn't belong out here in the wilderness, especially with no other boats at the dock. Maybe something mechanical?" He shook his head. "It'll come to me. Flash heard it too."

JC glanced at Flash. "Good-looking dog. I've got a mutt at home that spends more time on the couch than I do. So this is it?"

They came to the place where Roger Darby was attacked, now marked off by small orange flags and guarded by the rookie Sam Brown. JC looked around for a moment, noting the boardwalk over the marsh and the sandy game trails leading into the woods while the crime scene techs unpacked their equipment. "Bet we could bag us a hog or two back in here, couldn't we, Grady?" he observed.

"Wouldn't be surprised," Grady agreed, sipping from his water bottle. He winked at Aggie. "Of course, we'd end up in state prison."

Aggie said, "The blood-stained oar handle is about four hundred yards down that trail. The body is another fifty yards past it."

He grunted. "How far back does the trail go? Can we even get a body board back in there?"

"It's not too bad," she said. "Slow going."

JC nodded. "Even slower getting a body in than getting it out, I'd bet." He pushed back his hat and scratched his hairline. "So a guy attacks a park ranger, runs all the way into the woods to throw away the club, and happens to throw it fifty yards from where a dead body is buried. That's a mighty popular spot."

Grady said, "I thought the same thing." He nodded toward the boardwalk. "If you walk that way about ten minutes, you'll be directly across from the spot where Flash found the evidence. I think the guy might've tried to throw the club into the marsh from the boardwalk and missed."

JC glanced over his shoulder at his team. "Would one of you gentlemen be good enough to walk with Captain Grady and take some pictures from the boardwalk?" He looked back at Aggie. "That marshy sand should take some pretty good shoe impressions. Am I going to find any besides yours?"

Before she could answer, Sam Brown cleared his throat apologetically. "Well, sir, we had to get back there to bag the evidence and secure the site."

"I didn't see any tracks besides Flash's when I went in," Aggie said. "And it rained yesterday afternoon."

Sam Brown said, anxious to be helpful, "Sergeant Evers is waiting for you at the scene. He asked me to escort you the rest of the way in."

JC heaved a great sigh, obviously not looking forward to the trip. "All right, then, let's do it. Thanks, Chief Malone. You don't mind keeping your dog back here I'd appreciate it." He reached into his shoulder bag and took out a palm recorder, murmuring into it, "Arrived on the scene at 14:04, conditions clear, ambient temperature 89 degrees, winds from the north- northwest at 4 knots at the dock approximately three quarters of a mile away. Coordinates at point of entry are…"

Aggie walked away, raising her hand to Grady as he started down the boardwalk with the technician. Flash walked beside her as they moved down the trail, out of the way of the people with all of their bulky, important-looking equipment. Aggie waved a hand in front of her face to shoo away a sudden swarm of tiny bugs, and then dropped her hand down to caress Flash's ear. "Kind of weird to be the one answering the questions instead of asking them for once, huh, Flash?" Then she frowned a little. "Although, if I *were* asking them…"

Flash looked up expectantly, because Aggie had that look on her face that she often got when she was about to say something that Grady called "brilliant." Grady had also said that he and Flash should always pay particular attention to Aggie when she was being brilliant. But Aggie just shook her head in a dismissing, impatient way, and said, "Never mind. It's nothing." She sighed and pressed her water bottle to her forehead. "God," she said, "it's hot."

CHAPTER SIX

Steve Rider stared in disbelief at the television image of the fresh-faced young girl he'd just spent most of the day having fairly spectacular sex with. It was a school photo. The reason it was a school photo was because she was fifteen. *Fifteen.* In a way, that made her hotter, but Steve wasn't an idiot. He knew how much trouble he was in. She was fifteen, the cops were looking for her, and he had just taken her across state lines.

"Son of a bitch," he said, his lips dry.

It wasn't supposed to be this way. The chance of a lifetime had just dropped into his lap; they had a plan, a plan nobody could afford to screw up, a plan *he* couldn't afford to screw up, a plan that was going to make them all richer than most people could even dream about. But the plan was built totally around *no cops.* Now there were cops everywhere.

The guys were going to freak.

They had checked into the cheesy motel just off the freeway around dawn, when he got tired of driving and she wanted breakfast. She had three hundred dollars saved up, and that was going to look

like pocket change this time next week, so he figured why not live a little? Why the hell not?

This was why not. Because not one single thing
ever worked out for him. Damn it, not one thing.

Just then she came out of the bathroom, wrapped
in a towel with her long blond hair wet around her
shoulders. He couldn't stop himself. He swung on her,
grabbed her by the hair, dragged her in front of the
cheap wall-mounted television screen on the motel
room wall. She squealed, of course, but it died away
as she saw her own photo on the television, flashed
up once again just to make sure nobody missed it,
and heard the newscaster's voice drone, "Anyone
with information regarding the whereabouts of Tracy
Sullivan is asked to contact the Missing and Exploited
Children's hotline at the number displayed on your
screen, or the Killian, Maine, Police Department."
An abrupt change of tone, from somber to upbeat.
"Now, Amy, how about that forecast?"

Steve jabbed the off button on the remote control as though he was pulling the trigger on a gun.
The screen went black, but Tracy stared at it, wide
eyed, as though her picture was still up there. "Wow,"
she said, and her eyes took on an unsettling gleam.
"I'm famous."

It was all Steve could do to keep from backhand-
ing her. Instead, he tightened his hand on her hair
until she squealed again. "Ow!" she cried and he
jerked her head backwards.

"Are you freakin' kidding me?" he shouted, and
she quieted, rolling her eyes sideways to him and

reminding him, momentarily, of the cows on his grandpa's farm just before they were sent to slaughter. He loosened his grip. "Listen to me," he said, breathing hard. "Listen to me, this is bad. You told me you left a note for your folks, you told me they wouldn't care—"

She said, trying to twist away, "I'll text them, okay? I'll tell them I'm fine—"

Steve let her go long enough to grip his own head with both hands, trying to think. She stumbled back, then scrambled through the drawer of the battered bedside nightstand for her phone. *Her phone.*

He whirled in time to see her bent over her phone and he yelled, "Turn it off!"

She stared at him, and he snatched the phone from her. She cried, "Hey!"

He turned the phone off and thought about throwing it in the toilet, or crushing it with his boot heel. Then he remembered he had a phone too, and if the cops figured out who she was with—and how long would it take them to do that?—they could find it from anywhere, and his problem just got bigger.

He thought about leaving her behind, just walking out and leaving her standing there in the towel, while he got in the car and high-tailed it on down the freeway, but what would that solve? She'd only set the cops on him faster. No, she'd gotten him into this, and she could damn well see it through.

He said, "If you're not in the car in three minutes I'm leaving without you."

"But—"

He slammed the door on his way out of the room.

He took the batteries out of both phones and threw them in the dumpster, then disposed of the phones themselves by dropping them in the toilet tank in the men's room in the lobby. That might buy them a little time, he didn't know how much. What he did know was that now he was without a phone.

Tracy was waiting for him in the car, dressed in jeans and a skinny top, looking like a wet kitten all hunched over her backpack and watching him with scared eyes. "I didn't think you'd be this mad," she said in a small voice. "I didn't think it mattered. We were going to run away together anyway, weren't we? Why does it have to be such a big deal?"

"Because the cops are looking for you, bitch!" he shouted at her. "Because you told me you were eighteen and you're not! Because you're so fucking smart you decided to run away with a convicted felon who just broke parole for your sweet ass, *that's* why it's such a big goddamn deal!"

That shocked her into silence, and she fell back against the seat, staring at him with those big eyes as he slammed the car into gear and screeched out of the parking space. He burned rubber on his way out of the parking lot, which might not have been such a good idea because a fat woman in a swimsuit came around the corner from the pool just then, holding a toddler's hand. She gave him a hard look that told him she would remember the car. Like things could get any worse.

He pulled out onto the access street and Tracy added timidly, "We didn't check out."

He started to laugh. Right. Things by-God for damn sure couldn't get any worse.

CHAPTER SEVEN

Grady's rambling cedar house on Dogleg Island had been built in the forties by his great-grandfather, and added onto by each generation until little remained of its original structure. There were porches and decks that meandered up and down its three stories on every side, mismatched windows, doors that led nowhere. The detached garage had been converted into a tiny Key-West style cottage and used as a vacation rental off and on over the years. Aggie had lived there until she married Grady, and she still liked to go there from time to time when she needed to work and Grady wanted to watch the game, or sometimes just to be alone and think about things. One of the best things about Grady was that he understood that, and didn't mind.

Like many of the beachside houses, there was a crow's nest atop the roof, accessible via a set of stairs from the third-floor deck. From it there was a view of the ocean to the east and of the moonlit lagoon to the west, and this time of year it was the only place a cooling breeze could be found. Grady had built a deep curved bench nestled against the railing there, and Aggie furnished it with yellow weather-proof cushions that were solidly tied down against the wind. Now, freshly showered and wearing a soft nightshirt, she sat on the bench with her legs curled beneath her, her head tilted back to a sky that was so heavy with stars it almost seemed in danger of falling down. The starlight, the breath of the ocean, the salty breeze that parted the thick night air—she leaned into them, opening her pores to them, letting them wash away the remnants of the day in a way a shower and scented soap could not. She filled her eyes with starlight, trying to let go of the questions that were still marching around her head like petulant children, demanding attention. She wasn't entirely successful.

Flash lay beside her, his head on her lap, her fingers in his fur, thinking about how the sound of the ocean reminded him of the sound of Aggie's heart, and not much more than that at all. He knew that Aggie was thinking about the day, about the bad thing buried in the dirt, about the stick with blood on it. He wasn't sure why, but it was what she did a lot: think about bad things. In his opinion—and he sometimes got things wrong—she would be a lot happier if she would just think about the sound of the ocean, like he did.

"So Flash," she said, exhaling a soft breath. "What a mess, huh?"

Flash's ears pricked up. Aggie sometimes liked to talk things over with him, and he always listened. He learned a lot that way.

She went on, "I mean, what are the chances, right, that a couple of cops on their day off would decide to have a picnic on a deserted island and stumble right into the middle of a crime scene? None, that's what the chances are, none. So I'm thinking that whatever was going on there had been going on for some time. Drugs, maybe, or poaching, or, like Grady said, squatting. When we showed up, well, that was a problem, but it wasn't the real problem. Otherwise, the bad guy, whoever he was, would've either confronted us, like he did Darby, or pulled back. After all, it's a state park. We're not the only people to ever visit there."

Flash's attention quickened at the phrase "bad guy." He knew about bad guys, although it was a recent understanding and he was still trying to accumulate information on the subject. Bad guys hurt people, particularly Aggie. It was his job—his and Aggie's and Grady's, and that of all the other people who worked with Grady and wore green shirts—to keep the world safe from bad guys. So he listened carefully when their name was mentioned.

"No," Aggie went on thoughtfully, "it wasn't us that spooked the guy. We were nowhere close to where the body was buried. It had something to do with Darby. He was closer than we were, but it's not like he was right on top of the site when he was hit, and there's no reason to think he ever would have found that grave. If they'd just left him alone, left everybody alone, in fact, that body might have turned to dust before anybody found it."

Flash, if given the chance, might have argued that point. If he'd been allowed to continue to chase the horses, as he'd started out doing, he was pretty sure he would have caught scent of that dank, unholy thing sooner or later. But that was of course sheer speculation on his part. They'd never know now.

"He took the trash," Aggie murmured, stroking Flash's fur. "He went back and took the trash bag. Why would he do that?"

Flash swiveled his head toward the sound of the door below them opening and closing again, and he heard footsteps on the stairs. Grady came up the stairs with two bowls of ice cream in his hands, and Flash regarded him expectantly.

Grady said, "Because there was evidence in the bag. Am I right, Flash?"

Grady handed one of the bowls to Aggie, and all Flash got was a scratch behind the ears. Flash lowered his head to Aggie's lap again, disappointed but still hopeful.

"Evidence," Aggie agreed as Grady sat down beside them, "or some kind of ID. I've been going over and over it in my head, and I can't think of anything. Life jackets, scraps of wood, water bottles… I didn't see anything incriminating, did you? But someone thought it was important enough to get rid of. And then—this is the part I don't get—he left the actual weapon, the oar he hit Darby with, behind in the bushes."

"You start trying to make sense out of criminal behavior and you're on your way to the looney bin, sweetie," said Grady.

"Yeah, I guess." Aggie dipped her spoon thoughtfully into the ice cream. "You know what you need, Ryan Grady? A good woman."

"Too late," he replied. "I already found one. And the best part is, I was smart enough to marry her."

She licked ice cream off her spoon. "What I mean is, you need the kind of woman who does your laundry and remembers to buy groceries and makes sure you get more than ice cream for dinner."

He dug his spoon into his own bowl. "I had a woman like that once," he agreed, musing. "Her name was Mom."

Aggie chuckled softly. "Eat a salad now and then, will you?"

"Okay, I will. Set a date."

"Okay, I will." She ate more ice cream. It was already starting to melt, velvety and cold, just the way she liked it. "What a day, huh? From picnics to litterbugs to sharks to an attack on a park ranger to a body buried in the swamp. I don't work this hard when I'm getting paid for it. Anything on the computer?"

Ryan shook his head. "Just what we already know." They had stayed until exhumation was complete, just in case JC was able to make an initial determination about the cause of death, but no such luck. Though neither of them had cared to observe the actual recovery of the body, they'd seen enough to know that deterioration was advanced, as it naturally would be in those swampy conditions. It could take days to learn anything from the autopsy. "Female age eighteen to thirty, probably dead less than a week," he said. "No ID. Nothing on VICAP or NamUs yet, but it's early."

"I don't understand," Aggie said, leaning back against the cushions. "The grave was pretty shallow, which means that whoever disposed of the body wasn't all that concerned about a proper burial. Why didn't he just throw the body in the marsh? Between the alligators and, well, you know, natural decomposition, it probably never would have been found."

"The water is only a couple of feet deep in most places," Ryan replied. "At low tide, probably not even six inches. If it was low tide when they tried to dispose of her, there wouldn't have been even enough water to cover the body." He frowned and reached for his phone. "I should text JC. It might help narrow down the time."

Aggie slanted him a meaningful look. "Come on, Supercop, it's almost midnight. Can it wait?"

His lips turned down ruefully. "Right. And if JC hasn't already figured that out, I need to have his job."

He started to drop the phone back into the pocket of his cargo shorts, and then hesitated, staring sat it. "Damn," he said softly. He looked at her. "That's it. That's what I heard this afternoon. It was a phone. A text chime, I'm sure of it. Somebody was standing back in the bushes, texting."

Aggie lifted her eyebrows. "*That*'s worth texting the investigator at midnight about."

Grady did so, waited for the reply—which was nothing more than a simple *OK*—and turned his phone off with a nod of satisfaction. "Good day's work," he said.

Then he smiled and bumped her shoulder lightly with his. "You know what I love about you? That you can talk about alligators munching on decomposing bodies while eating ice cream and not miss a bite. No pun intended."

Aggie replied, "I told you, I'm tougher than I look." She licked another dollop of ice cream off her spoon and added with a dry downturn of her lips, "Not as smart as I used to be, but tough."

"Watch it. You're talking about the woman I love."

Aggie said, "So what happened to her stuff?"

Grady glanced a question at her.

"That's what I was trying to think of this afternoon," Aggie admitted. "Questions we need to ask… that was one of them. Whoever she was, she had stuff, right? Even homeless people have stuff. One-Armed Billy has a bicycle basket overflowing with stuff and he sleeps on the beach. And if she was a tourist, where's her purse? A woman that age—you said in her twenties, right?—she definitely didn't leave home without a cell phone. Find her stuff, and we'll be a whole lot closer to knowing what happened to her."

"Unless she didn't die on the island," Grady suggested.

Aggie glanced at him. "Why would anyone transport a body all the way to Wild Horse Island to bury it when they could just drop it in the ocean?"

"No clue. But I say find how she got there, and you'll find out what happened to her."

Aggie said, "Are you thinking homicide?"

He shrugged one shoulder. "Baby, I don't know. This is Florida. The FBI has an entire division devoted to bizarre and unusual crimes and they call it 'The Florida File.'"

She choked on a laugh. "They do not."

"Probably not," he admitted, "but they should have. The point is, all we've got right now is improper disposal of a body. It could be anything. People are weird."

"Yeah, I know." She licked the back of her spoon, and offered the remaining ice cream to Flash, who enthusiastically accepted. "But this is Murphy County. You just don't…"

She didn't finish the sentence, because both of them knew it would have been a false protest. Murphy County, where nothing ever happened. Murphy County, where a conscienceless killer had murdered three people, shot Aggie in the head and left her to die. Murphy County, where nothing was quite what it seemed.

Grady said, "My scenario? Illegal squatters, something went down—maybe homicide, maybe overdose, maybe something else—and one of them ended up dead. Whoever buried her got worried when Flash discovered that trash bag, and *really* got worried when the park ranger started poking around less than half an hour later. I don't know, maybe there was something in the trash we didn't see—a prescription bottle, an envelope—or maybe the dude was just paranoid. So he knocked Roger out, took the trash bag, escaped by boat. In his haste he dropped the club he used on Roger. Case closed."

"Except for the name of the victim, the manner of death, the name of the thief, the name of whoever attacked Roger Darby, and the motive for the crime," Aggie said.

"Right. Except for that. Good thing it's not our case, huh?" Ryan turned over his own unfinished bowl of ice cream to Flash and slipped his arm around Aggie's shoulders, drawing her close. "Look at those stars, huh? Are we lucky, or what?"

"We are." She rested her head on his shoulder. "At least we got to spend some time on the boat."

He admitted, "More than I planned, actually."

"Never did get to that champagne."

"It's in the fridge," he said. "I should have brought it up."

"No, let's save it." She sighed. "The best laid plans, right? But the first part of the day was nice."

"Yeah," he agreed softly, dropping a kiss atop her peach-fuzz hair. "It was."

"Tomorrow," Aggie told him. "We start eating healthy."

"Okay."

"I'm serious."

"I'm with you."

She closed her eyes for a moment, relaxing against him. "You know what I'm thinking?"

He traced the outline of her jaw lightly with the tip of his finger. "Something nice about me, I hope."

She thought, *Sharks, litterbugs, a broken oar covered with blood, a body in a shallow grave on a deserted island...* and she couldn't put it together. It happened like that sometimes, a sudden overwhelming fatigue, her poor battered brain simply refusing to work another minute. She had learned to accept it.

She sighed and sat up, rubbing her temples. "I'm tired," she said. "I don't know what I'm thinking. It's not our case. Going to bed. Are you coming?"

"In a minute." He held her elbow as she stood. "You okay going down the stairs?"

She said, "There's plenty of light. Don't stay up late, okay?"

Ryan caught Flash's eye and jerked his head toward Aggie. Flash gave the ice cream bowl one final quick lick and leapt down from the bench to join Aggie on the stairs, pressing close to make sure she didn't miss one. She hardly ever did, but still he wanted to be there, just in case.

That was, after all, part of his job.

Flash almost always had good dreams, even when his day included finding loathsome things buried in the swamp. Tonight he was stretched out on the rug at the foot of the big bed, because even with the air-conditioning it was too hot to sleep between Aggie and Grady, like he usually did, and he was dreaming about horses. In his dreams the horses had wild tails and hooves of thunder, with manes that streamed like clouds behind them. They ran together, he and the horses, while trees and bushes and a tall red life-guard stand whisked by, faster and faster with every step until the next time he stretched out his legs he actually left the ground and he was airborne. He sailed up into the sky with horses made of clouds, chasing a hat that spun on the wind just out of reach. Then Aggie tossed him a rope and just as he caught it with his teeth the anchor on the other end jerked him to the ground. Flash awoke with a start.

But it wasn't the fall that woke him. It was a sound, and as he looked effortlessly through the dark to the place where the only people who mattered in his life should have been peacefully sleeping, he knew that the sound had come from Grady. Grady sat on the side of the bed with his feet on the floor, breathing harder than was normal. In the moonlight his face looked shiny with sweat. Aggie sat up beside him, rubbing his shoulder, her voice thick with sleep. "Baby, what..."

"Nothing," he said, taking her hand. "It's fine. I'm sorry I woke you. Just a dream."

"Another nightmare?"

Flash had been about to get to his feet, but now he relaxed. He knew perfectly well that mares were female horses. So Grady had been dreaming about horses, too. How bad could that be?

Grady gave a brief shake of his head. "It's stupid."

"It's not stupid." She rested her cheek against his bare shoulder blade. "It's been going on for weeks. You should talk to someone about it. We need to try to figure out what this means."

"I can't even remember the dreams half the time. If I could, I'd tell you."

"The worst thing you can do is keep things buried. They only get bigger."

Grady glanced at her and she smiled back in the dark. "I did learn something in two and a half years of therapy," she said. "And who was it who made sure I never missed an appointment?"

He sighed and lay back down on the pillow, drawing her into his arms. "I know, hon. I just need to get back to work. Ten weeks of pushing papers would make anybody crazy."

She murmured, "Um, excuse me? That's pretty much what I do for a living."

He kissed her on the forehead. "Go back to sleep."

Within a few minutes, Flash could tell by the sound of her breathing that Aggie was asleep. Grady, however, was awake for a long time after that, and Flash tried to stay awake too, because no one knew better than Flash how bad the buried things could be. But before he knew it, Flash was dreaming of running with the horses again.

The best part about Flash's dreams was that he never tried to figure out what they meant.

CHAPTER EIGHT

The thing Aggie liked most about being police chief in a small isolated community like Dogleg Island was that it hardly ever involved homicide investigations, physical confrontations with violent suspects, or being shot at. At least, that was what she had been led to believe when she took the job. The thing she liked least was the monthly council meetings. Sometimes Aggie thought she almost preferred being shot at.

The downtown area of Dogleg Island consisted of two stoplights, three restaurants, and a handful of shops. The north side of the so-called commercial district was dominated by a sturdy two-story brick building that once had been a shipping warehouse. Now it was used as a town hall and community center, with a small maritime museum and the Dogleg Island Arts and Cultural Center on the second floor. Once a month the town council met around a scarred oak library table in a conference room across from the museum to review the business of running the island while Flash rested underneath the table and waited for someone to share a treat with him, which someone always did.

The room was paneled in dark wood with faded pictures of ancient mariners and schooners in full sail on the wall. It smelled like dust and hot, dry wood. The only air-conditioning was a window unit that barely chugged out enough cool air to keep the room livable, which was why they always met at seven in the morning. The town treasurer, the town clerk and the police chief all gave reports over coffee and pastries; any issues that needed to be addressed were discussed, and they all went about their days. The atmosphere was generally informal, as none of the council members was actually paid for his service, and brief, because most of them had businesses to run.

The council consisted of Pete Grady, chair; Jason Wendale, who with his partner Brett owned the Island Bistro; Bernice Peters, a retired school-teacher and one of the island's most active citizens, and Mark and Brian's father Walter McElroy. Today Aggie was presenting a detailed proposal outlining the advantages of having a full-time, paid lifeguard program that operated under the auspices of the police department with law enforcement author-ity that included the power to close the beaches in case of an emergency. She had worked on it for over a month, and with yesterday's water rescue still a topic of chatter around town, she thought she had a good chance of convincing everyone of the neces-sity for her plan...everyone, that was, except Walter

McElroy, who had not approved a single request from the police chief since he had been elected to the council two years ago. Today was no exception.

Almost before Aggie had finished handing out her spreadsheets, Walter said, "Too expensive. The town would have to underwrite the liability insurance. The police department can barely support the budget it has now." He glanced at his watch, clearly having somewhere more important to be. "I vote nay."

Aggie protested, "If you'll just look at the proposal, you'll see I've covered that…"

But unfortunately, when Walter spoke, everyone listened and—however incomprehensible it was to Aggie—they followed his lead. Bernice Peters shrugged. "The lifeguards we have now seem to do a fine job." And Jason Wendale, whose main goal in life was usually to annoy Bernice Peters, said, "Generally, I'm for anything that puts more boys in swim briefs on the streets, but insurance is a problem." And even Pete, who at least did her the courtesy of glancing through her papers, said, "I see here you only have the program partially funded by grants. Come up with the rest of the money and we'll take another look." He glanced around the table. "Agreed?"

There were murmurs of ascent, and Aggie glared at him. Pete was in charge of the volunteer lifeguard program, and they had discussed the need for full-time, paid guards more than once. She had expected his support, and not just because he was her brother-in-law. As for Walter McElroy, whose sons had been in the program most of their lives...clearly, she had misread her audience. This was her first official presentation to the council since she'd returned to work, and she was disappointed in herself.

With a motion and a second, the meeting was adjourned.

Aggie scowled as she stuffed her papers back into their folder. "What *is* it with that guy, anyway?" she demanded when no one but Pete, Flash and she remained. "He's never once voted for anything I brought up. What's he got against me?"

Pete smiled and handed her the last of the papers. "He just hasn't had a chance to come to know and love you like the rest of us do."

Pete was six years older than Grady, with close-cropped blond hair and eyes that were quick to twinkle. His left arm was covered with a colorful tattoo of a coral reef that Flash found fascinating, and he wore a gold stud in one ear that Grady said was left over from his biker days, although when Aggie had repeated that to Lorraine she had laughed so hard tears came into her eyes. It turned out that Lorraine, who was a cancer survivor, had given Pete the earring to commemorate her first all-clear checkup, and Pete had not taken it off since.

Pete and Lorraine had been Aggie's first friends in Murphy County, long before she thought of Grady as anything other than a good-looking nuisance, back when she used to take her dinner break at Pete's Place Bar and Grill every night that she was on patrol. They were family now, which somehow made it more acceptable to be annoyed with him than when they were just friends.

"And you were a big help," she told him. "Thanks a lot. You're supposed to be the chairman, not McElroy, but he's the one everyone listens to. What's up with that, anyway?"

Pete shrugged. "The power of the rich and famous. People think they're right just because they speak. This time, however," he added, "McElroy did happen to be right. Get your numbers together and come back. I'll make sure people listen."

They walked out together, Flash trotting between them. Aggie said, "What do you mean rich and famous?"

He gave her a quizzical look and then said, "Right. I keep forgetting you weren't here back then." He touched her shoulder, gesturing her toward the museum across the hall. "I'll show you."

Flash raced ahead, delighted, remembering the pirates and the amazing smells of all the old things there. He skirted a dugout canoe that was supposed to be five hundred years old and a giant anchor from the Spanish-American War, then went on to investigate a mannequin in cracked leather boots and a cutlass that stood on a display stand.

Pete guided Aggie to a display in the center of the room. The storyboard depicted famous shipwrecks along the barrier islands, with photographs of attempts to salvage them, maritime maps showing their locations, line drawings of some of the galleons that were purported to be at the bottom of the sea somewhere between Louisiana and the Caribbean Islands, and, in some cases, photographs of actual bounty that had been discovered by professional salvage companies. The far right panel featured a picture that was different from the others, though, and it was this one Pete pointed out. It clearly had been taken only a few years ago, and in front of this very building. It featured two men shaking hands while one of them, beaming, held a check up for the camera to see. A small crowd of other, official-looking people stood in the background. One of them she recognized as Walter McElroy.

Pete said, "The fancy-looking dude is Alan Brunelli, the New York billionaire. The guy he's shaking hands with is our mayor from about ten years ago. And of course you recognize our friend Walter."

Aggie was puzzled. "Alan who?"

"Come on, Ags, don't you ever read the gossip magazines? He married that actress, oh, you know who I mean, used to date Richard Gere. He gave her a rock the size of Egypt that everybody was talking about when they got engaged. Wait, here's a picture of her all decked out in the whole set."

He pointed to another photo of Brunelli and a gorgeous, wispy woman in a long white gown who looked vaguely familiar. The dress had clearly been designed to show off an emerald pendant the size of a robin's egg that she wore on a diamond chain, complete with matching earrings and a cuff bracelet that looked almost too heavy for her delicate wrist to lift.

"Whoa," Aggie said. "Are those real emeralds?"

"Like I said, a billionaire. They were a wedding gift from Brunelli, designed to match her engagement ring. See, it says right here the whole set was worth over thirty-five million dollars."

Aggie turned back to the picture. "So what's this picture doing in our museum? Did Mr. McElroy put it there?"

He chuckled. "Could be. But the official story is that it's part of our history. Brunelli and his wife were cruising from the Caymans to New Orleans when their yacht, the *Sweethaven*, went down about ten miles offshore."

"Oh, wait," Aggie said. "I think Ryan mentioned that yesterday. Not far from Wild Horse, right?"

He nodded. "Everybody got off okay, but they spent a day and a night on a lifeboat, and it was one of our rescue boats that ended up picking them up. That picture is of Brunelli presenting a check to our mayor at the time, in gratitude. That's how we got the pumper truck for the fire department, and were able to restore this building and acquire a lot of the artifacts for the museum. McElroy was one of Brunelli's lawyers at the time, helped him settle the insurance case. And that, the way I understand it, is how McElroy discovered our little piece of paradise and settled here."

Aggie was starting to understand. "So it's fame by association."

Pete nodded. "And that kind of influence has a long shelf life. McElroy doesn't even work for the billionaire anymore, and as far as I know hasn't traveled in those circles for years. But people still think of him as the man who saved Dogleg Island."

Aggie gave a grunt of amusement and turned toward the door. "Okay, got it. But just because I understand it doesn't mean I have to like it. Come on, Flash, let's get to work."

Flash, abandoning the intriguing smells of pirate treasure, raced to her, and Pete gave her a wink. "So come by for lunch and let me make it up to you. I've got an amberjack that was swimming in the ocean less than..." he glanced at his watch. "Four hours ago. I'm grilling it up with lime and cilantro on a Kaiser roll, mango salsa on the side."

"Wow, pretty fancy for the working crowd."

"Lorraine says we need to expand the menu. Speaking of which, she said to tell you she has some new swatches for you to look at."

Aggie smothered a groan as they started down the stairs toward the exit. Lorraine was Aggie's closest friend, but they couldn't have been more different. She had gotten it into her head that, since Aggie was a new bride living in a house that had been decorated by a man, she owed it to herself, and to Ryan, to add a few feminine touches. Aggie suspected Lorraine had been fantasizing about refurbishing Ryan's hodge-podge collection of second-hand furniture for years, and was just using Aggie as an excuse. Aggie said unhappily, "That amberjack had better be good."

"You're damn right. And Flash," he added, pushing open the door to the sunshine, "the burgers are on the house."

Flash bounded outside, tail wagging. Already he could tell this was going to be an amazing day.

But he couldn't help wondering why, as long as they were talking about pirates, Aggie hadn't mentioned the one that had been on Wild Horse Island yesterday.

CHAPTER NINE

Murphy County, Florida, encompassed 945 square miles of the Forgotten Coast, twenty of which were actually coastal, not counting the four barrier islands that were also in its tax base. The nearest freeway was an hour east, and the only state road with more than two traffic lanes passed through Murphy County for a mere fifteen miles. The biggest events the county hosted were the Seafood King festival in November, and the Fourth of July parade in the summer. There was a Holiday Inn at the marina and a couple of mom-and-pop motels along the highway, along with a fair share of fast food restaurants. Of the nearly 12,000 full-time residents, two-thirds were rural, scattered along the county's two hundred twenty-six miles of roadway in trailer parks, cluster communities, and farms. The other one-third lived in Ocean City, the county seat, and on Dogleg Island, which was accessible via the three-mile-long Cedric B. Grady Memorial Bridge. Both Ocean City and Dogleg Island had their own police forces, although Dogleg Island was only part time. The remainder of those 945 square miles and

12,000 residents were protected, night and day, by the forty-two sworn officers of the Murphy County Sheriff's Department. Ryan Grady was one of them.

Grady and sixteen other deputies were gathered in the department's cramped training room at 7:00 a.m. when Jerome Bishop walked in and took his place behind the small podium. He was greeted by a round of cheers, whoops, and fist pumps, a reaction that could be explained by the homemade banner taped across the back wall that read, "Welcome back, Sheriff Bishop!" There were clusters of balloons on either side of the sign, a couple of which had already been popped.

Bishop noted the sign, fighting with a smile, and let the cheers die down. He said, "I appreciate that, ladies and gentlemen. I really do. It's been a rough few months for us."

"We got your back, Chief," called one of the deputies.

"You can count on us, Sheriff," added someone else.

Bishop's dark skin did not betray his embarrassment, but the way he cleared his throat and fumbled to remove his glasses from his pocket did. "All right," he said, his voice gruff. "I've got to give this speech two more times today, so let me get going."

Jerome Bishop had a deep, rich voice that was made for public speaking, and he knew how to command a room. That, and his natural, almost intuitive understanding of what it took to make a good leader, had resulted in his being the first black man to be elected sheriff in Murphy County twenty years ago. He'd held the job until his wife's terminal illness forced him into retirement almost three years earlier, and he'd had every intention of staying retired. But intentions, like life, tended to change in unexpected ways, and here he was again, back where he'd started.

He still wasn't entirely sure it was a good thing.

"As you might've heard," he went on in his strong, deep voice, "the governor of the State of Florida has officially appointed me interim Sheriff of Murphy County…" There was another outburst of applause, which he ignored. "To serve the unexpired term of the former sheriff, who was indicted last month for a list of federal offenses I don't think I need to name."

Now a heavy silence fell over the room, and more than one glance was directed toward Ryan Grady. Grady did not look up from his phone. It was entirely possible he had not even heard the last words.

"Those of you who've stayed with the department through the whole mess will understand why my highest regards go to Sheriff Derrels over in Jackson County, who managed the administrative issues during the transition, and to you good folks of the Murphy County Sheriff's Department who stayed on during the storm that rocked this department, held your heads high, and did your jobs. You are without a doubt the finest group of peace officers in the State of Florida, perhaps in the country.

And…" He had to raise his voice to be heard over the applause. "You have my deepest respect, and my sincerest gratitude."

He waited until the cheers died down to go on. "At six o'clock this morning I was sworn in as sheriff of Murphy County. Before you leave this room, you'll take the same oath that I did, and you will be vested with the same powers and responsibilities that I have to enforce the laws of this country, county and state, and to protect the people who are in our care. This is not a matter to be taken lightly. I expect as much from you as I do from myself. If I didn't think you could live up to the job, you wouldn't be sitting here now.

"What all this means, folks," Bishop went on, "is that we all have jobs for another two and a half years, assuming we don't screw up. And every man and woman in this department is going to spend every working hour of the next thirty months proving that we deserve to keep those jobs."

That brought forth another round of cheers, and this time Grady glanced up, adding his voice and his raised fist to the others, although the gesture seemed a little absent.

"We've got a mess to clean up," Bishop said somberly, gazing at the assembly over the rim of his glasses. "This department has been crucified in the media, and over the past two years it's gone from bad to worse. We've lost half our sworn officers. We've been the target of a state investigation. I'll take my share of responsibility for all of that, which means

I'm going to fight twice as hard to get us back where we belong. But it's going to be an uphill battle, and that means PR is our number one priority and our full-time job. We are going to regain the trust and the respect of this community, and we're going to start in the schools, in the churches, in the garden clubs and the rotary club and the sewing clubs. We're going to go door to door if we have to." There was another outburst of approval, but Bishop spoke over it. "I want five ideas from each and every one of you about how to improve relations with the people of this county, and I want them on my desk by end of shift. Protect and serve, ladies and gentlemen, protect and serve."

He paused and looked out over the assembly soberly. "Most of you know what it's like to work for me. For you new recruits, let me be clear: the morals clause in your contract is not a joke. In uniform or out, you represent this department every time you set foot on the street, and everything you do reflects on me. You will treat the public with the same respect you treat your colleagues. You will not use profanity on the job, you will not tell off-color jokes. You will conduct yourself with dignity and propriety at all times. This means that if I see you in a bar after work, you'd better be stone-cold sober and out of uniform. If you feel like giving your kid's soccer coach a piece of your mind, think again. If you raise your voice to your wife, you better hope I don't hear about it, that's how serious I am, and if you're single, you do your looking outside this department, are we clear?" He took off his glasses and fixed the room with an unwavering stare. "This is a new day, ladies and gentlemen. You're either going forward with me, or you're going out. And if you think I won't fire you for misconduct in a heartbeat, you need to ask yourself where the man you're replacing went."

He paused a moment to let that sink in, then put his glasses back on. "Moving on. Some of you new recruits come from other law enforcement agencies, some are fresh out of police academy. Whatever your background, you will be considered probationary employees until you have satisfactorily demonstrated an understanding of the policies and procedures of the Murphy County Sheriff's Department and have been evaluated on basic law enforcement skills. In the meantime, you will have full arrest authority under the supervision of your field training officer. You will be assigned full-time duty and pay as soon as you complete fifty-two hours of field training, sixteen of which will be conducted in the classroom under the supervision of our new training officer, Captain Grady."

A full fifteen seconds passed in tense, uncomfortable silence before Grady realized that the attention of the room had turned to him. He quickly shut down his phone and sat up straighter.

Sheriff Bishop raised an eyebrow. "Something you'd like to share with the room, Captain?"

"No, sir, Sheriff." Grady got quickly to his feet, scraping his chair, and added, "I mean, yes, sir. New recruits, report to the training room at oh-eight-hundred hours. Field training officers, your assignments have been e-mailed to you. Report at twelve hundred hours to rendezvous with your recruits. Thank you, Sheriff." He sat down.

Bishop regarded him levelly for another moment before addressing the group again. "All rise, raise your right hand."

Chairs scraped, boots shuffled. Under ordinary circumstances, this ceremony would have been held after a triumphant election, with a marching band, a podium draped in bunting, guest speakers, and commemorative photographs. But even in the cramped room on an ordinary workday, the solemnity of the moment could not have been deeper, its import more clear.

In his deep, resonant voice Jerome Bishop said, "Repeat after me. 'I do solemnly swear that I will support, protect and defend the Constitution and Government of the United States and of the State of Florida…'"

When the echo of the last "So help me God" died down, Bishop stood there for another moment, his hands braced on either side of the lectern, regarding his troops. Then he gave a satisfied nod and said simply, "All right, deputies, let's get to work. Make me proud out there. Dismissed."

The men and women began to file out, and Bishop added as he turned for the door, "Captain Grady, my office. Five minutes."

CHAPTER TEN

The Dogleg Island Police Department was housed in a one-room storefront in a small strip mall on the edge of town that had once been a candy shop. It was barely big enough for three desks and a row of filing cabinets, and when all three women who worked at those desks were inside the office, they had to walk sideways to avoid bumping into each other. But its small size did have one advantage: it was easy to cool, and Sally Ann, Aggie's office administrator, kept the room at a constant 68 degrees in the summer.

Aggie leaned against the door and let the blast of cold air wash over her, lifting the edge of the short platinum wig she wore in a futile effort to allow some of the heat that had accumulated there to escape. Even as gooseflesh prickled her arms, her perspiration-slick scalp felt like a furnace. Her once crisp white shirt was sagging, her navy uniform pants damp and wilted, and it wasn't even nine o'clock.

She started to push away from the door and almost tripped over two boxes stacked beside it. "What's this?" She knelt down to undo the flap on the top box and Flash pushed in beside her, giving both boxes a thorough sniff. Finding nothing to attract his attention besides the smell of wet cardboard, pine air freshener and bait fish—along with the far more ordinary smells of tasteless packaged food, canned propane and bug spray, which were the contents of the top box—he trotted over to his water dish and began to lap up the contents.

"They were in front of the door this morning when I got in," Sally Ann said. "I thought you ordered them. Are you going camping, Chief?"

Sally Ann was a skinny, pigtailed, twenty-year-old in oversized glasses, dressed today for the interior climate in a fuzzy cardigan over her summer dress and ankle boots with socks. Only she could get away with it.

Aggie sorted through packages of instant oatmeal, MREs, mosquito wipes and sunscreen, looking for an invoice or bill of lading. At the bottom of the box were several containers of camp stove fuel, but nothing else.

"The bottom box is filled with bottled water," Sally Ann said. "Boy, was it heavy. That's why I just dragged it inside the door."

"What time did you open up?"

"Six forty-five, as usual," Sally Ann reported brightly.

"And the boxes were right in front of our door?"

"Yes, ma'am. Just like that, not even taped shut." She added, frowning a little, "You know, I did think it was a little odd that there wasn't even a mailing label."

Aggie shifted aside the top box to examine the bottom one. It contained nothing but four 24-bottle plastic wrapped packages of water, just as Sally Ann had said. She grunted curiously.

"Did you ask Maureen about these?" she asked.

"I did. She said she thought it would be okay to leave them there until you got in." Her tone was concerned as she added, "Did I do the right thing, Chief? I mean, I opened the boxes before I brought them inside, just to make sure there wasn't, you know, a bomb or anything."

Aggie made a face as she got to her feet. "New policy. Let's not open any boxes delivered to the Dogleg Island Police Department that we suspect might contain bombs, okay?"

Sally Ann's eyes grew big behind the glasses. "Yes, ma'am." She earnestly scribbled down the note and then looked at Aggie worriedly. "Is something wrong?"

Aggie studied the boxes thoughtfully for another moment. Camping supplies. There weren't that many places to camp around here; not legally anyway. She said, though it wasn't exactly what she was thinking, "Somebody probably just got the wrong door. I wonder where they came from, though."

Flash looked up from his water dish. He could have told her if she had asked him. There was only one place he knew of that smelled like bait fish and pine air freshener, and he was surprised that Aggie hadn't figured it out already.

But Aggie didn't ask him. She just added, "I'll track it down when I get a chance."

Relieved, Sally Ann turned to gather up her message slips. "Maureen is out taking a report on a fender-bender in the beachside parking lot," she said. "Judge Martin wants to reschedule magistrate's court for the twenty-first, Cassie Long came by to pick up her lost keys—well, found, now—and Darnell Watson called in a lost tag. I already copied the report to the Sheriff's Department. Nothing else important."

Aggie took the message slips from Sally Ann and dropped them on her own desk, two steps away. "Do we still have that uniform catalog?"

"Top left filing cabinet drawer."

"Whose idea was it to have navy blue uniforms in the summer, anyway?" She pulled open the cabinet drawer and found the catalogue as promised, filed under "C."

"Umm, yours, I think."

Aggie tugged uncomfortably again at the wig and pushed the file drawer closed with her shoulder. Sally Ann said, "You know, Chief, it's none of my business and, well, the wig is cute and all, but it might be cooler if you just wore your uniform cap. It's cotton, right?"

Aggie looked at her, raising an eyebrow. Sally Ann might be young, but she had a real knack for zeroing in on the obvious. "Right," Aggie murmured.

The door opened and Aggie looked around, her stomach automatically tensing when she recognized Jess Krieger, the publisher, editor and only full-time reporter for Dogleg Island's once-weekly newspaper. He usually stopped by on Friday to glance through their incident reports, but only breaking news would bring him out on a Wednesday. All she could think of was that he must have somehow gotten wind of the gruesome discovery on Wild Horse Island. The official policy was not to release any information on the body until a cause of death was determined, but that didn't mean word couldn't have gotten out somehow. Aggie hated dealing with members of the press, even the ones who were mostly fair to her, like Jess. She had had to do so far too often over the past two years.

"Good morning, Chief," Jess said, blotting his forehead with his arm. "Gonna be a hot one today, huh?"

Jess Krieger was in his fifties, with shaggy salt and pepper hair, a comfortable paunch, and an overall rumpled look. He had come to Dogleg from the *Miami Herald* ten years ago seeking a simpler life, and had found it as publisher of the little community newspaper that was sponsored mostly by ads. He enjoyed small-town life, didn't work too hard, and got along with most people. But the reporter in him was still alive and well, and he had won awards for his coverage of the notorious murder that had taken place on Dogleg Island two years ago. Aggie had learned not to underestimate him.

"Good morning, Jess." Aggie returned pleasantly. She took the catalog to her desk and sat down.

Jess glanced at the open boxes by the door and said, "Planning a camping trip?"

"You're full of questions today, aren't you Jess?" Aggie flipped through the catalogue until she found the women's styles.

"That's more or less my job."

Jess pulled up the rolling chair from Maureen's desk and sat across from her. Sally Ann edged past to bring him a cup of coffee.

"Thank you, sweetheart," he said when she placed the cup on the edge of the desk in front of him. Aggie suppressed a smile when she saw Sally Ann roll her eyes behind his back.

"What can I do for you, Jess?" she said.

"Okay, right to business." He put down the cup and took out his notebook and pen. "What can you tell me about the shark attack yesterday?"

Aggie's frown was mitigated by amusement. "Come on, Jess, you're usually sharper than that. It wasn't a shark, just a false alarm."

"So you're overruling the lifeguard who was on the scene?"

She blinked. "What? What are you talking about?"

"According to the victim..." he flipped a page in his notebook. "A Mrs. Elizabeth Singleton from Braselton, Indiana, the lifeguard who pulled her from the water said it looked like a shark attack."

Aggie shook her head. "Then she's mistaken. I talked to Brian myself and he was certain it *wasn't* a shark. Really, Jess, you need to check your facts."

"That's what I'm doing."

"Did you talk to Brian?"

"Tried to, couldn't reach him. Don't worry, nothing goes in the paper without a quote from the first responder."

"Well, the woman is obviously confused. When did you talk to her?"

"The victim? Yesterday after she was released from the hospital."

"She was probably still on pain meds."

He shrugged. "She seemed pretty clearheaded to me."

"Well, she was wrong."

"Still, I need a statement from you about public safety on our beaches."

"Dogleg Island beaches are among the safest on the Gulf Coast, and we intend to keep them that way."

He wrote that down. "Great. You always come through for me, Chief." He took a sip of his coffee and glanced around. "So. Arrest anyone interesting lately?"

"Sorry."

He tucked the notebook into the pocket of his wrinkled shirt and got to his feet. "Well, that'll do it for me, then. See you Friday."

"See you then."

At the door he looked back. "Say, what can you tell me about that attack on the park ranger yesterday? You know, over on Wild Horse?"

Bingo, thought Aggie. The real reason he was here.

Her smile was locked in place. "Sorry. Not my case."

He looked at her steadily for a moment, but she didn't budge.

He said, "Maybe I should talk to the sheriff's department."

Aggie agreed, "Maybe you should."

"It's probably not their case either."

Aggie just continued to smile.

Jess conceded the stare-down with a half-shrug and glanced at Sally Ann. "Thanks for the coffee, little lady."

Sally Ann scowled after him when he left. "Little lady," she muttered. "Who says that?"

But Aggie, gazing thoughtfully at the closed door, didn't reply. Instead she said, "Sally Ann, do we have an address on that Elizabeth Singleton?"

Sally Ann turned to her desk just as Aggie's phone buzzed. Aggie started to smile as she read the text from the sheriff's department, and by the time she finished she was beaming. Her day had just improved a hundred percent.

Sally Ann retrieved the address of the woman's vacation rental from Maureen's police report, jotted it down, and passed the paper to Aggie. There was a spring in Aggie's step as she started for the door. "Come on, Flash, let's go talk to a lady about a shark."

Flash was, of course, already waiting at the door, and bounded through it and into the front seat of the patrol car a good three strides in front of Aggie. Aggie slid into the driver's seat beside him, started the engine and turned the air-conditioning up full blast. Before she put the car in gear, though, she jerked off her wig, stuffed it into the storage compartment in the dash, and put her cotton uniform cap on instead. Immediately she felt ten degrees cooler.

When she got the text from Grady a few minutes later, she thought her day couldn't get any better.

She was right.

CHAPTER ELEVEN

Bishop glanced up from his computer when Grady came in, and gestured for him to close the door. Grady did so, surprised. Jerome Bishop had always been famous for his open door policy, and rarely felt the need to say anything inside those walls that could not be overheard by the whole department.

What he said now was, "Have a seat, Grady."

Grady took the chair in front of the desk and Bishop removed his glasses, sitting back from the computer. He said, "I didn't see any point in bringing it up at the meeting, they'll all hear soon enough. Briggs pled out. Life in a medium-security prison, no chance of parole."

Grady did not blink. "Medium security," he repeated, without expression.

Bishop regarded him steadily. "There's a reason they call it plea *bargain*. It's a negotiation. Each side gets something. We got to take down a half-dozen bad guys and save the state the cost of a trial. He got to not fry in the electric chair."

Grady said nothing.

"They're taking it to the judge this morning, but the DA is confident it'll hold. It's over."

Grady's expression did not change. "Okay," he said.

"My words were 'Thank you, sweet Jesus' and 'Hallelujah,'" replied Bishop. "There's never been a Florida sheriff on death row and I didn't want the first one to be from this department." He added, "I texted Aggie a few minutes ago. I figured she'd want to hear it from me."

Grady nodded, his face still revealing nothing. "She'll be relieved. A trial would have been hard on her."

"On both of you," suggested Briggs.

"Yes." Grady started to rise. "Thanks for telling me."

"That's not all."

Grady sat back down again. Bishop looked at him sternly across the desk.

"You're not getting paid overtime for yesterday," Bishop said. "It's not your case. It's the state's case and John Evers is the contact point in this department. You're not working cases for another two and a half weeks, are we clear?"

Grady said, "Yes, sir."

"You're lucky you're not under suspension," Bishop went on, scowling as he warmed to the subject. "You're lucky you've still got your rank, your *job*, when it comes to that. You're the best officer on my force and I'm not going to lose you to your own stupidity, so try to hold that particular characteristic of yours down to a minimum over the next two weeks, can you do that?"

"Yes, sir," replied Grady. "I'll try."

Bishop glared at him for another moment. "That having been said, and given the fact that you probably have a little more pull with the boys at the FDLE than John does, not to mention that you'll probably be called to testify in the case if it comes to that, I'd consider it a personal favor if you'd do some oversight on this thing on Wild Horse, in a completely unofficial capacity, of course. Give John the benefit of your experience, act as a consultant where needed, that sort of thing."

Grady nodded, keeping a straight face. "Yes, sir. Happy to."

"Your name will not appear on any reports. This is completely unofficial."

"I understand."

"I already spoke to Evers about it, he's glad to have it off his hands. Two and a half weeks, Grady. Keep your nose clean for two and a half weeks."

"You can count on me, Sheriff."

"So." Bishop waited, but Grady said nothing. He prompted, "What have you got?"

Grady looked blank.

Bishop said impatiently, "That's what you were doing with your phone, wasn't it, while you weren't listening to the speech I spent three weeks working on? Getting an update on the case?"

"Oh," Grady said. "No, no updates. I'll check on it for you, though."

"Good." Bishop looked at him narrowly. "You plan on keeping that beard?"

"It's not really a beard," Grady explained. "More like a fashion statement."

Bishop grunted. "The last thing I need is my deputies making a fashion statement." He picked up his glasses and turned back to the computer. "Get to work."

Grady stood. "You coming to dinner tonight?"

Bishop did not look up. "It's Wednesday, isn't it?"

"Aggie's making lasagna."

"I'll bring Chianti."

Grady added apologetically, "It's vegetarian. She's on a health kick."

Bishop hesitated, then shrugged. "I'll bring the wine anyway."

Grady turned for the door, then looked back. "You know who you should talk to about that community relations stuff, don't you? Aggie. She's the best in the business."

Bishop grunted but didn't look up. "You're right. I will. I still need five ideas from you."

"By end of shift, right."

Grady waited until he was well out of sight of the office to take out his phone and text Aggie.

You ok?

But he didn't exhale until he got the reply, *OK? I'm great! Champagne tonight!*

He typed back, *Gotcha covered* and added a throbbing heart emoji because he knew it would make her smile. Usually he would have smiled too, but not today.

Grady pocketed his phone, walked to the men's room, and closed the door. He leaned against it, closed his eyes and tried very hard not to put his fist through the wall.

Medium security.

CHAPTER TWELVE

If there was one thing Flash had learned in his short time on earth, it was that people were unpredictable. When a cat arched its back and hissed its ugly little hiss, you knew you were going to get scratched if you didn't move fast. When you came upon a snake in the bushes, all coiled up and glaring at you with its narrow pointy eyes, you knew to back away. But with people, you never could tell. They could be laughing and talking on the street corner one minute and step right out in front of a car the next. They could say, "I'm fine," and then burst into tears. They could offer a fellow a liver treat, and then pull a gun and shoot a chunk out of his ear. People. You never knew what they might do next.

The exception, of course, was Aggie. It was his job to know what she was going to do next, and he was hardly ever wrong. That was why he was so disconcerted when, on their way to what he was certain was going to be the lady with the shark, Aggie suddenly stopped the car, turned it around, and headed back the way they had come. "Who goes to work before Sally Ann?" she muttered.

Flash could think of lots of people. Joe the shrimp man for one, who parked his truck illegally in the vacant lot at the corner of Ocean and Main and who always had extra shrimp for Flash when they stopped by to give him a ticket. Then there was the guy who worked on the telephone lines, and the fellows who picked up the garbage, and Andy at the Kangaroo station across the bridge, and John Baker on Tarpon Drive who liked to mow his lawn in the summer as soon as it got light and who had gotten a noise ordinance violation warning from Aggie more than once. There were lots of people. It was Flash's job to know these things.

"I mean," Aggie said, "someone who gets to work practically in the middle of the night, and might have noticed somebody leaving those boxes in front of the door."

Well, that narrowed it down considerably. There was Joe the shrimp man, and...

Aggie pulled the car in front of the bakery that was right across from the police station. Flash's tail began to wag immediately as, even through the closed windows, he caught the scent of cinnamon and butter. He loved being right.

The bell over the door jangled when they walked inside the bright little shop filled with pies and cakes and mounds of pastries behind glass cases. Aggie called, "Hi, Mrs. Mosley! It's Aggie Malone."

From somewhere in the back a voice returned, "Be right there, honey!"

Mrs. Mosley the baker came bustling out with heat-flushed cheeks and a quick smile, smelling like baking bread and lemon frosting and all things wonderful in the world. She poured Aggie coffee from the pot behind the counter and started to take one of the cinnamon rolls out of the case but, to Flash's great disappointment, Aggie stopped her.

"You get to the shop about four thirty every morning, don't you, Mrs. Mosley?" Aggie asked, sipping her coffee from the paper cup.

"I have to," she said. "My sticky buns are our best seller and it takes them two hours to rise. People pay extra for fresh, you know," she confided, "and don't you let anybody tell you they can't tell the difference." She spread her hands in a gesture that was half-apologetic and half-proud as she indicated the bakery case. "We sold out an hour ago, but I've got some nice donuts sitting on the glazing tray, if you're sure you don't want to try one of my cinnamon rolls."

"Thanks, no," Aggie said. "You didn't happen to notice when you drove in this morning a couple of big boxes sitting in front of my door, did you?"

She frowned a little. "Why no, can't say that I did. You've got a nice bright light there and I'm pretty sure I would have noticed when I backed my car into its space."

"What about later? Did you notice any vehicles on the street, maybe stopped in front of the police station for a couple of minutes?"

She shook her head apologetically. "Sorry, hon. I was in the back from the time I got here until I opened up at seven. Is it important?"

"No," Aggie said, but Flash could tell she was disappointed. "Just trying to track down the owner of some lost merchandise. Thanks anyway."

But, to Flash's delight, the baker would not let them leave before pressing a bag of warm, cinnamon-sugar sprinkled donut holes into Aggie's hand. As soon as they were outside Aggie tossed Flash a donut hole, took one for herself, and put the bag in the front seat of the car. She leaned against the car door, sipping her coffee and munching the donut hole, squinting in the sun as she gazed up and down the street. "I know it's stupid, Flash," she said. "It's not important. I mean, we've got a DB and an attack on a park ranger that might be a little higher up the priority ladder. But I'd just like to figure one thing out. Just one." She took a sip of her coffee and sighed. "That probably means I'm going OCD on top of everything else."

Flash wondered if Aggie had forgotten about the lady and the shark. He finished the donut hole and looked at her expectantly, not begging, just wondering. But she didn't notice. Her attention was fixed on the Island Bistro restaurant on the corner. She stood up straighter, looked at the building, then turned and looked back at the police station. Then she smiled. "Modern technology," she murmured. "You gotta love it."

A few minutes later, they were in the back office of the Bistro, watching grainy black and white images flicker across a computer screen while Jason Wendale, one of the restaurant's owners, leaned against the wall a few feet away with his arms crossed and watched. When he and his partner had built the restaurant they had included a state-of the art video surveillance system, including four cameras that covered the parking lot and most of the surrounding street corner. Grady had scoffed at first, saying they had more money than sense, but at the time theirs was the only surveillance camera in town, aside from the one at a bank branch on Island Drive, and Aggie had been grateful for anything that made her job easier. A year later, on the advice of his insurance company, Pete installed cameras in his parking lot, and Grady stopped scoffing when the cameras caught a robbery suspect who'd come across the bridge and had been breaking into parked cars. Now about half of the downtown businesses had cameras, but the only one that covered the strip mall in which the police station was located belonged to the Bistro.

"I really appreciate this, Jason," Aggie said, clicking the mouse.

"Always happy to help lower the crime rate in my community," Jason replied.

Aggie clicked again to make the playback go faster. "It's not exactly a crime. At least, not that I know of."

"In that case, you owe me."

Aggie watched the images on the screen. So did Flash. Neither one of them saw anything except a staticy dark street with pools of light where the shops were located. The time stamp at the bottom of the screen read 4:41.

"I hear you're planning a big wedding reception," Jason said.

Aggie replied absently, "Where did you hear that?"

"I guess you'll be holding it at Pete's Place."

"He's family," Aggie said.

"I can give you a better price."

"Better than free?"

"Much better service, an unquestionably superior menu."

"We haven't even decided if we're doing it yet. Seems kind of hokey to me, having a reception six months after you're married."

"Oh, very on trend," he assured her. "You can take my word for that, I'm gay." He cocked a critical eye toward her and added, "Speaking of on trend, good choice to toss the wig. But if you're going to go bald, you really need to flaunt it. And wear a killer pair of earrings."

Aggie frowned and fingered the edge of her cap uncomfortably. "Cops don't wear earrings."

"Why is that, I wonder?"

"Because some perp could grab one and rip your ear off."

He considered that thoughtfully for a moment, then said, "About the date…"

"I told you, we don't have one."

"I'll work with you."

She took her eyes off the screen long enough to give him a skeptical look. "Why do you even want to do this? Pete's not your competition. You cater to two entirely different crowds."

"Right," he said. "He caters to the bar crowd; I cater to the wedding-reception crowd. It's about branding, darling, branding."

Aggie said, "We're more of the bar-crowd type."

"I would have voted for your lifeguard, you know."

Aggie turned back to the screen. "We're having it at Pete's Place."

"That would be the man who decided not to put it to a vote at all."

Aggie turned to look at him. "Now listen, Jason..."

Flash, watching the screen, suddenly barked.

Aggie turned back to the video. Jason straightened up and watched over her shoulder as headlights flashed off the camera and a pickup truck came into view. They watched the truck proceed down the street and slow to turn into the strip mall.

Aggie said, "Can we zoom in?"

Jason reached over her and tapped a couple of keys, bringing the focus in on a sign on the pickup's door that read "Captain Jack's Charters" followed by a phone number. Aggie leaned in, frowning, as Captain Jack himself got out, walked to the back of his truck, took out two boxes, and carried them to the police station, where he left them in front of the door. He then got back into his truck and drove away.

Aggie sat back, looking puzzled. "Captain Jack Saunders," she said. "Who would have thought?"

Flash, for one. In fact, he could have told her, if she'd asked.

"What's in the boxes?" Jason wanted to know. "Contraband? Doesn't surprise me a bit. What I don't understand is why he'd bring the evidence to your doorstep and leave it like a thief in the night. Do you think it's part of a twelve-step program? You know, make amends, make restitution…"

Aggie said impatiently, "It's not contraband and it's not evidence. It's camping supplies."

Jason wrinkled his nose in distaste. "Good heavens. Why would anyone want to go camping this time of year?"

That was a good question. Aggie got to her feet. "Thanks for your help, Jason."

He replied, "I can prepare a tasting menu for you. Tiny bites, absolute perfection, free of charge."

Aggie waved a dismissing hand on her way out the door.

"Think about it," he called after her.

Aggie held the door open for Flash and they made their escape.

CHAPTER THIRTEEN

It was risky to stop at Wal-Mart, but Steve didn't really see a choice. Besides, he figured the cops wouldn't be looking for them this far off the freeway, and anyway it was Tracy's picture that was all over the news, not his.

So far.

So he parked in the back in the employee parking lot and made Tracy scrunch down in the seat while he went inside. She whined about that because it was hot in the car and the alternator was so crappy he was afraid to leave the AC running when it wasn't in gear. He promised to be back in ten minutes and wheedled fifty dollars out of her, which she gave up reluctantly and not without another round of whining and complaints.

He was not gone ten minutes. It was more like thirty-five by the time he finally got somebody in electronics to activate the twenty-dollar phone with the ten dollars' worth of prepaid minutes he bought. He picked up two ham and cheese sandwiches and a six pack of Coke and nobody even looked at him twice.

He started dialing before he left the store.

Of course it took three calls before the person on the other end, not recognizing the number, answered, and even then he sounded terse and annoyed.

"Bro, it's me," Steve said, walking fast, head-down, toward the corner of the building. "Listen we got a small complication."

"Are you *insane?*" The voice on the other end dropped to a hiss. "Your face is all over the Internet, you're wanted for *kidnapping,* dude, and you call that a *complication?*"

Steve paused in his stride. "What? It is?" He cast a quick uneasy glance over his shoulder and added in a half whisper, "Shit!" He quickened his step, his head low.

"How could you be such a screw-up?" demanded the man on the other end. "I should've known better than to trust an ex-con! You couldn't stay out of trouble for another week? The biggest deal of your whole miserable life, and now you're bringing the cops straight to our front door!"

"Look, bro, just calm down. It's still on, we just might have to lay low for a while…"

"A while?" barked out the other man incredulously. "We don't have *a while.* Things are going south here with the speed of light, and we need to be out of here like yesterday, man!" He sucked in a sharp breath. "Okay," he said, "Okay, just forget it. It's over. Too dangerous. Jesus, I can't believe this!"

"Shut up, will you? Just shut up!" With a visible effort, Steve brought his tone down to something more reasonable. "Nothing's changed. This is still going to work. Forget laying low, we stay on schedule. You've got the goods, right? You're ready to go? Then what's the problem?"

"The *problem*," bit out the voice on the other end angrily, "is that it's over, *bro*. You're out, we don't need you. We'll find another way. You're too big a risk."

Steve gave a short bark of laughter, even though his blood was boiling. "Yeah, right, like you're going to just place a fucking ad on craigslist. Name me three other people who can get your stuff to Mexico and get you full price for it—in advance—without one, and I mean, not a single *one* chance of anybody tracing it back to you jerk-offs. No, let me make it easy. Name me just one person."

The brief hesitation on the other end was all the chance he needed.

"Listen to me, asshole," he said, rounding the corner of the building. "You're sitting on a fucking fortune that's worth exactly *shit* without me. We're doing this. I'm not going to let anything, I mean anything, get between me and my cut, got it? And I'm for damn sure not going back to prison just because you don't have the balls to execute a plan. So are you with me?"

There was silence on the other end of the line. Steve could hear his own heart beating in his ears.

Then came the voice, cold, angry: "You got the text, right? With the rendezvous point?"

Steve said, "8:30 Thursday, I memorized the address. You just be ready with the goods. We can do this, easy. You just hold up your end."

The voice on the other end of the phone said, "No more calls, no more texts. This is it."

Replied Steve, "Don't worry."

He disconnected the phone and, moving quickly into the back parking lot, placed it under the right back wheel of his own car. He got into the driver's seat, started the ignition, and slammed the car into gear before he noticed Tracy wasn't there. Before he could make the decision to leave without her— which was tempting—she opened the passenger door and flung herself inside. Her color was high and she was breathing hard as she opened the flap of her oversized purse. "Look!" she invited excitedly.

Inside was a virtual Aladdin's cave of frothy underwear, costume jewelry, and candy bars. There was no doubt in his mind that she had shoplifted them all. Steve stared in disbelief, then stepped on the gas.

"Jesus Christ," he said as he spun out of the parking lot, crushing the burner phone in the process.

CHAPTER FOURTEEN

I t made perfect sense, of course, Aggie decided. If a person didn't have a boat and needed to get to a remote island, where would she go? And if she were planning an extended stay on that remote island, she would definitely need some supplies. But Jason had a point. Who *would* want to go camping in Florida in August? Even at night the temperature didn't fall below eighty, and the no-see-ums made sleeping outside a misery. Besides, those weren't just camping supplies, they were survival supplies. At this point Aggie had far more questions and answers, and that was why she wanted to talk to Captain Jack.

The pier at Dogleg Island wasn't much to speak of. It was big enough to dock a half-dozen mid-size boats, but most people, like Grady, kept their boats at the marina on the other side of the bridge. Commercial fishermen dropped off their catches there, private mariners fueled up there, and a couple of tour boats left from there. Captain Jack had been running fishing charters out of the Dogleg Island pier for fifteen years.

Flash liked visiting Captain Jack, which he mostly did with Grady, but occasionally, when they were on routine patrol, with Aggie too. There were always interesting things to smell there, and usually interesting people there too. Today the last of the people were already making their way to the parking lot, some of them with coolers that smelled like fish, all of them looking sunburned and pleased with themselves. Captain Jack himself was on deck, watching his passengers depart and Aggie and Flash approach.

"Well now, if it ain't Chief Malone and her number one deputy," he said. "A good morning to you both."

His tone was pleasant enough, but it was hard to tell with Jack just what he was thinking. His face was leathery and his eyes squinty from years on the water, and he had a habit of chewing on toothpicks, which made him look as though he was perpetually grinning out of one side of his mouth.

Aggie said, equally as pleasantly, "Morning, Jack. How was the fishing?"

Jack shrugged. "So, so. One fella caught a couple of redfish, another hooked a flounder. "

Flash trotted ahead of Aggie and leapt lightly onboard, checking out the live wells and the bait buckets, and Jack gave a snort of what might have been amusement. "That dog of yours ain't stopped by nothing, is he?"

Flash wandered into the wheelhouse where the pine-tree-shaped air freshener hung, and Aggie agreed, "Not much."

Aggie stood on the dock, looking over at Jack, waiting for him to speak. She had learned to respect the taciturn, cautiously shuttered manner that was indigenous to the islanders, and had cultivated patience for it. But it was hot, and she knew perfectly well that Jack could keep her standing there all day if he had a mind to. So she said, "What's up with the boxes of camping supplies?"

He didn't blink. "Which ones would those be, Chief?"

"The ones you left on the doorstep of the police station at 4:56 this morning."

He shifted the toothpick to the other side of his mouth. "What makes you think I did that?"

"Video footage from a security camera across the street."

He said nothing; just squinted in her general direction and chewed lazily on the toothpick.

A trickle of sweat ran down Aggie's side, and the humidity was so thick she could practically see it. Even the water looked dark and unhealthy, leaving a froth of brown scum where it lapped against the pilings. She could no longer remember why it had seemed important, or even a good idea, to chase down the owner of those boxes.

She said sharply, "Come on, Jack, let's have it. I've got other places to be. Why did you leave the boxes?"

He was silent just long enough to irritate her, and then he said, "Couldn't figure what else to do with them, them being abandoned merchandise and all. Didn't want nobody accusing me of stealing 'em."

Aggie frowned. "Abandoned merchandise? You mean somebody left them on your boat?"

"Nah. I mean somebody paid me to deliver the stuff, and never showed up to claim it. Figured police custody was the safest place for it."

"Who was it?"

He shrugged. "Some woman. A paid charter. That's what I do, ain't it?"

"A fishing charter?"

He didn't reply. He didn't have to.

"Where did you take her?" Aggie asked, already knowing.

He shifted uneasily from one foot to the other. He turned his head, appearing to examine a bank of clouds forming in the western sky. Then he looked back at Aggie.

"Thing is," he said, with some deliberation, "I'm not a man to tell tales out of school. Can't afford to be. Mind my own business, expect other folks to mind theirs."

Aggie nodded encouragement.

"I figure a person pays his money, what he does after that is his own business, right?"

Aggie was wisely silent on that.

Jack went on, still chewing on the toothpick, "So a couple of weeks ago this woman shows up at the pier, weird-looking hippie-type, you know, baggie shorts with pockets all over, hair in braids, cotton backpack, and she pays me to take her out to Wild Horse Island."

Flash heard Aggie's heart skip a beat and he came quickly to sit near Jack, keeping an eye on him. Flash's heartbeat remained steady, but his alertness intensified, just like hers.

Aggie said, "Did she give you a name?"

He twisted his wrist dismissively. "Something with a K. Karen, maybe. Kelsey, Katie, something like that. Paid cash, what did I care? Thing is," he went on before Aggie could answer, "she gave me a hundred dollars and a list of supplies she wanted me to bring over to her this weekend, which I did. Only nobody was there, so I brought 'em back. Now you got 'em and I'm out of it. End of story."

Aggie looked at him intently. "Wait a minute," she said. "You took this woman to Wild Horse, and you just left her there?"

He scowled back at her just as intently. "That'as my job, wadn't it?"

Aggie said evenly, "There's no overnight camping on Wild Horse. You know that."

His brows drew together even more tightly. "Do I look like a damn park ranger? Anyhows, she had a permit. Leastwise, that's what she said. To study the horses."

Aggie blinked and Flash sat up straighter. "Horses?"

"From the university," explained Jack patiently, "at least that's what she said. Said she'd be there till Labor Day, which is why she needed the supplies. And that's what I'm trying to tell you. I went to drop off the supplies at nine o'clock on Sunday like she said, and nobody was at the dock. Thought about just leaving the stuff there on the dock, but that didn't seem right, what with wild animals and tourists and whatnot, so I nailed a note to the piling telling her I'd been there and I waited for her to call, but never heard nothing. I figure she found out living amongst the bugs and the snakes wasn't as much fun as she thought it'd be, and she got somebody from that university to pick her up. By rights that stuff was mine to keep, I reckon, but I run an honest business, don't need no trouble with the law. So I turned it over. Can't fault me on that."

Aggie said, "Did she happen to mention what university she was with?"

"Nah. Wasn't from around here, though. Some place up north, is my guess. Nobody but a damn fool foreigner would go looking for horses on Wild Horse Island."

Flash's ears pricked up in challenge at that, but Aggie looked thoughtful, so he let it pass.

Aggie said, "Do you remember what day it was exactly that you dropped her off?"

"'Course I do. July 31. That's how I knew when to bring the supplies. She packed in enough to last a couple of weeks, but said she'd need to resupply every two weeks. Two weeks exactly. Now, are we about done here? I got another charter in half an hour."

Aggie said, "So you never heard from her again after you dropped her off?"

He started to dismiss the question, then seemed to remember something. "Yeah," he grunted. "Matter of fact she called a couple of days after I dropped her off. I left her my card, you know, in case she changed her mind about staying. Figured it was only gentlemanly. But all she wanted was the water. Said she didn't have enough chlorine pills to last till Labor Day, so I should add bottled water to the list. And I did."

"Did she call you on your landline or cell phone?"

He removed the toothpick and spat a few wooden crumbs on the deck. "Ain't got no landline. Waste o' money, ain't it, since I'm never on land?"

Aggie inquired conversationally, "What made you decide to bring the boxes in today, Jack? Why not Sunday, when you first brought them back?"

He glared at her. "You ain't open on Sunday."

"We're not open at five a.m. either," she replied. "Why didn't you leave a note? Why all this subterfuge?"

He didn't answer, just tried to stare her down. Flash, in turn, stared him down.

"I got a business to run," he muttered, and started to turn away. "No time to stand here palavering."

"You know what I think?" Aggie said. "I think you heard about what happened to Roger Darby on Wild Horse yesterday and you got worried that maybe something dicey was going on over there. You didn't want to get involved, which is completely understandable, and since you couldn't get in touch with the woman who hired you, you figured the best thing to do was to get rid of the only thing that tied you to the whole situation, which was the supplies. You could have tossed them overboard, but you didn't, and I appreciate that. You're an honest man. "

"You're damn right." He squinted at her warily, waiting.

"Did you try calling her?" Aggie asked. When he didn't answer, she prompted, "Her number would have been on your phone if she called you. Did you call her back?"

"Yeah, I called her," he admitted testily. "Sunday from the dock. The next day too. Nothing. Just some message saying the voice box was full."

Aggie nodded. "I'll need your phone, Jack."

He scowled. "The hell you will."

"This is serious." It wasn't her place to give out information on a case that wasn't even hers, particularly when it involved an unidentified corpse, so she added only, "We think something might have happened to the young woman you dropped off on the island. You might be able to help us."

"Well, you're not getting my damn phone, not without a warrant you're not," he replied angrily. "And I've done all the helping I'm going to do. A man tries to do the right thing and look where he ends up. Now you and your dog get on outta here. I know my rights."

Aggie drew a sharp breath, frustration rising. "Jack, I can get a warrant, but if I do it could shut down your business for days. Give me the phone now and I promise I'll have it back to you as soon as I can. Don't make me do this the hard way."

"You can do whatever you damn well please." He swung away from her and stomped toward the wheelhouse. "I got work to do."

Aggie called after him, "Where were you between 12:00 and 2:00 yesterday afternoon?"

He didn't even turn around.

Aggie glared for a moment at Jack's retreating back, then looked at Flash, who was waiting expectantly near the rail. "Flash," she said, "keep an eye on him."

Flash turned to follow Jack and Aggie took out her phone, walking back down the pier as she looked up the number and dialed.

"'Who can find a virtuous woman?'" JC sang out when she identified herself. "'For her price is far above rubies.' What have you got for me, Aggie Malone of Dogleg Island?"

"Hopefully a break in the Wild Horse Island case," she replied. "At least a witness who might be able to help us identify the dead woman. But I need something from you first."

He said alertly, "I'm listening."

She told him about Captain Jack Saunders and the possibility of tracing the victim through the number she had left on his phone, and when she was finished he let out a whoop of delight. "Sweet Aggie Malone!" he declared. "That Ryan Grady sure married above his rank, didn't he?"

"Well, I don't know about that," she said, repressing a small smile. "The thing is, our witness has decided he doesn't want to cooperate without a warrant, and..." She heard the sound of an engine starting up and she whirled. "Son of a—!" She broke off and started running. "JC, I'll call you back."

She dropped the phone in her pocket and shouted, "Flash!"

While she was on the phone, Jack had cast off and started the engine, but he hadn't yet moved away from the dock. Aggie dived for the rope just as Flash reached the rail. She stripped the rope off the cleat and tossed it to Flash, who made one circuit around the rail support before leaping onto the dock with the end of the rope in his mouth. The boat began to edge away from the dock, taking up the slack in the rope, as Aggie snatched the rope from Flash and started to wind it around the cleat. She was tying the knot when she heard the gear lock in and felt a strong tug that almost pulled her off balance and into the water. Panic leapt to her throat. She finished tying the knot, praying it would hold, and shouted, "Jack Saunders, cut your engines! Cut your engines and disembark! That's an order!"

The line stretched taut but the knot held. The boat rocked in the water. Saunders called back,

"You can't give orders to a captain on his own boat!"

Aggie pulled her gun and got down on one knee in a shooter's stance. "Cut your engines this minute or I swear I'll fill this boat with so many holes she'll never float again! Do it now!"

The boat railing began to creak as it strained against the pull of the engines and the opposing pull of the rope. Aggie held her breath, but she also held her aim. In a moment the engines throttled down. "Return to dock!" she shouted. "Disembark with your hands above your head!"

Flash jumped onboard as soon as the boat was close enough, and kept Saunders in the pine-scented wheelhouse until Aggie had securely tied off again. He had done takedowns before but never on water and never, he had to admit, one that was this much fun. Captain Jack snarled at him but Flash had bigger teeth, and after he demonstrated as much, the captain gave him no more trouble. Saunders climbed sullenly onto the dock and raised his hands in the air. Flash kept a wary eye on him. After all, people, as he well knew, were unpredictable.

Aggie holstered her gun and snatched Jack's hands behind his back. She was breathing so hard she was practically wheezing, and she was soaked in sweat. "You are under arrest," she said, with difficulty, "for evading a police officer, interfering with an investigation, withholding evidence, and disobeying an order from an officer of the law. Damn it," she said angrily as she snapped the cuffs closed. "I *told* you not to make me do this the hard way."

121

Chapter Fifteen

Tracy had been a cheerleader back at Killian High, and one of the first things their coach had taught them was that cheerleaders, like dancers, had to have more than technical skill. They had to be able to act, to project, to reach out there and grab the audience and pull every single member in to the routine. Tracy was a good actress.

They pulled into Doug's New & Used Cars on the outskirts of a dusty little town called Bracken, New Jersey, around 5:00, which was a few minutes before closing. They'd been watching it from the Dairy Queen down the street most of the afternoon, baking in the heat while they sipped sodas in the car and Steve made a plan. At first Tracy hadn't liked the plan, had thought it was crazy and dangerous and flat-out refused to participate. But the hotter it got, and the more Steve talked, the more interested she became. Steve was nice—most of the time anyway—and sexy as hell, but sometimes she wondered how smart he was. So she added a few tweaks to the plan, and pretty soon it started to make sense. Pretty soon she thought it might work. Maybe it was still a little crazy, and way dangerous, but that was mostly what she liked about it.

So a few minutes before closing, when the secretary with the close-cropped gray curls and the salesman with the pit-stained pink shirt had gotten into their cars and driven off and no one remained inside the plain wooden structure with the "office" sign on the door except a balding, overweight man they'd decided was Doug himself, Tracy and Steve pulled into the parking lot and got out, making sure to slam the doors hard so that they could be heard inside. Through the plate glass window of the office shack they could see Doug look up hopefully from his desk, and then lose interest when a teenage girl and a scruffy young man in a faded Black Magic tee shirt got out. But he took a closer look at Tracy, who had pulled up her hair in a high ponytail, tied her tee shirt above her midriff, and unbuttoned the top button of her short-shorts, and he decided to come out anyway.

Tracy skipped ahead, waving and calling excitedly, "You're not closed, are you? Don't close yet!" While Steve followed more slowly a few yards behind, smoking a cigarette and pretending to be bored.

Doug met her with a tolerant smile in the small gravel yard in front of a row of freshly washed used cars. "What can I do for you, young lady?"

Tracy said breathlessly, "Thank goodness you're still open, mister! My daddy's right behind us, and he said for me to come ahead and get you to wait."

Doug's eyes flickered over her bare skin, and Tracy tried not to smile. "Is that right?" he said.

She nodded vigorously. "Today's my birthday! I just got my license and we're picking up my car!"

Now he looked puzzled. "What car?"

"That one." She pointed happily. "The blue 2013 Dart. The salesman showed it to us last week and Daddy told him we'd be back. Well, here we are! It's my birthday!"

Now he was starting to look more interested. The price tag on that little number was close to thirteen grand. "Well now," he said, smiling, "happy birthday. You sure picked a beauty. And your daddy's a mighty generous fellow."

"He feels guilty," she confided. "He got divorced from my mom last year and since then he's always giving me things. But he had to drive all the way over from Raintree after work today, that's why he's running late, so I got my boyfriend Razor to drive me over. That's Razor." She turned and waved gaily to Steve, and Steve lifted a laconic hand in return. Then she turned back to Doug, clasping her hands together in a plea and giving him the full benefit of her big blue eyes. "You won't close before he gets here, will you?"

Again his eyes flickered over her in an appreciative, completely instinctive way, and he smiled indulgently. "Well, now, don't you worry about that, little lady. Tell you what, why don't I go get the key and show you how the sound system works while we wait?"

"That'd be great!" She clapped her hands together and bounced on her toes with excitement. "Razor!" she called. "Come look at my new car!"

There was a spring in Doug's step as he went back into the building. When he returned with a broad smile on his face and the key fob on a paper ID tag dangling from his fingers, Steve was waiting just to the right of the door, a .22 hidden behind his back. Doug said, "All set, little la—" And Steve fired the gun.

Doug staggered and dropped to one knee as blood bloomed on his shoulder. Tracy screamed. Steve fired again, and this time Doug sprawled face-down in the gravel, whimpering and grunting out his breath. Tracy squealed, "You shot him! You didn't tell me you were going to shoot him! You really shot him!" while Steve scrambled in the gravel for the key that had flown from Doug's hand when he fell.

"Go!" he shouted, when he grabbed it. "Get in the car!"

But Tracy, flush-faced and bright-eyed, couldn't seem to tear herself away from the sight of the prone, writhing figure on the ground. Steve grabbed her arm and jerked her around and they half-ran, half-stumbled toward the blue Dodge Dart whose lights blinked, over and over again, when he repeatedly pressed the fob.

"Oh God, oh God," Tracy gasped, pressing her hands to her hot face as Steve backed the car out of the space, wheeled it around, and squealed out of the parking lot. "Do you think he's dead? You didn't tell me you had a gun! Where did you get a gun?"

"Of course I've got a gun, you crazy bitch! How else did you think I was going to pull this off?"

"Oh God, we did it! We did it!"

Steve glanced at her, his own eyes a little wild and his breath coming fast. "We sure as hell did."

The seat belt reminder chimed, and for the first time in her life Tracy ignored it. She felt a thrill tingling in her spine and her nether regions, a heat prickling through her skin. Her heart was pounding, her hands were shaking. She'd never felt anything like it before. She grinned at Steve. He grinned back. They'd done it.

Neither one of them had noticed the camera mounted under the eaves of the little office building that not only captured the image of everyone who went in and out, but also of anyone who approached within ten feet of the door. Within six hours their photos would be on every police computer in the state.

Next time they'd be more careful.

CHAPTER SIXTEEN

Jerome Bishop had been coming to dinner every Wednesday night for as long as Flash could remember, and he always brought dog biscuits. This made Wednesday one of Flash's favorite days. Flash ran to greet Bishop when he came in, claws skittering on the tile floor, and Bishop tossed him a dog biscuit while he was still six feet away. Flash caught it in midair and gobbled it down without missing a stride, which made Bishop chuckle.

Bishop kissed Aggie on the cheek and handed her a bottle of wine, saying, "Don't you look pretty tonight, sweetheart?"

Aggie was wearing a flowered sundress that swirled above her ankles, and had tied a chiffon scarf in the same pastel colors around her head, with the tails fluttering down her back. She had earrings that jingled and bracelets that jangled, and even Flash thought she looked pretty.

Flash sat in front of Bishop, waiting for the second biscuit he knew was coming, and Bishop bent to hand it to him, giving Flash's ears an affectionate rub before he straightened up. He said to Aggie, "Raise your right hand and repeat after me."

Aggie put the wine on a side table, raised her hand and said, "I do solemnly swear to support, protect and defend the Constitution of the United States and of the State of Florida; that I am duly qualified to hold office under the Constitution of the state; and that I will well and faithfully perform the duties of the office of the Deputy Sheriff of Murphy County, on which I am now about to enter. So help me God."

As soon she finished speaking, Grady popped the champagne cork behind them and said, "As witnessed by Captain Ryan Grady and Officer Flash, seven twenty-two p.m., August 16. Congratulations, baby. And congratulations, Sheriff. You just snagged the sworn loyalty of one of the finest peace officers ever to set foot inside this great state."

Bishop said, "Don't I know it?"

It was traditional for the sheriff to swear in members of the local police departments in his county as deputy sheriffs in order to facilitate law enforcement in emergency situations or when the authority of an arresting officer might be unclear because of city boundaries. Traditionally, those municipal police officers did not act outside their jurisdiction without the sheriff's request that they do so, but in Murphy County everyone worked as a team.

Aggie hugged him, smiling. "Welcome back, Sheriff. I wanted to be there to be sworn in with everyone else, but I couldn't get out of the council meeting. How does it feel, being back?"

"The best part was the cake in the break room," he replied, accepting the glass of champagne Grady offered him. "And this." He smiled and lifted his glass to her, and then to Grady. "To peace in Murphy County," he said, then added, "at least for as long as it takes me to finish my dinner."

They all clinked glasses and drank, and then Bishop lifted his glass again. "And to the woman of the hour," he said, eyes twinkling, "who not only gets the first break in a major case before the state investigator does *and* makes an arrest, but still finds time to run a police department, bake a lasagna, and look fresh as a daisy at the end of the day."

"Hear, hear!" said Grady and lifted his glass in a salute to her before drinking. Then he dropped his arm around her shoulders in a squeeze and added to Bishop, grinning, "Did I do good, or what?"

"Well," admitted Aggie modestly, "the lasagna actually came from the frozen foods section. But I did make dip. Besides, all I did was slap the cuffs on him. It was Flash who did the takedown."

Flash waved his tail proudly and grinned up at her. He liked hearing Aggie talk about the things he'd done almost as much as he liked doing them in the first place.

The truth was that the events of the morning had left Aggie exhausted, and she didn't want to admit to either of the men what a physical toll those few minutes of exertion had taken on her. She'd called for deputies to take Jack across the bridge to booking, and as soon as she finished the paperwork she had gone home and slept for three hours. It wasn't until she was changing into a fresh uniform that she found the crumpled note with Elizabeth Singleton's address on it and remembered why she had left the office that morning in the first place. On her way back to the office she had gone to the address, only to find the vacation rental house was empty. According to the maid who was cleaning it, the guests had checked out that morning. She'd ended up tracking down a home phone number for her and leaving a message, but by the end of the work day hadn't gotten a call back. So all in all her day had been only about thirty percent successful, with perhaps the most successful decision being the earrings, and those had been prompted by Jason.

She said, as Flash led the way to the living room, "I don't really think Jack is mixed up in that girl's death, do you? If only he hadn't been such a stubborn idiot about the phone."

Bishop replied, "With good reason. You don't want to know the kind of stuff he had on that phone."

She lifted an eyebrow. "Porn?"

"Kiddie porn," said Grady. "So whether he's connected to the dead body or not, he's facing charges."

Aggie screwed up her face in disgust and disappointment, and gestured Bishop to his favorite easy chair while she and Grady sat on the sofa opposite. In more temperate weather they liked to eat on the screen porch, or gather around the cedar table on the patio while Grady cooked something on the charcoal grill. But in August the only sensible place for anyone in Florida to be was indoors in the air-conditioning, and that was where they were staying.

Grady's living room had a tall bank of windows with a good view of the western sky, and one of the first things Aggie had done when she moved in was to arrange the furniture to take advantage of that view. The thunderheads that were piling up on the horizon promised a colorful sunset, if the rain didn't come first.

Aggie had set up a platter of vegetables and dip on the coffee table, which Flash glanced at and ignored. He wasn't wild about vegetables, although he would eat them if that was all that was offered, and he knew lasagna was coming later. Lasagna was one of his favorites, and well worth waiting for. So he sprang up onto the sofa next to Aggie when she sat down and settled in to wait.

Bishop said, "No word on the girl's ID yet, but JC said he'd let us know."

"I don't suppose she really had a permit to study horses," Aggie said.

Grady shook his head. "No such thing."

"They're trying to ping her phone," Bishop added, "but so far no luck."

"After two weeks, it might be dead," Aggie pointed out. Then she gave a quick, sharp shake of her head. "I just can't believe that about Jack. He seemed like a solid man."

"Solid men can still be perverts," Bishop pointed out. "And killers."

"Oh, come on. There's no way he killed that girl."

Grady sat beside Aggie and stretched his arm across the back of the sofa behind her, fingers cupping her shoulder. "Maybe not. We still don't know what really happened to her," he reminded her. "But I like him for the attack on Darby. He had the means to get to the island and a reason to be there."

"And a motive?" Aggie asked.

Grady shrugged. "So far, no."

"Did you check his charter schedule?" Aggie asked.

"Nothing after eight a.m. yesterday," Grady said. "And if you recall, his boat was not at the pier when we put in yesterday. He says he was out trolling the waters." Grady shrugged again. "Possible, I guess, but not looking good as an alibi."

"JC is coming in tomorrow to question him," Bishop added. "No rush, now that we've got him all cozy in our jail on the child porn charges."

Aggie shook her head. "It doesn't make sense. He went to all the trouble to return the supplies when a guilty man would have tossed them overboard, erased the evidence. I'm telling you, he's not involved in this."

"Maybe," agreed Bishop. "But he didn't get spooked until Darby was attacked yesterday. Why wait three days to be a good citizen, and why do it in the middle of the night without even leaving a note?"

"He has a police scanner in his boat, doesn't he?" Aggie said. "I think he heard about the attack yesterday and knew people would be poking around Wild Horse and he just didn't want to get involved. Especially since he had this secret life that he wanted to keep secret." Again she made an expression of disgust and took a sip of champagne as though to clear away a bad taste. "But he didn't hear about the dead woman. Nobody outside of law enforcement knows about that yet, not even that badger Jess Krieger. And if he *had* known about it, the last thing he would have done is draw police attention to himself by turning in the supplies. He would have cut and run."

"Yeah, that's what he claims, too," Grady said. "But I think it bears looking into a little further."

Aggie raised an eyebrow. "Is the sheriff's department working the case?"

"Well," said Bishop, "it's kind of a mutual cooperation thing. The state's running the death investigation, and we're giving an assist with the attack on the park ranger. And now that our only witness—or suspect, depending on how you look at it—has his own legal problems, I imagine there'll be a good bit of overlap."

Aggie looked at Grady. "So this mutual overlap thing, does it mean you're back working cases?"

"Who, me?" Grady lifted a hand in innocent protest. "No, no, I'm not working anything."

"Definitely not," agreed Bishop. "Captain Grady is officially off cases for two and a half more weeks."

"Unofficially, though," Grady said, straight-faced, "I'm interested."

Aggie inclined her head in tacit understanding and turned back to the sheriff, changing the subject. "I hear you've got some new recruits," she said. "How do they look?"

"Five men, three women," Bishop replied. "And I thank God for every one of them, but especially the women. I don't know how the department functioned with no female officers after you and Mo left. As for how they look, you'll have to ask Captain Grady that. He's in charge of the recruits, and I'm staying out of it."

Aggie cast a teasing glance at Grady. "So how do they look? Are any of them pretty?"

"Oh, I don't know. That Watson boy is kind of cute, if you like his type."

She elbowed him in the ribs and he grinned. "Every woman I see is fat and ugly compared to you, baby, you know that."

Bishop chuckled. "You're catching on to this marriage thing, Grady."

"What about that kid we met at the scene yesterday?" Aggie asked. "What was his name? Brown?"

Grady made a small grimace and dug a stalk of celery into the dip. "Not that impressed. He seems like he's got real screw-up potential to me." He crunched down on the celery and added, "This is good, honey."

He offered the uneaten part of the celery stick to Flash, who, with a long-suffering look, took it delicately between his teeth and began to methodically chew it up.

Aggie said, "I don't know. I liked him."

She swirled a carrot in the dip and Flash watched with interest. Carrots weren't half bad, especially when covered with dip. "He reminded me of myself when I first started out."

Grady smothered a chuckle. "If you'd bumbled around like that when you first started out you'd be out of the business by now—and probably the world's most famous lawyer." He paused to give her a quick playful kiss on the cheek. "The guy damn near shot off his own foot with a paintball gun today."

Both Bishop and Aggie stifled amusement while Grady went on, shaking his head, "I swear I don't know what they're teaching them in Academy these days. This is serious business, men out on the street with lethal weapons, up against road rage and drug dealers and *kids*, for God's sake, armed to the teeth, ready to blow your head off before you even get your weapon out. We're talking life and death here, and some of these guys still think they're back at home playing video games. They don't have any idea what it's like to fire your weapon at another human being. How it changes you. What it means." He broke off abruptly and drank from his glass.

There was a moment's tense silence, then Aggie said, trying to lighten the mood, "Come on, Grady, there's never been a teacher who didn't start off with the stupidest bunch of recruits God ever put on the earth, am I right, Sheriff? That's why they call them rookies."

Grady said, "Right." He drank again, fixing his gaze on the sunset beyond the windows.

Aggie met Bishop's eyes and he said easily, "Maybe a little less shop talk in front of the boss, huh? I don't want to have to review these guys with prejudice." He dipped a slice of cucumber in the creamy dressing and popped it in his mouth. He said "Good dip, Aggie. Hits the spot. It'd be even better with chips."

Aggie said to Grady, "Be nice to the Brown kid, okay? He's just nervous."

Grady forced a smile. "Anything for you, gorgeous." And he added, "No more shop talk, Sheriff. Don't know what I was thinking. What happens on the other side of the bridge, stays on the other side of the bridge." He lifted his glass to both of them, smiling.

Aggie said, "Well, I have a toast of my own as long as we're drinking." She lifted her glass again. "To the district attorney, the State of Florida, and the American justice system. To the end of the nightmare."

"I'm drinking to that, sweetheart," returned Bishop heartily, leaning forward to touch his glass to hers.

The two of them drank, but Grady just stared at his glass.

Bishop raised an eyebrow. "Problem?"

Grady said, "Not that impressed with the justice system right now."

Aggie turned in her seat to stare at him. "Come on, Ryan, are you kidding me? It's over. After everything we went through last year—the last two years, really—do you really mean to sit there and tell me you were looking forward to a trial?"

"Nope." He tossed back the remainder of the champagne, his face tight. "I was looking forward to the execution."

He put his glass on the coffee table and squeezed Aggie's knee briefly as he stood. "Sheriff's right, what this dip needs is a bag of chips. I'll get them. Do you want me to chop up the rest of the tomatoes for the salad while I'm in there?"

"Yeah, thanks." Her smile was a little slow in coming. "And check the lasagna for me, will you? The box said it should be golden on top, not brown. Don't let it overcook."

"Yes, ma'am."

Thunder rumbled in the distance as he left the room, and Flash raised his head to track a streak of lightning across the horizon. He loved storms, and could feel this one coming fast in the air.

"Looks like we'll be getting some rain," Bishop observed. "Lots of chop to the water coming over the bridge."

"Good," Aggie said. "Maybe it'll cool things off."

"It never does. Just steams up the windows and leaves everything hotter the next day." He nodded his head in the direction Grady had just gone. "So tell me the truth. What do you think of that beard of his?"

"It's not really a beard," Aggie replied. "More like a fashion statement."

He gave her a suspicious look and she smiled. "I like it," she clarified.

He grunted skeptically.

Aggie said, "So what's your theory on the dead girl?"

"Well, one thing's for sure, she didn't bury herself. Somebody wanted to make sure she wasn't found, and there's only one reason for that."

"Homicide."

"You know what they say, sweetheart. When you hear hoofbeats, think horses, not zebras. So for my money, that's what we're looking at."

Flash looked up alertly, wishing he'd been paying closer attention to the conversation. Horses, again? And just when he thought the best part of their adventure was over.

Aggie said, "Now we just have to figure out who, and why."

"Not 'we,'" Bishop reminded her. "The county doesn't investigate deaths on state-owned land."

She smiled. "Thank heaven for small favors, huh?" Then, "I heard about your suggestion box. Did you get any good ideas?"

Flash lowered his head to Aggie's knee again, disappointed that there was no more talk about horses, while Bishop screwed up his face and told Aggie about some of the suggestions he'd received, and Aggie laughed. The sound of Aggie's laughter always made Flash relax, and he was almost asleep when Grady came back into the room.

Grady had his phone in hand and was looking at it with an intense, slightly puzzled expression on his face. He said, "Hey guys, one more piece of shop talk if you're up for it. I just got a text from JC. They've tracked the phone number on Saunders's phone to a University of North Carolina grad student, Kayleigh Carnes. And we've got a cause of death. The ME found a skull fracture, possible blow to the left temple. But that's not what killed her. She died of post-internment asphyxiation." He looked up at them. "She was buried alive."

CHAPTER SEVENTEEN

Sometimes Flash liked to just be quiet and think things over. The best time for doing that, he'd found, was during a rain storm, when the ocean was loud and the rain thrummed on the roof, and the brilliance of the lightning reminded him of the power of his own thoughts. He liked the way the thunder rolled in the distance, like something playing at the back of your mind, and the way it rumbled closer and closer until suddenly it exploded, big and powerful and taking up the whole world. Understanding things, especially complicated things like people, was like that for him sometimes: rumbling around so far away that you hardly noticed it at first, then getting bigger and louder until all of a sudden it practically exploded in the front of his mind, the truth. Some of his best thinking had been done during thunderstorms.

So he lay on the rug in front of the balcony doors of the bedroom with his chin on his paws and watched rain bounce off the deck boards outside, thinking about things. He thought about sharks and hoofbeats, and things that chirped in the woods and made Grady draw his gun. He thought about pirates, and how some people could be both good guys and bad guys, which didn't make sense to him even though he knew it was undeniably true. He thought about the smell of fish and pine and how things weren't always what they seemed. He thought, though he didn't want to, about things that were buried.

He knew that part of their job, his and Aggie's and Grady's, was to figure things out. What he didn't understand, and maybe would never understand, was how they were supposed to do that when the good guys and the bad guys were so often the same person. It didn't seem fair.

Aggie came out of the bathroom in her night-shirt, smoothing moisturizer onto her arms and hands, to find Grady sitting up in bed, intently focused on the flickering of a video on his phone. The minute she came into the room he shut it down and put the phone aside, his expression changing from dark and brooding to easy welcome with such swiftness that it was startling.

"What're you doing?" Aggie asked.

"Just crap for work." He reached for her and added, "You smell good."

"Lilac and ginger."

Flash got up from the rug and jumped up on the bed to get a closer sniff of the lilac and ginger. It wasn't his favorite, and he jumped down again, stretching out on the rug by the balcony door where drifts of wild wet air occasionally forced their way through the cracks. He closed his eyes and relaxed into the storm, deciding that the best thing to do might be to just listen while Aggie and Grady figured things out. Sometimes it was easier that way.

Aggie got into bed and Grady ran his hands down her arms, gathering lotion on his fingers, then brought his hands to his face and inhaled deeply, rubbing the lotion on his face. She gave him an amused look as she pulled up the sheet. "You're going to smell like a girl."

"Can't think of anything I'd rather smell like." He drew her close and she rested her head on his shoulder.

"Fax me a copy of the ME's report when you get it tomorrow," she said.

"Will do. But it won't change anything. It was homicide, plain and simple."

She sighed, knowing he was right. "I guess."

Thunder rumbled and she snuggled closer. "I hope Bishop made it home okay."

Rain had started during dinner, but the storm hadn't moved in with force until an hour ago, bringing frequent bright lightning flashes and the kind of low rolling thunder that rattled the ill-fitting windowpanes of the old house in their frames. Grady reached for his phone and typed out a few words, showing her the text before he sent it. *Aggie says U OK?*

In a moment the phone buzzed back, and he showed her the reply from Bishop: *Go to bed.*

She smiled and smothered a yawn. "Hard day."

He kissed her head. "I'm so proud of you, baby."

She shook her head against his shoulder. "Don't be." She turned over, lying on her back, and looked up at him. "I couldn't have done it without Flash." Flash looked around and thumped his tail in acknowledgement. "And if Saunders had resisted, I couldn't have stopped him." She blew out a soft breath. "I'm still not one hundred percent, Ryan. Sometimes I wonder if I ever will be." She paused. "I forget things. I have a hard time putting things together. I'm slow. I didn't used to be." She looked up at him sharply. "And don't say I went back to work too soon."

"I didn't say that," he assured her. "I would never say that."

"Because I didn't. It's just that…everything is so hard."

"Why don't you hire a couple of off-duty deputies part time?" he suggested. "You know, just during the tourist season, to help out. I know three or four guys who'd jump at the chance."

She shook her head. "The council would never give me the money. They wouldn't even give me a lifeguard. Besides, I don't want them to think I can't do my job."

"There's no shame in asking for help."

She didn't answer.

He rubbed her shoulder gently. "You're not even six months post-op. Give yourself a break. You'll get there."

"What if I don't?"

"You'll still be the smartest woman I've ever met," he said. "And let's get real about this thing.

Even at half speed you're still a mile ahead of most people going full-on."

She reached up to link her fingers with his where they rested against her shoulder. "I love you. And I love my job. I just want to be able to do it."

He said, "Well, I'm glad one of us does."

"Does what?"

"Love the job. I swear to God, Aggie, I don't even know what we're supposed to be doing out there most of the time. What's the point?"

She shifted so she could look at him. "Is this about Briggs?"

She felt his muscles stiffen. "Maybe. A little. Damn it, he was my partner. I should have known. I should have…" His arm tightened around her shoulders. "I should have taken better care of you."

"You know nothing that happened was your fault." She placed a hand firmly on his chest and held his eyes steadily. "Nothing. None of us would be here if it weren't for you."

"I don't know, baby." Grady's voice was heavy. "Don't you think sometimes we're in the wrong business?"

"As opposed to what? Llama farming?"

"I could deal with that." He laced his fingers through hers, lining up their wedding bands side by side and watching the way the soft lamplight glinted off the gold. "Seriously, do you ever thinking about quitting?"

She replied without hesitation, "Never."

"You could go back to law school. Make a ton of money writing wills and handling divorces."

"I don't want to write wills and handle divorces." She looked up at him. "Are you trying to get me off the street, Ryan Grady?"

"Damn right I am. I'd like to get *me* off the street. It's crazy out there." He kissed her fingers. "What about when we have kids?"

"Not something we have to worry about for a few years," she reminded him.

"What I mean is…with both of us being cops, isn't that kind of like having both parents flying on the same plane?"

"I'm not going to quit, Grady. They'll have to fire me."

He squeezed her shoulder. "Nobody's going to fire you, babe." Then he mused, "I'd make a great stay-at-home dad. You should see me change a diaper, and I can pack a lunch and tie a hair ribbon like nobody's business."

She said, stifling a yawn, "Diapers, I'll believe. But your sister has boys. I don't see how you could have learned to tie a hair ribbon."

"I've been practicing," he assured her.

She chuckled softly into his shoulder. "Okay, Mr. Mom. You've got the job, as soon as you figure how we're going to live on one paycheck."

He sighed. "Right. That." Then he said, "I hate this classroom crap. I'm no good at it."

"You're just saying that because you don't want to do it."

"I'm saying that because one day I might have to work with one of the kids who was trained by me, and that scares the hell out of me."

She punched his ribs lightly. "Get over yourself, Grady. If you weren't the best man for the job, Bishop wouldn't have given it to you."

He kissed her and stretched out his hand for the lamp switch. "Night, baby."

She answered sleepily, "Good night."

Aggie felt, rather than saw, the light go out of the room, leaving a velvety blueness behind her eyelids that was punctuated, in a moment, by a sheet of lightning.

Grady said in a moment, "Hey, babe?"

"Hmmm."

"We still don't know where her stuff is. Backpack, phone…nothing turned up in the search of Jack's boat."

She sighed. "I know."

"It could be anywhere on that island. That's a lot of territory to cover."

"I know."

"Or it could be at the bottom of the ocean."

"I guess."

The words were barely a murmur, so Grady just smiled and said nothing else. He thought she was asleep when she said, "There wasn't a note on the dock yesterday. Captain Jack said he left one Sunday, but it was gone by the time we got there."

"Might have blown away."

"Or someone might have taken it."

"It's a public park."

"Yeah, I know. It's just that…"

"Go to sleep, baby. You're off duty."

She said, "Jack Saunders is a creep and a pervert and he makes me want to vomit in my mouth. But he did not bury that woman alive."

"Sleep," Grady repeated, and emphasized the command with a kiss on her forehead.

But Aggie was already asleep. It was Grady who lay awake for hours, listening to the thrum of rain on the roof and the roll of thunder in the background, until sleep finally overtook him and dragged him down again into the place of blood and terror from which, as hard as he fought, he knew he would never escape.

Chapter Eighteen

Tracy had been pouting for the last three hundred miles, scrunched up against the door, glaring out the window at the dead black countryside or pretending to be asleep whenever Steve spoke to her. She was mad because he hadn't told her about the gun. She was mad because he wouldn't tell her where they were going. She was mad because he refused to take the freeway to get there, creeping along instead at forty-five miles per hour along two-lane highways and backwoods country roads where, as he tried to explain to her, they were much less likely to encounter roadblocks or even state troopers. But mostly she was mad because he had left her backpack in the other car, back at Doug's New and Used Cars in Bracken, New Jersey. Steve was starting to think seriously about just pushing her out of the car and leaving her by the side of the road.

"My shampoo cost forty dollars a bottle," she informed him petulantly. "You can't just buy that stuff at Wal-Mart, you know."

He slammed his hand against the steering wheel and glared at her. "Are you shittin' me? Are you seriously busting my ass about *shampoo*?"

"What about my clothes?" she demanded. "I had a pair of Marc Jacobs sneakers in there! And the earrings my grandmother gave me for my birthday! And what am I supposed to do for bath products, can you just tell me that? Assuming I ever get to take a shower again." She slammed back against the seat, arms folded, lower lip pushed out. "First you take my phone, now you take everything else. I don't even have a lipstick!" And, as the full consequences of that struck her, her eyes suddenly swam with tears. "Oh, God. I don't even have lipstick!"

Steve made a hard right turn into the nearly empty parking lot of a CVS. The marquee sign said "Open Twenty-Four Hours" but, judging by the lack of activity inside the brightly lit space, most people in whatever small town they were in didn't care. Steve swung around to the back, as far away from the streetlight as he could get, and backed into a space across from the dumpster. He placed both hands on the steering wheel, stared straight ahead, and said, low in his throat, "Get your damn lipstick. And get a couple of Red Bulls while you're in there. And some chips or something. I'm starved. And listen, I need a screwdriver. We've got to switch out this tag before daylight comes."

She didn't move, just sat there with her arms folded, pouting. "I don't have any money."

"Since when did that ever stop you?" he shot back. "Besides, you've got money. I saw it."

"Not enough. You spent it all on gas and cigarettes and hamburgers."

He gave her a look that was filled with exasperation and impatience. "Don't you get it? It's almost over. By tomorrow night we'll never have to worry about money again, either of us. We'll be rolling in freaking money! Now will you get in there and get what you need before the cops in this one-horse hole in the ground wake up? And don't get caught."

But she just turned to look at him suspiciously. The colored lights of the store's marquee reflected from the pavement and shone across her face, making her look wicked, even a little witchlike, in the shadows of the car. It was not entirely unattractive. "What do you mean?" she demanded. "How much money? What are you talking about? Do you have a stash hidden away somewhere? Where is it? Did you rob a bank or something?"

"Jesus, what's with the questions?" he exploded. "No, I didn't rob a bank! Why would you say I robbed a bank? Jesus!"

"Well then, what were you in prison for? And what would somebody who just got out of prison be doing with money if he didn't rob a bank, huh? I'll bet you were never in prison at all."

"Maybe I went to prison for offing some blabbermouth girl that asked too many questions, did you ever think of that?"

She shrank back from him, her eyes flashing with tears and looking, briefly, so scared that he felt bad. He softened his voice, reaching across to caress her thigh. She jerked away. "Ah, baby, come on. Don't be like this. They put me in prison on a totally bogus wrap and I got out in two years, which only goes to show you it wasn't anything bad. I was selling stuff, that's all."

Her eyes went even bigger. "Drugs?"

"Not drugs." He seemed insulted by that. "*Stuff.* TVs, iPads, jewelry, that kind of thing. Only it turned out to be hot and I got busted, and it was totally bogus."

She looked at him skeptically.

"Here's the thing, baby." He edged closer, rubbing her thigh, giving her his most persuasive smile. "I've got this deal going now that's like nothing you ever even thought of, and when I say deal, I mean millions. *Tens* of millions, baby, can you dig that? All I've got to do is get some stuff—not even hot, totally legit—down to this guy I know in Mexico…"

She slanted a narrow-eyed glance at him. "You're sure it's not drugs?"

"Safer than drugs," he assured her, "easier than drugs. But the thing is, we gotta move *now.* And we gotta stay out of the way of the cops. Two more days, baby, that's all. So will you just give me a break and go get what we need so we can get out of here?"

She said, looking less scared and more interested now, "Mexico? I've never been there." She opened the door.

"Don't get caught," he cautioned her.

"I won't."

Steve gave her a few minutes, then eased the car around to the front of the building, lights off, so it would be easier to make a fast getaway when she came out. He saw her take out a bill to pay for the box of powdered donuts and the big shopping bag she had bought, smiling and chatting up the night clerk like she always did. The clerk put the donuts in the fabric shopping bag for her and handed her the receipt. She started toward the door, then slapped her forehead and turned back, like she'd forgotten the main thing she'd come for. Now she would go back and pick up the expensive stuff, slipping them into the bag one by one, and go back to the counter with something from the dollar aisle and pay for it, and the clerk would be so bedazzled by her tight shorts and cute smile that he wouldn't even think about the big shopping bag that was slung so casually over her shoulder. She was really good at this. Steve was glad he hadn't driven off and left her behind.

And then he saw the security camera.

CHAPTER NINETEEN

Flash and Grady began their day, as they usually did, with a run on the beach. Flash liked the way they started out in gray wet light and how, like magic, the day got lighter and lighter until the big yellow ball of the sun started flattening out at the edge of the sea, making the water sparkle and sending streaks across the sky. Flash had heard someone say one time that dogs couldn't see colors, which puzzled him. He saw magnificent colors all around him, and none more glorious than the sky at sunrise when he was running with Grady. He had finally come to the conclusion that people might not be able to see the same colors he did, which made him a little sad for them.

Grady didn't like to talk while they were running, which was okay with Flash. He and Grady had an understanding. Aggie liked to talk things over; Grady was more of the silent, thoughtful type. Sometimes it was good to just be quiet and do what you were doing; Flash could appreciate that. In fact, that was one of his favorite ways of being.

They paused briefly before leaving the beach to watch a helicopter bank out to sea, then took the path through the dunes that led to the street in front of their house. They splashed through puddles crossing the street and Grady paused outside their house to take off his shoes and dry Flash's paws with a towel they kept hanging on a hook for that purpose. The smell of bacon had been tantalizing Flash for three blocks and, sure enough, Aggie was scrambling eggs in a yellow bowl while bacon sizzled on the stove when they came into the kitchen.

"Five minutes," she warned Grady, and he grazed her lips with a kiss before bounding up the stairs.

"World's fastest shower," he called back.

Flash was already halfway finished with his eggs by the time Grady came back down, buttoning up his uniform shirt and glistening with shower water. He kissed Aggie again when she handed him his plate. "You look pretty," he said. "But what's with the…?" With a tilt of his head he indicated the wig. "I thought you said it was too hot."

She shrugged a little uncomfortably. "I don't know. I was too self-conscious. I just felt like everybody was staring at me."

"I know the feeling." He winked at her. "But you get used to it when you're good looking."

"How does it look out there?" she asked, bringing her own plate to the table.

Grady poured two cups of coffee and set one before Aggie's plate. "Not too bad," he answered.

"Standing water in the usual low spots. There was a Coast Guard chopper out."

"Oh yeah? I wonder what's up."

"Probably just maneuvers. I'll check it out when I get to work."

They sat down at the table next to each other, as was their custom, so that they both could see the television that was tuned to CNN in the living room, volume low. Aggie said, picking up her toast, "You look tired. Did you sleep okay?"

He shrugged. "The storm kept me awake."

Flash looked up from licking his dish. If Aggie had asked him, he could have told how Grady burst open the balcony doors at 4:30 a.m. and stood in the rain in his underwear, gasping and shivering until Flash had gone out and stood beside him, lending comfort. He could have told it, but, oddly, he was not sure he would have. It was one of those things that was understood between him and Grady. Maybe it had something to do with things that were buried; maybe it was just that people were unpredictable. He didn't know. He just knew that if Aggie had asked, and if he had been able to answer, as much as he loved her, he wasn't sure what he would have told her.

Fortunately, before she could ask, Grady said, "What does your day look like?"

"Pretty ordinary. I need to do some work on the budget, get a head start on the end of month reports. I thought I'd check on Roger Darby this morning." She took a forkful of eggs. "I want to ask him about that note, too, as long as I'm there." Before Ryan could point it out, she said, "I know it's not my case, but I'm curious. I need to do some follow-up on that water rescue, and…" Her phone buzzed and she took it out of her pocket, smiling as she read the message from Lorraine: *See U today?* She sent back a reply and said, "Lunch with Lorraine. Say, Ryan, how do you feel about redecorating the living room?"

"Does it involve a new 68-inch flat screen?"

"No, I don't think so."

"Then whatever you girls decide. Listen, I was thinking about taking JC out for a beer after work. You want to join us?"

"Yeah, maybe." Her attention was on the television. "Text me. And don't forget to copy me on the autopsy. Have you been keeping up with this?"

She gestured with her toast to the television where a reporter was saying, "…this disturbing video footage of a shooting at a CVS in Windham, Pennsylvania, in the early hours of the morning. As you can see, this man shoots out the video camera behind the main register but neglects the one in the pharmacy, which captured his companion, believed to be fifteen-year-old Tracy Sullivan, stripping the store shelves of various items. The man, who police have identified as twenty-eight-year old Steven Rider, a convicted felon recently released on parole, holds a gun on the cashier until he empties the cash register, and then shoots him three times, as you can see here. The two, who have been dubbed Bonnie and Clyde since they began their crime spree yesterday at a used car dealership outside of Bracken, New Jersey, got away with an undisclosed amount of cash."

Grady turned back to his breakfast and said, "Yeah, I think I saw a bulletin yesterday. The girl is only fifteen, hooked up with the dude online. They thought she'd been kidnapped at first, but doesn't look like it now."

Aggie said, biting into her toast, "And you really want to have kids?"

Grady winked at her. "Dozens."

"It's your job to keep them out of federal prison then."

"Fortunately, I'm trained to do just that."

Aggie gave a short shake of her head and angled the remote control to turn off the television. "If the video footage is so disturbing, why do they keep showing it over and over again? That's what I'd like to know."

Grady glanced at his watch. "Speaking of disturbing things, I'd better get going. I've got a bunch of knuckleheads across the bridge waiting for me to teach them how to make a routine traffic stop."

Aggie said, "There's no such thing as a—"

"Routine traffic stop, I know." He finished his coffee and wadded his napkin beside his plate. "Thanks for breakfast, honey," he said as he stood. "Dinner is on me."

"We're having leftover lasagna."

"I'll bring dessert, then."

She gave him an exasperated look. "Ryan, we're trying to eat healthy." She took their plates to the sink, adding grudgingly, "Maybe you could pick up some ice cream on your way home. Chocolate chip. No, salted caramel."

"You got it." He kissed her, tasting of coffee. "I love you."

"I love you, too." When one of the tools of your trade was a Glock semiautomatic, you always remembered to say that. That was one of the first things Aggie had learned when she had decided to share her life with someone else. "Be careful out there."

"Don't work too hard." He turned toward the door.

"Don't worry."

Grady dropped a hand to Flash's head on the way out, ruffling his ears. "Take care of my girl for me, bud," he said, just like he did every day.

Flash grinned up at him, assuring that he would do exactly that, just like he did every day.

No one, not even Flash, could have guessed how very unlike every other day this one was going to be. On the other hand, never knowing how a day was going to turn out was one of the things he liked most about his job.

CHAPTER TWENTY

Flash and Aggie did their usual morning patrol, stopping to tag a car that had been illegally parked overnight in the beachside parking lot, and to run the tag on another one that appeared to have been abandoned across from the church, but in fact had just run out of gas. The owner came staggering up with a gas can not long after his information came back clear, and Aggie and Flash helped him get his car started and sent him on his way. They got out of their patrol car at Beachside Park again when they saw One-Armed Billy pushing his bike up from the sand. Aggie stood beside the car with her arms folded in disapproval, sweating in the muggy air, but Flash waved his tail happily. Billy was wearing his big straw hat with red Christmas tinsel around the brim, and he smelled like peanut butter today. When he was close enough he tossed Flash a foil-wrapped miniature peanut butter cup. Aggie snatched it out of the air before Flash could catch it.

"Chocolate is bad for dogs," she said. "You know there's no camping on the beach, Billy."

He grinned at her, his front teeth smeared with chocolate. "You ever catch me camping?"

"If I ever do, it's a two-hundred-dollar fine," she said. "Have you got two hundred dollars?"

"No, ma'am," he admitted, "I don't. But if I did, I sure wouldn't be sleeping on the beach." And he cackled like that was the funniest thing he'd ever heard. Flash couldn't help grinning back, but Aggie didn't smile.

"Where'd you get the candy, Billy?" she asked.

"Same place I got the flowers," he replied proudly, twisting the rust-spotted handle of the bicycle this way and that to show off the plastic flowers tied to the basket. "Down at the dumpster on Twenty-Fifth. They sure do spruce up the old gal, don't they? Make her look brand new."

"In Ocean City?" Aggie winced. "Billy, I've told you, it's dangerous to ride your bike across that bridge, especially at night. Do I have to tell the sheriff's patrol to keep an eye out for you?"

"I got reflectors, don't I?" he returned, somewhat belligerently. "You told me to get reflectors, and didn't I go out and acquire me some?"

Aggie thought it was probably best for both of them if she didn't look too closely into how, exactly, he had "acquired" the reflectors. She returned the candy to him and said, "It's not a good idea to eat what you find in the dumpster, Billy. Why don't you go by the Open Pantry next door to the church? They have all kinds of food there, and it's free. All you have to do is ask."

"Yeah, and who's gonna cook it for me?" He stripped the foil off the peanut butter cup and popped it into his mouth. "Anyhows, I got plenty of food. Good stuff, too." He reached over his shoulder, fumbled in the pocket of his backpack, and drew out a stick of what appeared to be beef jerky. He offered it to Flash. "See? Not chocolate."

Just as Flash was about to take a step forward, Aggie held out a staying hand. "We've got to go, Billy," she said. "Try to stay out of the sun. It's going to be a hot one today."

"Don't you worry about me, Miss Chief," he replied, mounting the bike again. "I got it made in the shade." He cackled again mightily as the bike wobbled off.

Aggie shook her head as they got back into the car. "It takes all kinds, Flash," she said.

Flash thought that was one of the main things that made life so interesting.

Flash thought they would go back to the office then, but Aggie surprised him by turning left onto Island Road, which was the main road off and on the island via the bridge. They didn't cross the bridge, though. They went past the two-pump gas station with its attached quick-mart and adjacent liquor store, and turned right onto a sandy lane whose green street marker identified it as Pine Street. It took Flash a while to figure out why Aggie would want to go there.

Pine Street was a residential neighborhood of median-income families just across the bridge and barely, as some of the old-timers might observe spitefully, on the island at all. It was where you wanted to live if you worked on the mainland but couldn't quite afford the inland houses closer to the beach, or if you worked on the island and were willing to pay a little more in order to avoid the commute across the bridge every morning. Aggie's hairdresser lived in this neighborhood; so did the cable TV guy and the local UPS driver, both of whom worked across the bridge.

Roger Darby lived with his wife Shirley in a modest two-bedroom wood-sided cabin at the end of the street. It was surrounded by a grassy yard that was shaded by some of the tall pines for which the street was named. Both the grass and the flower beds that lined the driveway would look better in cooler temperatures, but it was otherwise a pleasant, well-maintained home. The siding was stained a deep brown and the windows were shaded by Bahama shutters in a lighter tan color. Two cars were parked in the under-house carport, a green Hyundai and a small, somewhat battered pickup truck. Aggie went up the stairs to the front door, which was painted tan like the shutters, and Flash went with her.

"Hi, Mrs. Darby," Aggie said when Shirley Darby opened the door. "I hope it's not too early. I wanted to stop by and see how your husband was doing."

Shirley Darby was a small, plump-faced woman with tightly curled, wren-brown hair and a big, warm smile that, on this day, showed the signs of anxiety and fatigue. Nonetheless, the smile only got bigger as she opened the door wide and gestured Aggie inside. "Chief Malone, how sweet. And you brought your dog."

Flash hesitated at the threshold. Aggie thought he was just being polite, which he tried to do whenever he remembered, and she said, "Is it okay if he comes in?"

"Oh my, yes." She made another big sweeping gesture with her hand. "Roger has done nothing but talk about how that dog saved his life."

Aggie came in and Flash followed, looking around carefully as he tended to do in strange places. It was a nice house, with sand-colored walls and a kitchen that was open to the living room, with blue countertops that matched the blue-flowered sofa. There was a coffee table in front of the sofa that was littered with small gold foil candy wrappers, and Shirley Darby hurriedly swept them away into her hand. "Sorry about the mess," she said. "They're Roger's favorite, but I'm afraid I sat here and ate almost the whole bag last night. You know how you do when you're stressed. Can I get you some coffee?"

"No thanks," Aggie said, "I won't stay. I was hoping I could talk to Roger for a minute, though, if he's awake."

"Oh." The other woman looked distressed, or at least as distressed as someone with her naturally buoyant personality could look, and her hand fluttered uncertainly to her throat. "Oh. I guess it would be all right. I mean, I could check. Please sit down, Chief."

She started to leave the room, then looked back. "It's just that…" She bit down on her lower lip, looking torn. "He's been so upset since that investigator told him about the dead girl. I found him up this morning before dawn, pacing up and down the deck, and to tell you the truth, I don't think he'd been to sleep. I'm really worried about him."

"My wife is always worried about me."

Aggie turned to see Roger Darby coming into the room from the hallway. The smile he gave his wife was weary but affectionate, and he added, "It's good to see you, Chief. Have a seat."

Roger Darby was in his early sixties; his hair was starting to thin and his shoulders were beginning to round, and today the pallor of his skin and the hollow dark circles beneath his eyes made him look much older. He was dressed in jeans and a tee shirt, but both looked as rumpled as though he'd slept in them. The back of his head had been shaved and was covered with a large gauze bandage.

Aggie took a seat on the blue-flowered sofa, saying, "I hope I didn't wake you. I probably shouldn't have come so early." Flash preferred to look around, and he did so cautiously.

Shirley fussed around her husband, trying to take his arm to lead him to a chair, but he waved her away. "No, I'm fine. Just a little headache. The doctors said I'd have one for a couple of days."

"Ten stitches," Shirley protested. "It took ten stitches."

He gave her a fondly tolerant look as he made his way across the room, moving stiffly. "This one," he said. "You'd think nobody's ever been hurt on the job before."

He lowered himself carefully into the chair across from Aggie while his wife hovered anxiously. He smiled up at her, squeezing her fingers in a gesture of reassurance. "Maybe some coffee, honey," he said. "Chief Malone?"

Again, Aggie demurred, and Shirley hurried off. The affection in Roger's eyes followed her. "That woman is the salt of the earth," he said, turning back to Aggie. "I don't know what I'd do without her. I don't like to see her so upset." His expression grew somber as he said, "Do you have any idea how something like this could have happened, Chief? Or who the dead woman was?"

Aggie didn't think it would further his recovery to share the details, so she avoided the question. She leaned forward, her hands clasped between her knees. "I know the state investigator already asked you this, but you didn't notice anything unusual on the island this summer? No sign of overnight campers, a boat that shouldn't be there?"

He said apologetically, "Like I said, I don't patrol every week."

"We think she'd been buried less than a week," Aggie said. "So whatever happened to her would have been recent. Are you sure you don't remember anything unusual?"

"I'm sorry. The usual hikers, picnickers. A few boats have been in and out, but this is the time of year for them. Some divers, bird watchers. You know I have a lot of area to cover here so I don't usually spend time talking to folks." He looked regretful, chewing his lip. "Maybe I should have."

"So you were there Monday, right? Picking up fees?"

He nodded hesitantly. "I usually get there about ten in the morning."

"Did you happen to notice a note pinned to the pier?"

He blinked, then frowned. "A note? What kind of note?"

"So you didn't see anything."

Flash came over and sat beside Aggie's feet, watching Roger Darby. His wife bustled around the kitchen, clattering cups, running water.

He said, "No. Should I have?"

She said, "It's probably nothing. We're just tracking down leads on who might have buried the woman."

"And what about the person who hit me?" he asked. "Any leads on that?"

"I'm sorry. We think the two things are connected, though. Maybe he was afraid you'd find the grave. You were off the path."

He murmured. "Right. That's probably it."

She said, "Why were you off the path? You never said."

He looked confused for a moment. "Oh. I heard something moving in the palmettos. I thought I told you that. It was probably the guy with the club. I must've walked right to him."

She nodded. "We had deputies searching the island until dark, but the best guess is that he got away before we got there."

"It doesn't seem right, that something like this could happen here." His voice was heavy. "I guess the world is changing."

"Well, the good news is," Aggie assured him, "so is police work. We can answer questions now we didn't even know how to ask ten years ago, so don't worry. That investigator who talked to you the other night? He's a little goofy, but Grady says he's the best in the state. We're going to find out what happened on that island, and we're going to get the guy who did this to you."

He said, "Do you think so?"

"Absolutely." She stood, and so did Flash. When Roger started to get to his feet she waved him to remain seated. "I've got to get back to work, Mr. Darby." She called into the kitchen, "Good-bye, Mrs. Darby. Let me know if you need anything."

Shirley Darby waved with one hand as she took a carton of milk out of the refrigerator. "Thanks for stopping by, Chief."

Roger said, "Chief, will you do me a favor?"

She inclined her head toward him, feeling bad about the anxiety she saw in his eyes.

"Can you let me know what you find out?" he asked. "I've got to tell you, I don't think I'm going to be able to sleep until I know what happened."

Aggie said, "Sure." Again she gave him a reassuring smile. "Take care. I'll be in touch."

They left the house, and Flash was glad to be out in the sunshine again. It wasn't that he disliked Mr. Darby—after all, Flash himself knew a thing or two about being hit on the head, or at least about being shot in the ear—but the smell of hospitals always made him feel bad. He didn't like to be reminded of the kinds of things that put people there.

When they were in the car Aggie sat there a minute, gazing at the house. "He's keeping something from us, Flash," she said. Her voice sounded sad. "I hate it when they do that."

So did Flash.

CHAPTER TWENTY-ONE

According to the Coast Guard, the report of an overdue vessel was first logged at 8:45 p.m. August 16. Offshore conditions were stormy, with swells ten to fifteen feet and frequent lightning. A cutter was deployed and an H-65 SAR helicopter was called in from Mobile. The search continued throughout the night. Coastal sheriff's departments in the Seventh Coast Guard District were notified and bulletins from those departments went out to the appropriate emergency response agencies. Grady didn't learn about it until 9:45 a.m.

"Every new recruit in the Murphy County Sheriff's Department will ride the road for the first two years of his employment here," Grady said, clicking through the PowerPoint presentation that had been boring when he'd sat through it himself ten years ago and hadn't improved much since then. "Ninety percent of this time will be spent on routine patrol, answering calls and responding to requests for assistance from a fellow officer." He clicked through another slide. "The types of calls we get most frequently here are, in order: motor vehicle

accidents, domestic disputes, larceny, assault." *Click.*
"The overall crime rate in Murphy County is 2.8
percent. Of this, less than one half of one percent
are violent." Click. "If you make ten arrests a month,
eight of them will be for DUI." He paused the computer and consulted his notebook for the names of
the recruits he hadn't quite gotten around to learn-
ing yet. "Addison," he said, picking the first one
he saw. "What is the policy of the Murphy County
Sheriff's Department regarding minor traffic violations for a driver with no previous violations in the
past three years?"

A young man shot to his feet. "Assuming the
violator has no outstanding warrants and does not
appear to be in violation of any other laws or ordi-
nances, federal, county or municipal, and gives
the law enforcement officer no reason to believe
a vehicle search is indicated, we give him a warning, sir."

Grady could barely repress a wry smile. He wondered whether the young man would still be showing that kind of enthusiasm after two years on the
road, including nights, weekends and holidays. He
wondered if he had ever been that eager.

He glanced at the notebook again. "Davis, what
is the definition of a minor traffic violation?"

Davis stood. "That would be one in which the
speed of the vehicle is not in excess of ten miles over
the speed limit, or as determined by road conditions, and doesn't present any immediate apparent
danger to life or property."

Grady started to click to another slide, then abruptly turned the projector off. "All right, new scenario. You're on patrol, word goes out that there is a manhunt in progress. You spot the vehicle in question on a two-lane road at nine p.m. in a sparsely populated area twelve miles from the county line. Traffic is light. What is the procedure?"

Hands shot up. He started to give it to one of female recruits, because he'd noticed that, in general, they gave the right answers almost twice as often as the males, and he thought it wouldn't hurt the rest of the class to be reminded of that fact. But at the last minute he changed his mind and said, "Brown, take your shot."

Sam Brown started to stand, looked at Grady nervously, and said, "Do you want me to stand, sir?"

A few grins went around the room, and Grady gave a dismissing wave of his hand. "Just tell us the procedure, Brown."

He cleared his throat, blushing a little. "I radio in my position and a description of the vehicle. I wait for instructions from my commander."

"Good," said Grady, remembering that Aggie had asked him to be nice. "Your instructions are to initiate takedown when you deem it safe. Backup is on the way. Four units are three minutes out." He nodded his head. "Go."

Brown said, "I initiate pursuit. Lights and sirens."

Grady's jaw tightened. "All right. Let's assume our criminal is also a good citizen who respects the law enough to pull over." A few more grins went around the room, and Brown's flush deepened. Grady said, "Now what?"

Brown said, "I turn on my takedown lights. I radio my position. I approach the vehicle."

Grady said sharply, "Where's your sidearm?"

"In my hands, sir, steadied on the target. I call for the suspect to exit the vehicle with his hands above his head." Brown paused, waiting for further instructions.

But Grady just nodded. He said conversationally, "Are you married, Brown?"

"No sir."

"Kids?"

Brown looked uneasy. "Um, no."

Grady said, "Well, I hope you've at least got a mama who loves you, because it'd be a damn shame if nobody claimed the body after we haul it all the way down to the morgue." His voice rose on the last word and he abandoned the attempt to sound even-tempered as he got to his feet. "Damn it to *hell*, Brown, you made about six mistakes just now, and every single one of them ends up with you being shot full of holes. Do you think this is a game? Do you think I'm standing up here every day trying to pound this stuff into your head because it's fun? Because I've got nothing better to do? I'm trying to save your life, for God's sake, and I'd appreciate the hell out of it if you'd at least do me the courtesy of meeting me halfway!"

Grady drew a breath to continue what he now recognized was well on its way to being a tirade when he saw, through the corner of his eye, the sheriff standing at the window of the training room door. Bishop raised his hand in a small beckoning gesture, and Grady clamped his teeth together. He said to the class, "There are twenty-seven citable traffic offenses that carry a fine of $150 or more. Find a piece of paper and list them all before I get back."

He left the recruits scrambling for a clean sheet of paper and he went out into the hall, closing the door behind him. He greeted Bishop with a forced and rueful smile. "Sorry about the language, Sheriff. Is there a penalty box?"

"There is," returned Bishop, unamused, "but somehow I get the feeling I'd be doing you a favor by putting you in it."

Grady's expression dropped into seriousness. "I'm not sure I was cut out to be a training officer."

"Too bad." Bishop looked him up and down, sternly. "You're the only one we've got." He jerked his head toward the classroom. "How much longer in there?"

Grady glanced at his watch. "Fifteen minutes."

"Good. John Evers is in court today, so I'll need you to sit in on the interview with Saunders. JC is going to be at the jail at ten thirty."

"Yes, sir. No problem."

Bishop started to leave, but turned back, remembering. "I thought you'd want to know," he said, "we got a bulletin from the Coast Guard this morning. Two island kids took their boat out yesterday afternoon and didn't come back. Name is McElroy. Do you know them?"

Grady stared at him. "Do you mean Brian and Mark McElroy?"

"That sounds right."

"Damn," Grady muttered, disturbed. "Yeah. I know them. They're both lifeguards, never met two better sailors. They won their class in the regatta two years straight. I can't believe it. Do you mind if I take a few minutes to call the Coast Guard station when I finish here, see what I can find out? I won't be late for the jail."

"Go ahead. Let me know if there's any news. We've got extra patrols along the coastline, and I'm sending the rescue boat to search the shore, but that's all we can do at this point." He paused, directed his glance again toward the classroom door, and added, "Take it down a notch in there."

Grady replied, subdued, "Yes, sir."

He went back into the room and closed the door.

CHAPTER TWENTY-TWO

Aggie and Flash got the news as soon as they walked into the office. Sally Ann's eyes were big as she handed Aggie the bulletin from the Coast Guard. "Do you think they're okay, Chief?" she said, her voice tight. "I mean, I just saw Mark last week on the way to work, and I can't believe...I mean, they were both such good swimmers...are, I mean. What I mean is, they're okay, don't you think, Chief?"

Mo, who was known to spend as little time in the cramped office as possible, even in the heat of summer, was waiting in front of her desk. "Sherriff's Department is patrolling the coast roads on the mainland, just in case they made it ashore that way," she reported. "I thought maybe you'd want to organize some volunteers to search the beaches."

Aggie looked up from the bulletin, and a single blink replaced the shock in her eyes with purpose. "That's a good idea, Mo. Start calling everyone on the volunteer lifeguard list, have them meet you at Beachside Park. Sally Ann, get me the Coast Guard station on the phone." She glanced again at the paper in her hand. "It doesn't say anything here about the location of their emergency beacon. They had to have deployed an emergency beacon."

But less than a minute later, after a brief but concise conversation with the commander of rescue operations, she learned that neither emergency beacon nor radio distress signals had been picked up from the missing vessel. At one point in the early morning hours the chopper's FLIR had picked up a heat signature some four miles off shore, but by the time their cutter reached the coordinates it was gone. For all intents and purposes, the boys had vanished.

Aggie hung up the phone, her expression troubled, and said, "Sally Ann, check Facebook and Twitter, see if either of the boys posted anything yesterday, and if so, what time."

Sally Ann spun her chair around to face her computer, already typing. "What about Instagram?"

"That's good, and what's that other one?"

"Snapchat?"

"Right. And start tracking down their friends, see if anybody talked to them yesterday. Mo, same for you."

Mo held up a hand of acknowledgment from behind her desk, still on the phone.

"I'm going to their house," she said, moving toward the door where Flash sat alertly, waiting for her. "I know this is a lost-at-sea, but for now we have to treat it like a missing person too. Call me if you get anything."

The Beach Walk community was one of the first so-called subdivisions on Dogleg Island, and ten years ago, when a spate of vicious hurricanes had made beachfront property undesirable, it had been the most prestigious area in which to live. The plan had been to install a golf course, which had turned out to be ecologically unfeasible, and build a country club which, without the golf course, had seemed pointless. So what had started out to be an exclusive gated golf community had ended up being mostly unsold lots, which was a bonus for those residents who'd chosen to build there anyway and who enjoyed the quiet island life. Ordinarily Aggie would not have guessed Walter McElroy and his sons to be the type who appreciated the isolation, but Brian had mentioned to her once that the only amenity they really cared about happened to be the one that had actually come to pass, and that was the canal, complete with private dock and boathouse, that ran behind their house. From it you could fish for mullet, seine for shrimp, or be sailing in the Gulf within ten minutes, according to Grady, who sounded a little jealous when he said it. Theirs was the only house on the canal, so they could come and go as they pleased, and the only thing beyond it was the lagoon.

The house itself was a white clapboard Cape Cod style, whose obvious signs of wear illustrated why modern builders now preferred the hulking concrete block, Mediterranean-looking monstrosities that were so common up and down the Florida coastline. The blue shutters were faded, the paint showed bare wood in places, and symmetrical rust spots indicated the placement of nails on the deck railing. An American flag, a little faded from the harshness of the Florida sun, hung limply from a tall pole atop the crow's nest.

All in all, it did not look like the home of one of the island's most prominent citizens.

The day was getting more and more steamy, and Aggie felt her shirt start to cling to her armpits the minute she got out of the car. Flash, impervious, jumped out behind her and raced to explore his environs. Aggie looked around for a moment, squinting in the sun, and then walked toward the house. Flash joined her just as Walter McElroy answered the door.

Aggie said, "I just got the Coast Guard notice about the boys. I want you to know that law enforcement will be working closely with Search and Rescue to try to pinpoint their last known location. May I come in and talk to you for a moment?"

Walter McElroy looked haggard in a rumpled shirt and khakis. His eyes were bloodshot and his face shadowed with a grayish bristle of beard. He opened the door wider, and Aggie and Flash stepped inside a room that was chilled with air-conditioning and seemed dark after the brightness of the sun. When Aggie's eyes adjusted she couldn't help noting that this was definitely a bachelor's home: wood paneling, leather recliners, a wicker sofa and chair upholstered in a well-worn orange tropical print. It smelled of stale coffee and recycled sweat.

McElroy said, "Chief, I appreciate you coming by." His voice sounded hoarse, weary beyond defeat. "I've been at the Coast Guard station all night, just got home an hour ago. I told them everything I know. I don't see how you can help."

Aggie started to say something officious about multi-agency endeavors, land, air and sea, about no clue being too small, about every resource being deployed. But then she looked into the eyes of a brokenhearted father and she said, gently, "Mr. McElroy, I won't pretend to know how you feel. I worked with both of the boys and consider them friends. My brother-in-law was their coach. My husband helped train them. I want you to know we're all here for you. Just let us know what you need."

Walter McElroy's shoulders sagged, and he actually seemed to stagger a bit, the way a person would when he'd been carrying around an extra weight and was suddenly relieved of it. He said, a little hoarsely, "Thank you." He gestured abruptly to the sofa. "Can I get you coffee?"

Aggie started to refuse, then remembered how comforting the gestures of routine hospitality could be. She said, "Thank you. That would be great."

Aggie looked around the room while Walter went to the kitchen, and so did Flash. There were built-in bookshelves flanking the big-screen television, and they were decorated mostly with framed photographs of the boys. A few showed them as children, with a pretty woman Aggie had to assume was their mother. Almost all were nautical in nature, featuring the boys on boats, holding up fish they'd just caught or swim medals they'd just won, standing beside their surfboards or posing in their dive gear. Aggie recognized the picture she'd taken with Flash and Brian in the lifeguard stand. Flash was sitting in the lifeguard chair, watching the water, and Brian was standing beside the stand, wearing his reflective glasses and signature white baseball cap, grinning at the camera. She spent a little more time studying the next photograph, puzzling over what it was that seemed familiar to her. She recognized the boys as teenagers standing on the deck of a ship surrounded by ten or fifteen crew members, all of them mugging for the camera. It was one of the young men standing next to them that she recognized; she was sure she had seen him around here before but couldn't place him.

Walter came back into the room with two mugs of coffee in his hands. "Sorry," he said, "I should have asked if you wanted cream or sugar."

Aggie took the mug he offered. "Black is fine." She looked back at the photograph. "Was that taken around here?"

"No. We used to vacation in Maine every summer when the boys were younger. That's where they learned to dive. That was taken onboard the *Hialea*, a salvage ship they worked on a couple of summers. I say worked. It was more like volunteered. But they loved it. Who wouldn't? Well, if you were a teenage boy who loved the water the way those two did. Do." He took a gulp of coffee. "I'm sorry. I'm rambling."

She said, "Do you know who the other people in the photograph are?"

"No, I never met them. The boys would go out to sea six weeks at a time. They probably mentioned some names, but I don't remember."

She directed his attention to a copy of the picture of Mr. Brunelli presenting the check to the mayor she had seen in the museum yesterday. "Pete was telling me yesterday how much you and Mr. Brunelli had done for the island. I never knew before."

He made a low disgusted sound in his throat. "What a joke. I don't even know why I keep that picture. That man ruined my career. He fired the firm two months after that picture was taken. No reason, just because that's what billionaires do. Of course, the partners blamed me, let me go the next week. They paid me off with a big severance check, but it wasn't enough to retire at forty and put two boys through Ivy League schools, that's for sure. Everybody thinks Brunelli is such a hero. He's just a self-centered jerk with too much money."

Aggie said, "Where is the boys' mother?"

"She died when they were in junior high," he said. "Icy road, drunk driver."

"I'm sorry," Aggie said, sitting on the wicker sofa. "It must have been hard, raising them alone."

"They're good kids," he said gruffly. "Always have been."

He seemed to notice Flash for the first time and looked surprised. "Oh," he said. "Your dog."

Flash came over to Walter and offered his head for stroking. He had learned from Aggie that diplomacy was a tool, just like the radio in their patrol car or the handcuffs and gun and Taser Aggie wore on her belt. And sure enough, Walter McElroy seemed to soften a little as he patted Flash's head, and even smiled, though tiredly. "I've got a picture of him over there on the shelf," he told Aggie.

"I know," Aggie said. "I was just looking at it."

McElroy let his hand drop, and Flash went back to Aggie, sitting beside her on the floor. Walter McElroy took the leather recliner opposite her but did not relax into it. Instead he sat stiffly near the edge, his hands wrapped around the coffee mug, waiting for her to speak. Aggie tried to put him at ease. "I'm sorry we haven't had a chance to get to know each other before this, Mr. McElroy. It seems as though I've known the boys since I moved to Murphy County, but until you joined the town council, I don't think you and I had ever met."

He didn't answer.

She tried again. "You're from New York originally, right?"

"New Jersey." His tone was curt. "Look, Chief, I know you're trying to be nice, but my kids are missing and I just can't make small talk. If there's anything you can do to help, great. If not, I really just came home to shower and change clothes. I need to get back in case…" He drew a sharp breath. "I want to be there when they find them."

Aggie said, "I understand. The Coast Guard will call you the minute anything changes. They'll also call me," she pointed out gently, but firmly, "and the sheriff's department. We're all working together on this."

He nodded, lifted his cup to drink, and then lowered it again without tasting the contents. "What do you need from me?"

Aggie said, "Can you tell me when you saw them last?"

"They were getting ready to take the boat out yesterday morning when I left the house. I don't know what time they actually got underway. I told the Coast Guard."

"Did they tell you which direction they were heading?"

He shook his head. "There's no reason they should. They're out on that boat just about every day they have off. I had a golf date yesterday morning after the council meeting. I didn't get home until after one. The boat was gone by then."

Aggie said, "Did you hear from them at all yesterday?"

His lips tightened. "They're grown men. Just because they live here doesn't mean they report to me twenty-four seven."

Aggie said gently, "I'm just trying to get an idea of the time line."

He squeezed his eyes closed briefly in a gesture of regret and gave a short shake of his head. "I've been up all night. I know you're trying to help, but I can't even think straight right now. I didn't hear from the boys yesterday. I'm doing some legal business for Wright-Harris Boat Yard, and I had a meeting with them across the bridge at three. Afterwards I met some friends for cocktails and dinner. I got home about eight, but neither one of them were here. To tell the truth, it took me about fifteen minutes to even think to look for the boat. It had started storming around dark, and it never occurred to me they would still be out. I tried calling them, got voice mail. They didn't answer my texts. After about the sixth or seventh try, I had to admit something was wrong. I called the Coast Guard." He looked at her with eyes that were filled with dread. "Is it true they call off the search after twenty-four hours?"

"No," Aggie said firmly, "it's not. There's absolutely no reason to think the boys didn't just have radio trouble, or get off course somehow. They may have even made it to shore somewhere up or down the coast, which is why we're also searching on land. But unless we have some idea what time they left or where they were headed...well, there's an awful lot of ocean out there. I was hoping one of them might have called a friend, or sent a text or an e-mail, anything that might have a time stamp on it. We're trying to track down some of their friends now, but if you can give me a more complete list, it would be a big help."

He said, "I can try. But everyone keeps their address book on their phone these days...I can try."

"What about girlfriends? Was either of the boys seeing anyone in particular?"

"No. Mark was seeing some girl who was down here on vacation earlier this summer, but I don't think they kept in touch. Brian dated a girl in graduate school, but it started to cool off this summer. I haven't heard him talk about her in over a month."

"Still, if you could find the names and phone numbers of the girls they were seeing, it could be a help."

He rubbed his thumb across his forehead, as though trying to massage a weary brain. "Yes. Okay, I will."

"When you came in yesterday afternoon, or even last night after you got home and realized they weren't back yet," Aggie suggested, "did you look for a note? Maybe an e-mail telling you what time they planned on being back?"

His eyes reflected a mixture of frustration and regret. "No. No, we don't do that kind of thing. Look, I didn't tell them where I was going yesterday either, okay? We keep different schedules, if I need to know where they are, I call them and they do the same. They're twenty-six years old, Chief. When I was twenty-six, I'd been married two years and was already handling million-dollar accounts. I don't keep tabs on them. Jesus."

He drew in a sharp breath and ran his fingers over his face. When he looked at her again his expression was bleak. "You think you're a good parent. You think you're an ordinary family. Then something like this happens and the police are asking you questions you can't answer and you realize you were doing everything wrong, you don't even know your own kids." He blew out a helpless breath. "What is ordinary, anyway?"

Aggie gave him a moment of sympathetic silence. Then she said, "They're good kids, smart kids. You should be proud of them. You have nothing to feel guilty about."

He didn't reply, so she said, "Do you know if there was a particular place they liked to dive?"

He looked startled. "What?"

"My husband said there were some wrecks around here that divers like to explore," she said. "Maybe they mentioned one to you?"

He shook his head. "No. No, I don't think the boys have been diving all year. They used to like it, but lost interest I think. Who knows why?"

Aggie said, "Did you check their computers? There might be something there that could help."

He said, "Mark keeps everything on his phone, but Brian has a laptop he uses for schoolwork. I'll get it."

Aggie put her untasted cup of coffee on the coffee table and followed him up the stairs, Flash close by her side. She felt a stab of sympathy when she saw him hesitate outside the door of the open room, and then square his shoulders before entering.

It was much the kind of room Aggie might have expected from a young single man living with his parents. There were posters on the walls instead of art, most of them of underwater scenes. The bed was covered with a navy blue corded spread and flanked by bookshelves that held a variety of things besides books—souvenir beer mugs, old license plates, a baseball glove and a soccer ball, to name a few— and the matching dresser and desk were equally well worn and cluttered. Aggie did not see a laptop computer. She didn't see a television set or any other electronics, either, which struck her as a little odd. Brian seemed to be a young man of relatively spartan tastes.

Walter opened drawers, searched the closet, looked in the nightstand and under the bed. Flash sniffed around the room himself but didn't find anything of interest at all, so he returned to Aggie. Walter muttered, "I'm sure he kept it on his desk. I saw it just the other day."

He went across the hall to what was presumably Mark's room and performed the same search, but also came up empty.

"Maybe in his car?" suggested Aggie.

Walter gave a short shake of his head. "He rides a motorcycle, a street bike, no room for saddlebags. Mark uses a moped to get back and forth to work."

Aggie said, "Could he have taken it with him?"

"On a boat?" Walter frowned. "That doesn't make sense."

He hesitated, sighed, and ran his hand through his thinning hair. "There's another possibility," he said. "He might have sold it."

Aggie looked at him, puzzled.

His lips tightened. "We've been letting go of a lot of things lately. The jet ski, the Land Rover, both the boys' cars. Things have been rough since the crash. I had to refinance the house, we've been living on savings, even took the Florida bar exam so I could start seeing clients again. But too little too late, I guess. This year..." He swallowed hard. "This year I had to tell Brian I couldn't keep up the tuition on graduate school. He took it pretty hard. He's been trying to get a teaching job, but no luck. He sold a lot of stuff on eBay this summer for spending money. The laptop was a nice one; he might have done the same with it."

Aggie didn't know what to say. It was hard to feel sorry for someone who thought hardship was having to sell three of his cars and a jet ski, and whose "poverty" vehicle was still nicer than the one she drove when she was off-duty. But it only proved how hard it was to know what was really going on beneath the surface of another person's life, and it wasn't her place to judge.

She turned toward the stairs. "Don't worry about the laptop, Mr. McElroy. We're checking social media and talking with the boys' friends and coworkers. I'll let you know the minute we find out anything helpful. The lifeguards are already rallying at Beachside Park to comb the beaches in case they come ashore that way. They're both sturdy seamen. I have every reason to believe in a good outcome. "

He nodded stiffly and opened the door for her.

Aggie turned to shake his hand. "Try to get some rest, Mr. McElroy. I'll be in touch."

"Thanks for coming by, Chief." He shook her hand without much enthusiasm. "I'd appreciate it if you wouldn't repeat what I mentioned about the financial situation. In a small town like this...well, things can get blown out of proportion."

She gave him what she hoped was a reassuring smile, but couldn't help wondering why, at a time like this, concern about his financial reputation would even cross his mind. Clearly the rich—or the formerly rich—inhabited an entirely different world from her own.

As far as she was concerned, that was just fine.

CHAPTER TWENTY-THREE

Aggie called as Grady was logging in his weapon at the jail. He held up a finger for patience and stepped away from the window to take the call. "Hey," he said. "I called the office and Sally Ann said you were at McElroy's. How is he?"

"Not good," she said. "Anything I should know?"

"The Coast Guard had a report about half an hour ago from a fisherman who might have seen their boat yesterday afternoon about six miles southwest of Dogleg."

"Southwest? What's out there?"

"Nothing but open sea," he replied grimly.

Her silence was heavy. "Nobody's been able to raise them on the radio or on their phones," she said. "That's not good, is it?"

"Not the best," he admitted. "But their phones could be out of range or damaged in the storm. And we don't even know if their radio was working before they left."

Aggie said, "Sally Ann is checking social media to try to get an idea of what their day was like yesterday."

"That's a good idea."

"Any chance they might have weathered the storm onshore somewhere?"

"The Coast Guard combed the shore last night. If they were anchored anywhere near here they would've been spotted."

She sighed. "God, I hate this."

"Me, too, babe." Then he said, "Look, I'm at the jail. I've got to hand over my phone, JC is waiting for me."

"Are you talking to Saunders?"

"Yeah."

"Let me know if you find out anything."

"Same for you." He started to disconnect when something occurred to him. "Hey, Chief, you should check with Pete. One of the kids might've said something to him about where they liked to dive."

"On my list," she replied. "I doubt it though. Their father said they hadn't been diving all summer. If that's what they were doing yesterday, it must have been a spur of the moment thing."

"Bad timing, if it was," he said. Then, "Gotta go."

"Later," she said.

He disconnected and passed his phone through the window to the impatient-looking clerk. JC was waiting for him on the other side of the security door.

"We are cloaked in righteousness and well able to defeat the enemies of the Lord," JC greeted him. He was dressed today in baggy shorts, sandals, and another bright tropical print shirt, the green canvas messenger bag worn across his body like a bandolier. "Are you ready to answer the call of battle, my friend?"

Grady said, "You know something, JC? Half the time I think you just make this crap up."

"Half the time," agreed JC amiably, "you'd be right."

They started down the corridor to the interview rooms. This part of the building, away from the inmate population, housed mostly administrative offices and, except for the concrete block walls and metal doors, wasn't that different from the sheriff's office a few blocks away. It even had the same smell of coffee and microwave dinners that clung to the walls Grady had just left.

"So," JC said, "Thanks to your lovely spouse—a far, far better woman than you deserve, by the way—we have a preliminary profile of the victim." He took some papers from his bag and passed them to Grady. "Meet Kayleigh Carnes, twenty-three, teaching assistant at UNC Raleigh. We notified the family; they're on their way down."

Grady frowned at the picture of the pretty, dark-haired young woman who smiled at him from the student ID photo at the top of the page. "Damn," he said. "That's young."

"'You have cut short the days of his youth,'" replied JC somberly. "'You have covered him with shame.' Didn't make that one up."

Grady said, "So what's the covered with shame part?"

"For one thing, she lied to her family about what she was doing this summer. They thought she was staying on campus, working on her dissertation," JC said. "For another, she lied to her professor about where she was going. She was supposed to be doing some kind of research project in the Outer Banks."

"Where there really *are* wild horses," Grady observed. "At least that explains why nobody reported her missing. Any idea why she would lie?"

"Grant money, her professor thinks. The competition is pretty fierce and money tends to go to the people who are discovering something new, not just studying what somebody else has already discovered. And since it's illegal to set up any kind of permanent research station without a permit, and since you can't get a permit without evidence that there's something there to research..." He shrugged. "Catch 22."

"Jesus," Grady muttered. "That's a pretty stupid thing to get yourself killed over."

"My guess is she didn't plan that part."

Grady flipped through the pages. "Did you e-mail this to me?"

"I did, with a courtesy copy to the good Chief Malone. By the way, are you working this case, or what?"

"Kind of," Grady replied uncomfortably. "It's complicated."

"Well," JC said, undeterred, "if you were working the case you'd probably be interested to know that we've been pinging her phone for two days and we've got nothing. Which means it's either dead or..."

"At the bottom of the ocean," Grady said.

"That'd be my guess," said JC. "And *that* means that unless we can get a confession from Saunders, here, this investigation is pretty much dead in the water. So to speak."

"Not going to happen," Grady said.

"How come?"

"He didn't do it."

"Are you sure about that?"

"No," replied Grady. "But Aggie is."

JC paused outside the interview room to give Grady a speculative look, then he flung open the door. "Captain Jack Saunders," he declared to the unshaven, disgruntled-looking man who was scowling at them from the other side of the wooden table that bisected the small room. "'For all have sinned and come short of the glory of God,'" he pronounced, "and, you, my friend, have come shorter than most."

He dropped his satchel on the table and pulled out a chair with a loud scrape. Then he sat down, swung one sandaled foot up onto the tabletop, and folded his hands across his chest, regarding the other man companionably. Saunders's belligerence became slightly mitigated with uncertainty as he took JC's measure. Grady, watching the show from a few feet away, hid a smile behind his knuckles as he pretended to rub his nose.

"My name is Jim Clark from the Criminal Investigations Division of the Florida Department of Law Enforcement," said JC pleasantly, "and I'd like you to keep one thing in mind. The wages of sin is death. Let's hope it doesn't come to that for you. Now, let's talk."

Sally Ann looked up from her computer when Aggie and Flash came in, her expression both regretful and puzzled. "I've checked all of Brian's and Mark's social media," she said. "They haven't posted anything since Tuesday, either one of them."

Flash helped himself to a long drink of water, then found his place on the cool linoleum beneath Aggie's desk. Aggie squeezed around her desk to get to Sally Ann's, looking over Sally Ann's shoulder at the screen. "That's odd, isn't it?" she said. "I mean, don't most kids post something somewhere at least once a day?"

"Oh, a lot more than that," Sally Ann assured her. "Brian posted two or three pictures a day on Facebook alone, and Mark used to send out a couple of Tweets an hour."

"What kinds of things did he say?" Aggie asked absently, using Sally Ann's mouse to scroll down Brian's time line.

"Stupid things. Jokes, mostly. Brian tweeted things like weather conditions and pictures of girls on the beach."

Aggie frowned a little as she straightened up. "That's funny. Brian didn't post anything about the rescue Tuesday. You don't make a save every day. Looks like that would have made the cut."

Sally Ann reached for her message pad. "That reminds me. That Elizabeth Singleton returned your call while you were gone. And this came in from the FDLE."

She handed Aggie a stack of papers, and Aggie nodded as she glanced at them. "Kayleigh," she said. "Saunders said it was something with a 'K.'" She took the papers over to her desk.

"Do you want me to get Ms. Singleton on the phone?"

Aggie glanced up from her reading, blinking. "Who?" Then, "Yes, sure. And get a twenty on Mo, will you? I need her back in town as soon as the volunteers are dispatched. We can't leave the town unprotected, and..." She had to pause, remembering that Brian was the person she would have ordinarily trusted to head up a project like this. She finished simply, "One of the more experienced guards can head up the search."

Aggie brought up the Coast Guard website on her computer and scanned for updates. Finding none, she turned back to the report on Kayleigh Carnes. Twenty-three years old, originally from Asheville, an environmental anthropology and eco-studies major at UNC. Aggie flipped a page, looking for the autopsy report.

"Chief?"

Sally Ann held up the receiver of the phone, and Aggie punched a button on her own desk set, bringing her focus back to the present. "Ms. Singleton? This is Chief Malone from the Dogleg Island Police

Department. We're just doing a follow-up on the incident at the beach Tuesday afternoon."

"Oh." The woman sounded both puzzled and relieved. "Oh, yes, that's nice of you. I'm fine, thank you. I drove back home yesterday, didn't get your message until late last night or I would have called back sooner. It really was just a scratch, I told that young man not to make a fuss, but he was so nice, insisted on calling an ambulance."

"Well, I'm sorry your vacation here was ruined, but I'm glad to hear our people took such good care of you." Aggie glanced through JC's telephone interview with Kayleigh Carnes's advising professor. Conscientious, dedicated, ambitious. "I was just curious—you talked to the editor of our paper, Mr. Krieger, right? And you told him you thought it was a shark attack?"

She laughed a little. "Goodness, no, I never thought it was a shark. I didn't know what I bumped into in the water, but it was the lifeguard who said he thought it was a shark. I thought he was joking at first because anybody could tell the cut on my leg didn't look anything like a bite. But then everybody started talking about a shark and people started running out of the water and...well, you know how panic spreads. But I never thought it was a shark."

"The lifeguard?" Aggie took her attention off the report for just a moment, frowning. "You're sure that's who it was?"

"Like I said, I thought he was joking. But he was very nice. Really thoughtful and concerned."

Aggie absently turned to a page in the report filled with pictures, trying to make sense of what Elizabeth Singleton had said. The photos had apparently been taken from Kayleigh's student page, and each one was carefully labeled, including the names of everyone who appeared in each photograph. Asterisks noted the names JC had already interviewed. He was thorough. There she was receiving an award of some kind, there she was with her volleyball team, there she was in the airport with a group of other students preparing for a field expedition to Greece. Aggie started to turn the page. "Thank you, Ms. Singleton..."

She stopped, looking at the picture of Kayleigh at the airport. Jeans and hiking boots, dark hair braided beneath a cowboy hat, and a backpack swung over one shoulder. She stared at it.

"...for your cooperation," Aggie finished quickly. "I hope you'll come visit us again soon. Good-bye."

"Mo says she's on her way back to the office," Sally Ann started to report.

"Get her back on the radio," Aggie said. "Tell her to find One-Armed Billy and bring him in. And make sure she brings his bicycle too."

CHAPTER TWENTY-FOUR

JC had coffee brought in for himself and Grady—after first offering to do the same for the interviewee—and, after tasting it, declared himself ready to stay at this the rest of the day. The interview had already gone on an hour and a half, and Saunders was showing signs of wear.

"You can't hold me here forever," Jack Saunders challenged, working up to a righteous anger which, considering his circumstances, would be difficult to achieve. "Not without charging me, you can't. Twenty-four hours, that's all you get. Everybody knows that."

"Actually," replied Grady pleasantly, "it's forty-eight. Also, you have been charged. We just haven't charged you with the murder of Kayleigh Carnes. Yet." He glanced at JC, sipping his coffee. "I love a perp who knows a little bit about the law, don't you?"

"They're so much more interesting to talk to," agreed JC. "They always have something informative to say."

Saunders glared at Grady. "You know I didn't kill that girl. I didn't kill nobody. You know that."

"Honestly," Grady said, his gaze level, "I don't know whether you killed her. But so far you haven't told us anything to make us think you didn't."

"So here's a theory," JC said, leaning back in his chair with his hands folded behind his head. "You delivered the young lady to the island on July 31, just like you said. She called you up, ordered the supplies just like you said. Only she *didn't* pay in advance, like you said." He glanced at Grady. "How about that?"

Grady nodded thoughtfully. "I like it."

"So you went and did her shopping for her, drove all over town in the heat, probably had to go across the bridge…" He glanced questioningly at Grady.

"Oh yeah," Grady assured him. "Those MREs came from Outback Outfitters, and they're not cheap either."

JC nodded. "Hell of a lot of trouble. So you get it all packed up and loaded on your boat, use your own gas to haul it over to the island on a Sunday morning—might even have missed a charter or too, who knows what that cost you?—and when you get to the dock she's there waiting to take delivery of the stuff, only she's not quite so ready to pay for it. Maybe she doesn't have the cash, maybe she thinks you charged too much—where did you say the receipt was, again?"

"I told you, I lost it." Saunders sounded less angry than uneasy now.

JC shrugged and picked up his coffee cup. "Doesn't matter. Now, you claim you tried to deliver the goods, but she never showed so you left a note nailed to the dock. The problem is, our park ranger, the one you knocked over the head when he came snooping around day before yesterday—and I've got a theory about that, too, don't let me forget—anyway, according to this text I got from Chief Malone, the park ranger, who's very good at his job and who came by to collect the fees the very next day, didn't see a note. Maybe some tourist took it, though I can't think why anyone would. More importantly, our ranger didn't see any sign of a young woman pacing the dock waiting for a delivery of much-needed supplies, so I'm thinking—well, I have to think—that while you two were arguing about money on Sunday, maybe there was some grabbing and shoving going on, a little slip and fall, she hit her head, you thought she was dead. Only she wasn't. She didn't die until she was buried under two feet of dirt, too weak to dig herself out or even know what was happening to her. Maybe she tried to scream for help, we'll never know. Because she choked to death in her own grave, and this is where the tragedy comes in: if you had just left her there, if you had just walked away, she'd probably be alive today and you wouldn't be sitting here talking to me about murder charges, am I right, Captain Grady?"

Grady nodded. "Very likely."

JC sipped his coffee. "So then I figure you got to stewing about it, worrying maybe you'd left evidence behind, so the next day you went back, which happened to be the same day my man Grady here, conscientious citizen that he is, called in the park ranger about illegal campers. Well, that's when it all starts to go downhill for you. Maybe the park ranger gets a little too close for comfort, or maybe you were afraid he'd seen something, so you take a swipe at him with the club and leave him for dead. And he might've *been* dead by the time anybody found him if Captain Grady and his wife hadn't come back. I'm sure you didn't count on that."

Saunders sneered. "You got it all figured out, ain't you? Only one problem with your theory. I didn't come back Monday. Anybody could've seen my boat if I had've and it wasn't docked at Wild Horse, now was it, *Captain?*"

Grady pretended to think that over. "You have a dinghy, don't you, Saunders? I'm pretty sure I've seen it. And there were signs that a small boat had been pulled up onshore on the leeward side of the island when we got there."

Saunders looked disturbed by this information, and JC pressed his advantage. "The only thing I don't understand," he said, "and maybe you can help me with this, Mr. Saunders, is why you went to all the trouble to drag her body into the woods when you could have just dumped it off the dock. Mind explaining that for me, Mr. Saunders?"

"No, I can't explain that to you because that's not the way it happened," Saunders replied angrily.

JC smiled. "Just how did it happen, then, sir?"

"I told you I didn't do it! You can sit here and come up with your fancy-ass theories all day long, but that don't mean shit in a court o'law!"

"Well, sir," admitted JC with a sigh, "you're right about that." He closed the cover on the legal pad upon which he had been doodling elaborate abstracts of flowers and animals and skyscrapers. "I guess you and I just wasted all those years in law enforcement school, huh, Grady? Clearly we don't know anything about the law."

"I guess," agreed Grady. "Of course, one good thing came out of all this." He sipped his coffee, his eyes cool. "We got a worthless perverted freak off the streets, and for my money the children of Murphy County are safer for it."

"You can't pin that on me!" Saunders flared. "You got nothing on me! That was illegal search and seizure! What a man does in the privacy of his own home is his business! You think I don't know my rights? You got nothing!"

The door opened and both lawmen looked around as a deputy approached the table.

"Excuse me, sir," he said, "but Chief Malone is on the phone."

Grady started to rise, but the deputy turned to JC. "She asked me to give you a message. She said…" He took his notebook from his pocket and read, "Ask Saunders what color Kayleigh's backpack was."

JC inclined his head toward Saunders. "Well?" he invited.

Saunders scowled. "I don't have to tell you anything. I'm tired of answering questions. You can talk to my damn lawyer."

JC opened the legal pad again and made a note. Grady, sitting next to him, could tell that the note was nothing more than a drawing of a floppy-eared dog with off-center eyes. JC said to Saunders, "Didn't you say you had a boat moored at the pier on Dogleg Island?"

Saunders returned a suspicious look. "So?"

JC glanced at Grady. "Is anyone watching that boat?"

Grady replied, "Not to my knowledge."

"It'd be a shame if anything happened to that boat," said JC, "especially since he's going to need it to bond out of here."

"To tell you the truth," replied Grady, "once word gets out about this whole child porn thing, there's no telling what people might do. Of course, if anything *were* to happen, the sheriff's department would conduct a very thorough investigation." Grady sipped his coffee. "Once we got around to it."

Saunders glared at them. Silence ticked on. The deputy stood by, waiting to write down the reply.

"Pink," spat out Saunders angrily at last. "Tell her the damn backpack was pink."

CHAPTER TWENTY-FIVE

Flash watched as Aggie, wearing a pair of plastic-smelling blue gloves, unpacked the contents of Billy's pink backpack and laid them out on the desk, one by one. Mo took pictures with a camera that flashed every time she pressed the button, and occasionally Aggie laid out a ruler on the desk beside something and lined it up. Billy hovered anxiously by the door, saying, "That's my stuff. You said if I found it I could keep it, Miss Chief, you always said that. Be careful with my stuff. It's mine." The whole room smelled like him, which was just fine with Flash, but occasionally Sally Ann would dab at her nose with a tissue and breathe through her fingers.

Aggie said, "Don't worry, Billy. We're not going to break anything. We just want to make sure we get pictures. Are you sure you don't want a sandwich or something?"

"I should get my bike," he fretted. "I can't just leave my bike. I should go get it."

"Your bike is fine," Aggie replied. She pulled out a bag half-filled with foil wrapped miniature peanut butter cups, which Flash noted with interest, and placed it on the desk. "No one is going to steal it from in front of the police station. Besides, I can see it from the window. Do you want to stand over here and keep an eye on it?"

Maureen said under her breath, "Lord, child, I don't think my nose could stand that. Leave him be."

Aggie told her, "Be nice."

Billy shifted anxiously from one foot to another. "I'm worried about my bike. Somebody could steal it. Don't hurt my stuff. It's mine."

He had been saying things like that for the past half hour and growing more and more agitated. Aggie said they had to be patient with Billy and help him when they could, because he had been in a war and had a steel plate in his head. This was something Flash could not imagine, but he thought it might be even more interesting than being shot in the ear. He wanted to go over and offer comfort to Billy, but he also wanted to see the next thing Aggie brought out of the pack. He was torn.

So far there was half a bag of miniature peanut butter cups, six organic beef jerky sticks, four gluten-free protein bars and two organic vegan dark chocolate bars with cranberries and almonds. There were two white tee shirts, three pairs of ladies' underwear, a pair of white athletic socks, and a rain poncho in a small zippered pouch. There was a handful of individually wrapped wet-wipes, some sunscreen, mosquito repellent, two paperback books, both of them about wild horse populations in America, and a bottle of hand sanitizer. There were also two large shatterproof bottles of Jack Daniels whiskey, one of them mostly empty, and an open package of cigarette papers. As hard as Aggie looked, she did not find anything that might be suitable for smoking in those papers, but that didn't surprise her. By his own admission, Billy had had the backpack for a while.

She searched the outer pockets and found two packets of biodegradable toilet tissue and a folding toothbrush. Then, inside a zippered pocket concealed by a flap, she felt something else. She unfastened the pocket and drew it out.

"Wow," she said, holding it up. "Not very practical for a camping trip."

The bracelet was composed of eight strands of green jewels in a heavy black setting, wide enough to be called a cuff but almost too big to be pretty. It looked antique, almost ancient, and yet, to Aggie, bizarrely familiar.

Mo peered closer, putting the camera aside. "Those real emeralds?" she demanded.

"Emeralds," Aggie repeated thoughtfully.

"Wow," Sally Ann said. "She must've been rich."

Billy lunged forward, extending his hand. "That's pretty. It's mine."

Aggie closed her hand around the bracelet, holding it away from him. "Who found it?" she demanded.

He lowered his eyes and backed off. "I'm worried about my bike," he said. "That's my stuff."

Aggie said, "Sally Ann, get on the computer and see if you can find a picture of Alan Brunelli's wife, the one they have over at the museum, with her all decked out in her wedding jewels."

Sally Ann said excitedly, "Oh, my gosh." She started typing, and less than fifteen seconds later triumphantly turned the screen around for everyone to see.

"Well, will you look at that?" Mo bent in close to have a better look. "You think that's the same bracelet?"

Aggie said, "Can you zoom in, Sally Ann?"

Sally Ann turned the screen back around, made the adjustment, and then swiveled it back for Aggie to see. Aggie looked at the heavy emerald cuff in her hand, and then at the one on the screen.

Mo frowned. "Can't be. This one here is all black. The one in the picture is silver."

"Platinum," corrected Sally Ann. At Aggie's inquiring look, she explained. "The caption on the picture said they were Columbian emeralds set in platinum."

"How in the world would a grad student from UNC get her hands on something like this?" she murmured.

She put the bracelet on the table, lined up against the ruler. "Get a couple of shots," she told Mo. "Front and back."

Aggie stepped back from the desk, her hands on her hips, looking over the display while Maureen took the pictures. "No phone," she observed. "No wallet, no cash, no ID. All that organic trail food—what *is* vegan chocolate, anyway?—and half a bag of peanut butter cups."

"And a million-dollar bracelet," added Sally Ann.

"Maybe," Aggie pointed out. "We don't know for sure." She regarded the lineup thoughtfully. "All those healthy, organic snacks. What was she doing with a bag of peanut butter cups?"

Flash edged closer, sniffing the peanut butter cups.

"No chocolate, Flash," Aggie told him.

He knew that, of course. He sat down, keeping watch over the items on the table.

"Guess she got tired of all that healthy stuff," observed Maureen, moving in for a closer shot of the watch. "Started jonesin' for some real food."

Aggie glanced at Billy. "Was the candy in the pack when you found it, Billy?"

"Most of it," he admitted reluctantly.

"What do you mean, most of it?"

"Well, I ate some."

Aggie said, "What about the booze?"

He avoided her eyes. "It's my stuff," he muttered.

Aggie gave him a steady, patient look. "What did I tell you, Billy? I said you could keep what you found in the dumpster as long as it wasn't drugs or booze. Didn't I say that?"

"I didn't find it!" he burst out. "I bought it with money! It's mine!"

He took a lurching step forward and Maureen reached for the baton on her belt. Aggie held up a staying hand.

"How much money was in the wallet, Billy?"

Again he shifted his eyes away.

Aggie picked up the two bottles of whiskey and handed them to Maureen. "Log these as evidence, will you, Mo?"

Maureen took the bottles and Billy cried, "A lot! Okay? A lot of money. I spent it. It was mine. You never said money wasn't mine!"

Maureen fixed an accusing look on Aggie, which she met stare for stare. "Okay," she admitted in a moment. "So we need to be clearer on the 'finders, keepers' policy." She turned back to Billy. "What did you do with the wallet?"

He shrugged. "Threw it back. Didn't need it."

Aggie said, "And this was when?"

He thought about it. "Before the rain."

"The day of the rain," Aggie insisted, "or the day before?"

Again he was thoughtful. "Morning," he said. "Morning before it rained."

"And this was at the dumpster behind the Twenty-Fifth Street mini-mart, right?"

He nodded.

Aggie turned to Sally Ann. "Sally Ann, find out when trash pickup is—"

She was already typing on her computer "On it."

Aggie said to Billy, "What did you do with her phone?"

"Didn't find no phone, wasn't no phone. What'd I do with a phone, anyhow?" Billy licked his lips, staring at the bottles in Maureen's hands. "Can I have my stuff back now?" His tone was wheedling.

Aggie said, holding his gaze, "We really need that phone, Billy. Are you sure you don't know where it is?"

"I need my stuff," he said. His voice rose an octave with desperation. "Please? Can I have my stuff?"

Aggie looked at Maureen. Maureen's expression was decidedly unhelpful. "This is definitely," Aggie said, almost to herself, "what you might call one of the finer points of the law."

Aggie took the two bottles of whiskey from Maureen and set them on the desk. "Okay, Billy," she said, "consider this a gift."

He lunged forward and retrieved the bottles.

"But," she continued somberly, "the rest of this is evidence. We have to keep it."

Billy cried, "But it's mine! You said—"

Sally Ann turned from the computer. "Trash pickup is Friday," she said.

Aggie took out her phone and scrolled for a number. "Mo," she said, "take some money out of petty cash and go buy Billy a new backpack. Any color he wants."

Mo gave Billy a skeptical once-over. "You sure you want to use public funds that way? I'm paid to uphold the law, you know."

"Yeah, well, since most of those 'public funds' came out of my leftover lunch money, I think we're entitled to use a little discretionary judgment. Sally

Ann, call the Twenty-Fifth Street mini-mart and see where their security cameras are located."

"Yes, ma'am."

Billy said, clutching the bottles, "I need my stuff back. I've got to go. Somebody might steal my bike."

"JC," Aggie spoke into her phone. "Aggie Malone with the Dogleg Island Police Department. I think we've located Kayleigh Carnes's backpack and its contents. Call me when you get this."

Billy said, "Can I have my stuff now? It's time for me to go."

Aggie dug into her pocket and came up with a crumpled twenty and a ten. She handed them to Maureen. "Officer Mo is going to take you shopping, Billy. I have to keep this stuff, but she's going to buy you all new stuff, okay?"

Maureen looked at the money in her hand, frowning, and then returned the twenty to Aggie. "I got some money," she grumbled.

Sally Ann, still on the phone, dug into her purse and waved a ten-dollar bill at Maureen. Maureen took it, looking disgruntled. "I'll take him shopping, but I'm not putting him in my car," she told Aggie.

Aggie smiled at Maureen. "God bless you, Maureen," she said sweetly.

"Yeah, well, that and $4.25 will buy me a cup of coffee," said Maureen, pushing her way toward the door. She jerked one shoulder toward Billie. "Come on then. But don't walk too close to me. Six feet behind. That's the rule."

The door closed behind them and Aggie stood beside Flash, studying the items lined up on the desk. "What is wrong with this picture?" she murmured.

Flash could have told her, but he didn't have to. Aggie was one of the best people he knew at figuring things out, and besides, she already knew the answer. She just had to remember it.

CHAPTER TWENTY-SIX

"You know, Grady," JC said as they walked back down the hall toward the exit. "What you need to do is come work with me at CID."

"Oh, yeah? Why is that?" They reached the property window and passed their claim sheets and badges through the window to the clerk.

"Better pay, for one thing."

"I'm onboard with that," Grady said. "Don't think I could get onboard with all those dead bodies, though."

"It's not so bad," JC said. The property clerk returned and passed a receipt through the window. JC signed it and she pushed his possessions through. "You get used to the smell. Most of the time it's pretty easy duty. And people hardly ever shoot at you."

Grady watched as JC retrieved his weapon, checked the magazine, and tucked it into his shoulder holster. Noticing his look, JC pointed out, "I said, hardly ever."

Grady signed for his gun and phone while JC checked his messages. "I need to call Aggie," Grady said. "She wouldn't have interrupted an interview unless she had something."

JC smiled and lifted a finger, his phone to his ear. "Too late," he said. Then, "Hello, beautiful lady with a gun! What have you got for me?"

Grady gave him an annoyed look, then holstered his own weapon and checked his phone. Nothing but bulletins and updates and a revised copy of tomorrow's duty roster. He tried to eavesdrop on JC's conversation, but the man was deliberately—and uncharacteristically—taciturn on the phone.

Finally, JC disconnected and dropped the phone into his pocket. He glanced at Grady. "You want the good news or the bad news?"

Grady said impatiently, "How about both?"

JC strode for the door and Grady kept up. "The good news is," said JC, "we are about to break this case wide open. The bad news is..." He winked at Grady as he pushed open the door. "I'm in love with your wife. Do you know where the mini-mart on Twenty-Fifth Street is?"

The look Grady gave him was unamused. "I do."

"Good." JC tossed him a set of keys as they stepped out into the sun. "You're driving."

Jess Krieger fell into step with Aggie as she left the office. The backpack and its contents were securely packed in an evidence box waiting for pickup, and Aggie was on the phone with Grady.

"We've got video," Grady said, and there was no disguising the triumph in his voice. "We have to get it back to the office to play it, but the chances are one hundred percent that we're going to find a picture of whoever dumped Kayleigh Carnes's backpack, and when that happens we're going to nail his ass. Also, I've got a team of recruits sorting through the dumpster to find her phone, tent, notebooks, iPad, whatever. Baby, you are a genius. Give yourself a raise."

Aggie said sadly, "Thanks, but I'd feel a lot more like a genius if a twenty-three-year-old girl weren't dead."

Grady was silent for a moment. "We can give her justice, and bring closure for her family. That's pretty much the job description."

She sighed. "I know." That was when she looked up and saw Jess Krieger stalking her. "Gotta go, babe. Call me the minute you find something."

"You got it. Love you."

"Me, too."

She disconnected the phone and increased her pace. Krieger had no trouble catching up with her.

"Big news day, huh, Chief?" said Jess as she turned for her car.

"Is it?"

Flash sensed Aggie's tension and moved closer. She dropped a reassuring hand to his head as she pushed the button on the remote to unlock the door of the SUV.

"Any update on the McElroy boys?"

"The lifeguard corps and other volunteers are combing the beaches. You should talk to them. It would make a good human interest story for you."

"Already on it," he said. "Unfortunately, unless they're found in the next twelve hours, it won't make Tuesday's paper. We'll do a big feature next edition, though, color photographs, retrospective, everything."

Aggie stared at him. "That sounds like an obituary."

He said, unapologetic, "It's a weekly newspaper."

Aggie jerked open the door for Flash and he jumped in.

Jess Krieger said, "What can you tell me about the murder on Wild Horse Island?"

She swung around to face him. "*What?*"

He glanced at his notepad. "Twenty-three-year-old UNC student Kaleigh Carnes, buried alive..."

Aggie took a breath. Sweat trickled down from her scalp and stung her eyes. She said, "You've been on the FDLE website."

"It's my job."

"That girl has a family," Aggie said tightly. "They only learned she was dead twelve hours ago."

"Then help me," he said. "Help me tell a fair story. I told a fair story when you were brought up before a grand jury on charges of shooting a law officer, didn't I? I told a fair story when your husband was named in an officer-involved shooting and almost brought up on charges for endangering lives during an emergency. Talk to me, Chief Malone. I just want the truth."

Aggie leaned against the car, feeling the heat of the side paneling sear through her uniform. The brilliance of the sun danced off the sidewalk and the asphalt in bright sparks of heat. She said, "The Dogleg Island Police Department is working with the Murphy County Sheriff's Department and the FDLE to provide whatever resources they can to assist with this case."

He jotted something down. "I was just by the park service office," he said. "Nobody there but the part-time clerk, and she said Darby is on indefinite medical leave. I've been trying to get an interview with Darby, but he won't return my calls. What information can you give me regarding the connection between the attack on Roger Darby and the death of this girl?"

She stared at him, torn between admiring his reasoning and resenting his impudence. "I can give you absolutely no information. The state of Florida is in charge of that investigation." Aggie blotted perspiration from her face with her forearm. The sidewalk actually seemed to shimmer before her eyes for a moment. She said, "Look, Jess, I'll make you a deal. You come by my office tomorrow and we'll sit in the air-conditioning and talk as long as you want to. But right now, two boys are missing, and I've got a job to do."

He gave a considering tilt of his head. "Ten o'clock? My deadline's at one."

"You got it."

He took a foil-wrapped piece of candy from his shirt pocket and saluted her with it before he turned to go. "See you then."

Aggie stared. "Where did you get that?" But it was a foolish question. Suddenly, standing there in the white hot glare of the sun, she knew. And she had known, some place far back in her mind, for some time now.

He glanced at the peanut-butter cup he was unwrapping. "This? There was a whole bowl of them on the desk at the park service. Want one?"

Aggie shook her head and got into the car, watching in the rearview mirror as Krieger walked away. She started the engine and turned on the air-conditioning full blast, and only then could she fully exhale. "Oh, Flash," she said softly. "Now I know what was wrong with the picture."

Flash settled down on the seat and relaxed as Aggie put the car in gear. He'd always known she'd figure it out.

Chapter Twenty-Seven

Tracy wanted a shower. Tracy wanted to wash her hair. Tracy wanted to pee in a real toilet and sleep in a real bed and eat something that didn't come in a paper bag. After a while it was easier to give in to her than to listen to her whine, and besides, Steve's eyeballs were starting to feel like sandpaper after driving all night on one-lane country roads, getting lost twice, and backtracking almost a hundred miles to avoid what might have been a routine DUI checkpoint, or it might have been a roadblock set up solely to stop them. After that he was more than ready to get off the road, so he followed the signs to a mom-and-pop campground, and at 2:00 a.m. rolled right past the check-in gate with the lights off and pulled into an empty tent camping spot that was practically in the woods. Tracy was already asleep, so he leaned the seat back, closed his eyes and slept until daylight. When he woke, Tracy was gone.

He found her outside the women's showers, her hair all wet and lank around her shoulders, carrying the tote she'd gotten at CVS with her stolen beauty products inside. As he watched she turned toward the payphone on the corner of the building, digging inside the bag for change. He moved quickly toward her.

Two women were coming down the path toward the showers with towels over their arms. They stopped talking and gave him a suspicious look when they saw him, and Steve didn't blame them. He hadn't shaved in three days, his clothes had been slept in more than once, and though they couldn't have known it, he had a gun tucked into the back of his jeans. He smiled and nodded politely to them. "Morning, ladies," he said. Then, raising his arm to wave at Tracy, he called, "Hi, honey! You about ready for breakfast?"

Tracy whipped her head around guiltily, but before she could so much as draw a breath, he was on her. He kept the same easy smile on his face even as he seized her arm hard above the elbow. "Who're you calling, baby?"

She tried to pull her arm away, but he dug his fingers into her skin and lowered his voice to a growl. "You even think about making a fuss, and I'll blow your fucking head off."

She looked up at him with eyes that were big and terrified. Her hair smelled like herbal shampoo, and she was wearing eye shadow and a pretty pink lipstick. Maybe it was that, or maybe it was the way those made-up eyes filled suddenly with water, but he eased his grip.

"My mom, okay?" she said, her voice high and tight. "I wanted to talk to my mom."

This time when she tried to pull away he let her. She folded her arms over her chest, her head lowered and her voice sounding wet and sniffley. "I had to dry off with paper towels. I don't have any clean underwear. I'm tired of sitting in the car. And you stink. Would it kill you to take a shower? I mean, there's such a thing as being *considerate*, you know. And don't swear at me. I hate it when you do that."

About a dozen things went through Steve's head, but he didn't see how saying any of them would cause anything but trouble, right here in front of the women's showers with another woman and her two little rug-rats coming down the path. So he put on his best sweet-talking voice and dropped an arm around Tracy's shoulders. "Ah, baby, you know I don't mean it. But you can't be calling people, and I don't have time to take a shower. We need to get on the road." She shrugged away his arm, but not in a violent away.

He ducked his head, trying to wheedle a smile from her. "Anyway, you smell good enough for both of us. Don't cry, baby. We're almost there."

She stomped off, arms still folded across her chest, pouting. He kept up with her. "Come on, darlin'," he said. "Be sweet. I don't want to fight. We're almost home. I'll buy you breakfast at McDonald's."

"I'm tired of McDonald's."

Steve thought hard. "I'll let you drive."

She looked at him, her eyes lighting up. "Really?"

And that's how they ended up on I-10 with a broken taillight, wanted for murder and fleeing for their lives.

CHAPTER TWENTY-EIGHT

Roger must have seen them drive up, because he opened the door as soon as Aggie reached the bottom of the stairs.

"Chief," he said. "Flash." He sounded surprised, and his smile was more nervous than welcoming. "Come on in out of the heat. Shirley just went across the bridge to get my prescription filled, but she should be back before long."

If possible, he looked even more stressed than he had a few hours earlier. The bruised circles under his eyes were even more pronounced, and he kept wiping his palms on his jeans, as though they were sweating. His gaze darted over Aggie's shoulder before he closed the door, but he kept the smile in place.

Aggie and Flash walked into the cool, pleasant room and were immediately enveloped by the smell of simmering onions and beef. It made Aggie's stomach rumble.

"What smells so good?" she asked.

"Shirley put a roast in the Crock-Pot before she left," he said smiling. "The only problem with that is that after you smell it cooking all day, you're about starved by suppertime."

"I should do that for Grady," Aggie said. "He'd like a nice home-cooked meal now and then."

He gestured her to the sofa. On the table in front of it was a bowl of miniature peanut-butter cups, and beside it a small pile of tiny crumpled gold foil wrappers, just as she remembered from the last time she'd been here. "Have a seat," he said. "What brings you out?"

Aggie said, "Thanks, but I can't stay. I just stopped by because I promised to keep you updated on the case."

He sat on the edge of the sofa, looking concerned. "Did you find out who she was?"

Aggie nodded. "Her name was Kayleigh Carnes, a twenty-three-year-old graduate student from UNC. Apparently she arrived on the island July 31 and planned to stay until Labor Day. That's illegal, of course, so she probably had to be pretty circumspect about it."

She paused. "The thing I don't understand is how she managed to stay off your radar for almost a month. I mean, you walked the trails every other Monday, right? And you didn't see anything suspicious?"

He shook his head slowly. "Nothing that raised a flag. Of course," he added quickly, "I don't go inland, where the prairie is. Too much territory for one man to cover."

Aggie nodded. "Still, looks like you would have noticed signs of campfires, or latrines, or something."

His expression remained blandly apologetic.

Aggie said, "We found out how she got there. Jack Saunders—you know, who runs the fishing charter?—he took her over. He came back to deliver supplies last Sunday but she never showed. He said he nailed a note to the dock telling her to call him. You're sure you didn't see it when you were there Monday?"

He shook his head. "Like I told you, I didn't notice anything. Of course, I wasn't looking for it."

"Still," Aggie said, "it would be pretty hard to miss, being right there on the end of the dock next to the fee box."

He said nothing.

Aggie said, "You know, I understand what it's like living with a head injury. Sometimes I still have trouble remembering things. So if something comes to you, even though you didn't tell JC, no one would think you were withholding anything. We'd understand."

He just looked at her with that nervous expression of forced pleasantry on his face.

Aggie said, "I thought you'd want to know the cause of death. There was a skull fracture, but the actual cause of death was asphyxiation. She was buried alive."

The pleasant expression vanished. So did the color in his lips. "What?"

Aggie said, "We were able to find some of her possessions, and we have a lead on the remainder. In fact, the sheriff's department just took possession of video from a surveillance camera at the location where her backpack was found, and we're pretty sure that whoever killed her and disposed of her things is on that video."

Roger ran an unsteady hand over his face. "Buried alive?" he said hoarsely. "That's what happened to her? She was…buried alive?"

Aggie took a step toward him. Flash pressed his shoulder against her knee, watchful. "I'm not in charge of this case, Roger," she said gently. "I'm just trying to help out. So let me ask you again, is there anything you want to tell me?"

He just looked at her, his eyes twin dark pools, his breath coming in shallow, uneven puffs through flared nostrils.

Aggie tried again. "I mean, if you met her, if you talked to her…she might have said something, something that might not even seem important to you, but that might help us bring her killer to justice."

He just stared at her, face showing nothing but shock.

Aggie took out a card and offered it to him. "This is my cell phone number," she said. "If you think of anything, anything at all, you call me, okay?"

He made no move to take the card. Aggie placed it on the table, next to the bowl of candy.

Aggie turned toward the door. When she was halfway, there he said sharply, "Chief."

She looked back.

He was still on the sofa, white faced, dark eyed. And when she looked at him, all he said was, "I'm sorry I can't help you."

Aggie nodded, and left.

CHAPTER TWENTY-NINE

JC and Grady watched the video on the big screen in the training room while eating chicken nuggets and French fries. "Man, I love these new security systems," JC said. "Everything's digitized. Plug in a flash drive and you've got a week's worth of footage. Remember the old video tapes that used to record over themselves every twenty-four hours?"

Grady replied, "Sorry, before my time."

"Right," replied JC, who was nine years older. "You're just a baby." He swirled a nugget in mustard sauce and popped it in his mouth. "Trust me, it was no fun."

Grady ate some French fries and tried not to imagine the look on Aggie's face if she could see him now. He promised himself to eat a piece of fruit later, if he could find one. He said, "You know, I could get a couple of rookies to scrub this footage for us, if you need to get back."

"Or I could take it back to the office with me. You know you're just as anxious as I am to get a look at who dumped that backpack. Are you a betting man?"

"Can't afford it." Grady helped himself to a couple of nuggets. "Are you still thinking Saunders?"

"We'll soon know. Damn, look at the size of that rat, will you?" He pointed to the screen with a French fry.

The security camera was not pointed directly at the dumpster, but was positioned to monitor the employee parking lot and the back entrance. The dumpster was, however, situated only six feet from the back door, and even with the grainy nighttime quality of the picture they had a good view of every rat, raccoon, and armadillo that scurried over the edge of the container.

"We had a black bear get trapped in one of those last year," commented Grady. He picked up his paper cup of soda and swirled the ice around, then took a sip. "A lot of people are putting their dumpsters inside fences now."

"A black bear can climb a fence."

"Not if you put a roof on it."

"Then it's a box, not a fence."

Grady shrugged and finished off his nuggets. The recording had ninety hours' worth of footage on it, but they were watching it at four-times acceleration, slowing the video down only when people came into view. They watched employees and delivery trucks come and go, they watched trash being dumped and cigarettes being smoked, and a couple of times a drunk staggered by to relieve himself against the side of the dumpster. Once they slowed the footage and leaned forward intently when a late-model Ford pulled up beside the dumpster and a man got out, looking around furtively. But all he did was toss what appeared to be a couple of empty vodka bottles into the container, and he drove off. Grady copied down the license plate number anyway, intending to put it on the DUI watch list.

JC said, "Who do I call to see if the evidence box is back from the island yet?"

"I'll check on it." Bored with sitting, Grady gathered up their trash and started to rise.

"Hello there," JC murmured, leaning forward to click the mouse. "What have we here?"

Grady watched as a pickup truck came around the corner of the building with its lights off and pulled up close to the dumpster. The time stamp read Wednesday, 4:12 a.m. A man got out and came around to the back of the truck, lifting out two large black bags. Grady stopped the footage as the man's face came into profile. "What the hell?" he said, leaning in for a closer look.

JC looked at Grady just long enough to assure him they were seeing the same thing, and Grady started the playback again. They watched him toss both of the bags into the container and walk back to the open driver's side door. Just before he got inside, though, he cast a furtive look over his shoulder, and the camera caught him full-face. Grady froze the video.

For a moment neither of them spoke. Then Grady said, "I don't get it."

JC did not have much in the way of a helpful answer to offer. "Four o'clock Wednesday morning.

Our witness says he went dumpster diving that morning, most likely before the store opened at seven. My guess is we're going to play this video through and not find anybody else tossing garbage into that dumpster before the bicycle guy comes and takes the backpack out, what do you think?"

"Yeah," murmured Grady, disturbed.

"One of the bags probably had the backpack in it, and the other, heavier one had the tent, sleeping bag, camp supplies," JC said. "It probably settled to the bottom, which is why the homeless dude only found the backpack. We're going to need fingerprints from the bags."

JC took the mouse to restart the video, but they both turned at a crisp voice behind them. "Grady." Sheriff Bishop was at the door. "We've got a jumper on the bridge. Get your gear and suit up. The rescue boat is leaving in six minutes."

Grady was a member of a five-man dive team certified for emergency rescue operations, and as such he was always on call. He was at the door before Bishop finished speaking. Bishop started to follow him, but his attention was caught by the face frozen on the screen opposite him. He said, "Is that…?"

"Yes, sir," JC said sadly, clicking the mouse. "It's Mr. Roger Darby. Our new prime suspect."

Flash's mood was not as excited as it usually was when they pulled into the parking lot of Pete's Place. It was the height of lunch hour and they were forced to park in back by the delivery dock, which was okay because all the great aromas of what was cooking that day wafted out, along with the boom of music and the sound of busy people. That was not what dampened Flash's mood. It was Aggie, and her dark thoughts, and the difficulty of figuring out how good people could also be bad guys. Thunder rolling around in the back of his mind, far away.

On the drive over, Aggie kept her phone on the console, close at hand, but it didn't ring. Before she turned off the engine, she called up the Coast Guard website on her phone, then the sheriff's department. Neither had any updates on the missing boys. She said with a sigh, "I need to talk to Grady, Flash." But she needed to talk to him as a friend, not as a colleague, and it would have been unfair to dial his number. She didn't have anything official to report except a hunch about some candy wrappers, and that would mean nothing until the video was examined. In the meantime, all she could do was wait for him to call her, and do her job. But she missed him.

Aggie and Flash walked around to the front of the restaurant, where a much subdued Sherry greeted them at the hostess stand. "Chief, have you heard anything?" she said anxiously. "No one here can believe it. I mean, Brian and Mark were like, *gods* when it came to sailing. They knew everything. They're okay, don't you think?"

Aggie managed a smile. "I think they are, Sherry. But I need to talk to anyone who might have seen Mark before they left yesterday. Could you put the word out? And I know Pete's in the middle of the lunch rush, but could you tell him I'm here?"

Sherry said, "Sure thing, Chief. Do you want to sit upstairs?"

Aggie regarded the stairs that led to the upper deck, and felt suddenly incapable of climbing them. "Can you find me a place on the patio, Sherry?"

Sherry led them to a table at the back of the patio near the hostess stand, where a powerful ceiling fan whipped the perspiration from Aggie's face and the blare of the music was somewhat muted. A labradoodle and an Australian shepherd occupied adjacent tables, and Flash gave them each wary looks before taking his place on the bench opposite Aggie.

"What can I get you to drink, Chief?" Sherry asked.

Aggie took a deep, luxurious breath. "Sherry," she said, "I'd like a mojito served in a great big glass, double rum, double sugar."

Sherry regarded Aggie uneasily. "Sure, Chief."

"And…" Aggie raised a hand as she started to turn away. "I'd like it served poolside at my resort hotel in Cancun. Meanwhile, I'll take a lemonade, and bring Flash the usual."

Sherry's smile was relieved. "Be right back."

Aggie was looking at her phone, trying to think of a way to compose a text to Grady, or if in fact she should send one at all, when Lorraine came up behind her, a swirl of peaches and patchouli scent and paisley chiffon. She hugged Aggie's shoulders and pressed her cheek against hers and said, "Oh, honey, isn't it awful about the boys? Have you heard anything?"

Flash couldn't help noticing that she forgot his ice water. Next to the hamburgers, the ice water at Pete's Place was the best thing on the menu. But he could tell by her scent, and the quick nervous way that she moved and looked, that there would be no ice water today. That was okay. They all had heavier things on their minds.

Aggie put her phone away. She said, "I'm sorry, nothing yet. But the search is still active, and you know that even in the worst case scenario those boys have survival skills that most people don't. There's every reason to be optimistic."

Lorraine sat across from Aggie, next to Flash, and Flash leaned his head against her shoulder. She stroked him absently. "I heard you have lifeguards combing the beach," she said. "That's good. Pete and I are planning to go see Walter as soon as the lunch rush is over." She smiled faintly, looking weary and tense. "He can be an arrogant cuss and full of himself, but the boys were—are—dear to us."

Aggie said, "I'm trying to get an idea of what time they left yesterday. Did Mark come into work?"

Lorraine shook her head. "He was scheduled, but he called in sick. He went home early the day before, too, so I figured he'd picked up a bug."

Sherry set a glass of lemonade in front of Aggie and an aluminum bowl of water—no ice—on the floor for Flash. Aggie smiled her thanks, then said to Lorraine, "Can you get me a copy of the schedule for Tuesday? I'd like to talk to everyone who worked with Mark. Maybe he said something that would give us a better idea what their plans were yesterday."

Lorraine said, "Sure, that's a good idea. I have it on my phone. I'll text it to you." Then Lorraine took a breath and straightened up her shoulders, forcing a smile. "Mind if we talk about something else for a minute?"

Flash got down and went to sit beside Aggie. He knew she needed him more now.

Aggie sipped her lemonade. "Oh please, let it be about reupholstering furniture. I can't tell you how much I want to talk about fabric swatches right now." But then she looked at Lorraine, and a tiny coil of dread formed in the pit of her stomach. She put down her glass. "This isn't about decorating, is it?" she said.

Lorraine just looked at her, sad and tired. The dread grew bigger, tighter, colder.

Flash edged closer to her, and Aggie put her arm around him, wrapping her fingers through his fur. She looked at Lorraine, and she knew. She said hoarsely, "The cancer's back, isn't it?"

Lorraine's smile was tight and dry. "Wouldn't you just know? Twelve years living like a saint, eating broccoli and wearing sunscreen, and the next thing you know some smart-aleck doctor is telling you you've got a mass on your lungs. What pisses me off is that I could have been smoking a pack a day all this time while chugging gin on the beach." She gave a rueful shake of her head. "All those wasted years."

Aggie tightened her arm around Flash. He put his head on her shoulder. Aggie brought her fingers to her lips to cover one shaky, indrawn breath. "Okay," she said. "Okay." Another breath, and she sat up straight. "When do you start treatment?"

She forced a tight smile. "Next week. I can't wait."

Aggie formed her fingers into a fist, pressing hard against her lips. "I should have come by yesterday, like I told Pete I would. That's what you wanted to talk to me about, isn't it? Not fabric samples. I should have been here for you, but I was too damn busy...God, Lorraine, I'm so sorry! Can you forgive me?"

"Stop that," Lorraine said sharply. She waved a hand before her face. "I only have so many tears to spare, you know, and we haven't even gotten to the hard part yet." Her expression gentled as she added, "Honey, I'd only just found out yesterday. I hadn't even told Pete yet, and he would have been furious if I told you first. After all, fighting cancer is kind of our thing." Her smile was brave and proud and funny, and it helped as Aggie swallowed back her own tears.

"How is Pete?" she asked.

"My hero," replied Lorraine immediately. "My rock. And breaking into a million pieces inside, just like Grady was when you were sick. God, Aggie." She drew a deep, soft breath. "We are so lucky to be loved by these men. And so cursed to love them back."

Aggie did not reply. Some things were understood too deeply for words.

Aggie reached across the table and grabbed Lorraine's hand, squeezing her fingers hard, and managed a fierce, determined smile. Lorraine smiled back, even though her eyes went a little misty.

"Hey." Half-laughing, Lorraine pulled her hand away to dab at her eyes. "At least we get to go wig shopping together. That'll be fun, huh?"

Aggie's phone buzzed. She ignored it, and it buzzed insistently again. She grabbed it impatiently from her pocket and read the message. Stared at it. "No," she said. Then, *"Damn it."*

She looked helplessly at Lorraine, "I—there's a jumper on the bridge. We have to close off traffic. I—God, Lorraine, I'm sorry but…"

Flash jumped down from the bench and started toward the door.

Lorraine said impatiently, "Like I don't know you're the chief of police? Go, for heaven's sake. I'll be here."

Aggie got up and hugged her friend hard. "I love you."

"Go," Lorraine repeated, hugging her back. "Do your job."

Aggie had no choice. She ran back out into the sun, where Flash was waiting for her.

CHAPTER THIRTY

Flash had observed that there were some people, Aggie chief among them, who had the almost canine-like ability to separate themselves from events of the past and focus entirely on what was required in the present. He could feel the pain in her heart and taste the anguish in her throat, but for the next few minutes it was as though she, herself, was barely aware of them. She slammed the car into gear and barked out orders on the radio, dispatching emergency vehicles, calling in volunteer firemen and EMTs, positioning ambulances, and all the while driving with lights and sirens toward the intersection of Island Drive and the Cedric B. Grady Memorial Bridge at a speed that caused Flash to lean into the door to keep his balance.

The Cedric B. Grady Memorial Bridge, named for a heroic Grady ancestor, was the only connection between Dogleg Island and the rest of the world, and the order to close it was never given lightly. The last time the bridge had been closed was during the April hurricane. No hurricanes were on the horizon now; nonetheless, Aggie had the same sick, terrified feeling in the pit of her stomach now that she had had then. Some things you never got over.

Mo approached from the south as Aggie came from the east, sirens blaring. Aggie executed a hard U-turn to bring her vehicle nose-to-nose with Maureen's across the intersection, effectively blocking access to the bridge. Flash dug in his claws on the seat to maintain his balance as Aggie slammed the car to a stop. She reached for her radio mike and for an instant, just an instant, she was transported back in time four months to the roar of rain pounding on her roof, blue lights flashing, dark waves pounding over the causeway, slamming against her vehicle and blinding her with water. *You'll never make it across that bridge...*

With a single sharp inhale, she picked up the mike and said, "Dispatch, secure from Dogleg Island. Westbound traffic is blocked at Island Drive. All emergency vehicles have been deployed, ETA five minutes. Please advise."

To her surprise, the voice that came back to her was Bishop's. "Dogleg Island, stand by."

Within three seconds, her phone rang. It was Bishop. "Aggie," he said, "no point in broadcasting this, but the jumper is Roger Darby."

The breath left Aggie's lungs in an audible gasp, leaving little air for the word she choked out. "What?"

"I'm coming up on the site now, and it doesn't look good. If you can get his wife out here it might help. We've got a crisis intervention team on the way, but by the time they get here it might be too late."

Aggie said urgently, "Sheriff, let me talk to him. I think…" She managed another choked breath. "I think this might be my fault."

"Aggie, I don't…"

"I'll have Mo call his house, but I think his wife might be on the bridge, heading home," Aggie went on quickly, her breath coming hard and fast. "Can you have deputies check cars? Sheriff, let me help. I think…I think he'll talk to me."

Bishop said, "Aggie, listen. It was Darby on the surveillance video. This is starting to look real bad."

Aggie pressed her lips tightly together, gripping the phone. In a moment Bishop, said, "All right. Come across. No lights or sirens."

"Thank you, sir."

"But Aggie," he added quietly just before she disconnected, "be careful. The divers are still ten minutes out."

Aggie traversed the bridge in the emergency lane at a steady thirty-five miles per hour, her armpits sticky with sweat despite the air-conditioning. In the background the radio crackled traffic instructions and emergency vehicle deployment. For over a mile she saw nothing but brake lights, and then the conflagration of strobing blue lights as sheriff's department cars bisected the bridge, creating an island of emptiness in the middle of the bridge about a hundred feet long. A team of deputies was directing an ambulance into position while others went up and down the lines of cars, instructing the drivers to stay inside. Sheriff Bishop stood outside his car, squinting in the sun, waiting for her. Aggie and Flash got out and hurried across the blistering pavement to him.

During the worst of Aggie's struggle with PTSD after she'd been shot, she had developed a paralyzing fear of bridges, and she still wasn't entirely sure she was over it. Being here so high with nothing but hot blue sky around her and nothing but bright blue water below her left her feeling light-headed and disoriented, as though the shimmering road beneath her feet might dissolve into nothingness at any moment. There was a pressure in her chest and a pounding in her ears. A hot wind dried the perspiration on her face and tasted like exhaust fumes.

She had almost reached Bishop before she saw the two deputies leaning over the concrete barrier of the bridge, and just beyond them, positioned on the ledge on the other side of the thick metal guardrail posts that topped the concrete barrier, a man in a wind-buffeted blue tee shirt. Her throat convulsed and she choked on her own saliva, her eyes magnetized to the sight. Bishop came over to her, his face creased with worry. "Maybe you'd better stay back," he said. "I tried to talk to him, but it only seemed to make him more agitated. We need to keep him calm until we get the rescue team in place."

Aggie managed, "How long...has he been out there?" The muted roar of idling engines mixed with the sound of blood rushing through her ears made even her own voice hard to hear. She leaned in close to hear Bishop's reply.

"A motorist called it in about twelve minutes ago. He was already on the ledge when I got here."

Again Aggie tried to swallow, and again had difficulty. "I was at his house less than an hour ago. I have to talk to him."

Flash started across the pavement toward the barrier. Bishop looked at Aggie intently. "Can you do this?"

She said hoarsely, "I don't know." But she followed Flash anyway.

As every dog knew, there were only two kinds of things in the world: good and bad. There were only two kinds of feelings: love and fear. What Flash knew, but couldn't entirely understand even in his deepest private thoughts, was that the good things and the bad things somehow were the same as the feelings. Life got very, very complicated when you forgot about that, even when it didn't always make sense.

For example, there were all kinds of fear. None of them were good, but not all of them made people do bad things. There was the fear he smelled on Aggie when she crossed the bridge, and the fear he smelled on Grady when he woke gasping in the middle of the night, and the fear Flash smelled on Lorraine because she was sick. Then there was the fear that made a bad guy point his gun at Aggie and made the man with the bandage on his head climb over the guardrail on a bridge. The thing most people didn't understand was that fear and anger and violence and hatred all smelled the same to dogs, because they all came from the same dark place of bad things. In a lot of ways, they *were* the same. This was what confused Flash. How could Aggie, who was the best person he knew, and Grady, who was the second best person, sometimes smell like the worst thing he knew? And how could people like the man on the bridge, who almost always smelled like fear, sometimes do good things? Flash thought if he could understand the answer to that he would know everything in the world worth knowing, and that was why he was so eager to cross the bridge, to try to find out.

The concrete guard barrier was four feet high, topped by two heavy metal rails of reinforced steel, each a foot apart. On the other side of the bridge only a narrow ledge looked out over a thirty-foot drop into the Gulf. That was where Roger Darby stood, balanced on the ledge, clinging to the metal rail with one hand. The two deputies, stationed on either side of his position but too far away to reach him, looked at Aggie with stressed, sweaty faces when she approached. Flash put his paws atop the concrete barrier and looked between the rails at Roger. Aggie stepped up onto the shoulder of the bridge and grabbed the rail with one hand, resting the other on Flash's neck. A gust of wind ruffled Flash's fur backwards over her hand and instinctively her fingers tightened around his collar. The bridge seemed to have a life of its own, breathing with the hum of distant traffic, swaying faintly, almost imperceptibly, with the currents below. She tried to focus on the man who hung so precariously over the ocean only a few feet away from her. On him, and nothing more.

She said, "Roger. It's Aggie Malone."

He turned his face to look at her. It was tear-streaked and terrified, his eyes dark wounds against pale doughy skin. "I didn't kill her," he said. "I didn't kill Kayleigh."

"I never thought you did," Aggie said. A gust of wind seemed to take her words away so she repeated, more loudly, "I never thought that. Don't do this, Roger. Come back over the rail and let's talk about this. Please."

He said, "I can't. If Shirley finds out…I can't face her, I can't tell her what I did. She's a good woman. I can't put her through that."

"Do you know what you'll put her through if you fall?" Aggie demanded. Her hand was gripping the rail so tightly she could feel the ache in her shoulder. "Have you thought about that?"

He seemed to hesitate. Then he squeezed his eyes shut so tightly that Aggie thought he was gathering the courage to jump, and instinctively she let go of Flash's collar and reached her hand through the bars toward Roger. One of the deputies lunged forward and grabbed her arm, pulling her back. He was right, of course. There was no way she could physically stop a man twice her size from jumping, and the attempt would only result in her being pulled over with him. It was hard to remember that, though, when someone you knew was poised on an eight-inch ledge looking down on the Gulf of Mexico.

Roger did not jump. He said, not looking at her, "I was such a fool. Such a stupid, reckless fool."

The deputy who had grabbed her leaned close, speaking quietly in her ear. "The rescue chief says it's too dangerous to have him climb back over by himself. They need to get him to put on a body harness. They want you to keep him talking, if you can, until they can get here with one."

Flash put all four paws on the pavement and stood close to Aggie. Aggie nodded to the deputy and turned back to Roger. "Just tell me what happened, Roger. We know you didn't kill Kayleigh. You didn't even know she was dead. But you knew her. You gave her the peanut butter cups, didn't you?"

He almost smiled. "She loved them. I brought her some every few days. Other things, too. Batteries, matches, fresh fruit. Things like that."

"It sounds like you were a good friend," Aggie said.

Again he screwed his eyes shut. "I was a fool," he repeated, grinding the words out.

"For letting her camp on the island?" Aggie said. "Come on, Roger, that's a minor offense. It's not worth…this."

For a moment he didn't speak. Aggie could see his chest rising up and down, and could actually hear the folds of his shirt snap against his body with each whipping gust of wind. He said, not looking at her, "I spotted her campsite on routine patrol, and I went looking for her. I found her swimming in that little cove down from the hiking trails. She was swimming naked, and she came out of the water just like that, not in the least bit embarrassed, and she took her time looking for a towel while I told her she was camped illegally and would have to leave. She didn't even try to get dressed the whole time I was talking, just dried herself off with the towel, then started brushing her hair, and telling me about how she was working on a really important project for the university and how grateful she'd be if I let her stay, and if I did let her stay maybe she would…we could…I started to walk away. I meant to walk away. I told her to get her things together and I would take her to the mainland, and then I started to walk away so she could get dressed. But I came back.

"I felt so bad afterward. I didn't think I could live with myself, I felt so bad. The next day I swore I was going to do the right thing, tell my supervisor what had happened, but I didn't. I went back to the island. And I kept going back. After a while I even managed to convince myself it was okay, what we were doing, that she was enjoying it too, and it was like a summer fling, a little secret between us. Sometimes we'd even talk afterwards, and like I said, I'd bring little presents…but it was business, wasn't it? Just business for her. And the part of me that knew that, deep down, hated myself."

Aggie felt a little sick. She thought about Shirley, with her mousey brown curls and her big smile and a roast simmering in the Crock-Pot. She thought about how twisted and torn relationships could get, just like the inside of some people's minds. And then Flash nudged her knee, and she heard a boat engine approaching from the opposite side of the bridge. The engine throttled down, and stopped. She looked down to see the red rescue boat with divers inside floating quietly into view beneath the bridge. One of the divers was Grady.

Even from that distance she could see the shock in his eyes when he saw her, but it was almost immediately replaced by something else: quiet confidence, reassurance, shared strength. He gave her a small nod, a simple, *I've got your back*, then he wet down his goggles and pulled them on. Aggie watched as he positioned his regulator and slipped silently into the water. The diver on the other side did the same, and they held onto the boat, watching the bridge.

Aggie dropped her hand to Flash's neck, breathing easily for the first time. She said, "When was the last time you saw her, Roger?"

"Friday. Friday morning. She was all excited about something she'd found, but she wouldn't tell me what it was. I figured it had something to do with her horses. She said maybe she'd show it to me tomorrow, but when I came back the next day she wasn't there. I'd seen a small boat moored there earlier in the week so I figured she must have some friends around, somebody who picked her up. I kept thinking she'd come back, but it was the weekend... well, I couldn't have some tourist stumbling over her campsite, I couldn't have anybody knowing what I'd done, so I packed up her stuff and took it with me. I kept it in my shed, thinking she'd come back and I'd give it to her. But she never did. When Grady called about finding the trash, I was afraid there might be something there, you know, to give me away, so I came as quick as I could. That's all I ever thought about, being caught, Shirley finding out, my boss... and then, she was dead..."

"And it was much, much worse than you imagined," Aggie said gently, almost to herself.

"I didn't kill her." His voice was thick and wet with tears. "I threw out her stuff because I knew how it looked, knew I couldn't be found with it. But she was alive the last time I saw her, I swear it."

Aggie said, "I believe you."

Two EMTs came across the bridge with a canvas safety harness and rigging, followed by four firemen and more deputies. Aggie said, "Roger, you need to let us help you get back over the rail now. I know you don't want to do this. I understand why you thought it was the only way out, but it's not. Now that we know the truth we can help you. Just don't let this get any worse."

He shook his head, the wind drying the tears on his face. "I can't. I can't live with this, can't carry this around, can't face what I've done to my wife. You don't understand. I'm not a brave man. I can't."

Aggie saw him start to flex his fingers in preparation for letting go. Aggie's heart leapt to her throat. She said, "Roger..."

Flash gave a sudden soft bark, and Aggie whipped her head around to see a deputy escorting Roger's wife Shirley across the road. She was wearing shorts and a tee shirt with kittens on it and a look of stunned disbelief on her face. But when she saw Aggie and Flash and the deputies at the bridge, she started to walk faster, and then she pulled away from the deputy who was escorting her and started to run. She cried, "Roger!"

Roger turned his head around, saw her. He looked at Aggie with despair in his eyes.

"If you do this it will be her last memory of you," Aggie said quickly, urgently. "She'll never get the picture out of her head, not ever. Is that what you want? To punish her for what you did? Don't let her see you do this!"

Shirley screamed again, "Roger! Roger, no!"

Aggie saw Roger Darby's shoulders slump in defeat, and he started to cry. Aggie moved out of the way when the EMTs arrived with the harness, and lent a comforting arm to Shirley Darby as she pressed against the rail, sobbing. The last thing she saw before the rescue workers pulled Roger over the railing and back to safety was Grady, pushing his goggles back, looking up at her, his lips relaxing into a faint smile of relief.

CHAPTER THIRTY-ONE

Tracy broke the taillight when she hit a small tree backing out of the camping space. Steve winced when he felt the thud, but didn't bother to get out and check for damage. He'd already switched out the license plate for one registered to a Taurus in Ohio, and all he was interested in was getting out of the campground without being noticed. That proved to be no problem, and after that Tracy actually appeared to be a pretty good driver. Steve began to relax and enjoy letting someone else take the stress.

The problems began when they crossed into Florida and got on I-10 westbound. "So where are we going?" Tracy insisted. "You just keep giving me directions, but you won't tell me where we're going."

"You'll know when we get there." The last gas station they'd stopped at had a boiled peanut stand beside it, and Steve had bought a big cupful. He munched on the soft salty peanuts now, discarding the soggy shells in the ashtray.

"Yeah, well, I don't know what high school you went to, but if you think this is the way to Mexico, you're an idiot. I-10 goes to California, not Mexico. I learned that in eighth grade."

He scowled sharply at her. "Yeah, well, did you ever hear of El Paso, bitch? That's in Texas, and it's just across the border from Juarez, and that's in Mexico, and I-10 does go there, so just keep driving."

She swung her head to look at him. "Texas?" Her voice was high and incredulous. "El Paso, *Texas?* That's where we're going? Do you know how far that is? *That's* where we're going? And don't call me bitch!"

A horn blared as Tracy let the car drift into the left lane. Steve lurched for the wheel, grabbed it, over-corrected, and the back tires spun onto the shoulder. The Styrofoam cup of peanuts sprayed over the front seat. Tracy squealed. Steve's face was glistening with sweat when the tires finally grabbed the road and the car was back in its lane again. He sank back against the seat, cursing. Then he heard the siren.

"Oh, God." Tracy's big terrified eyes flew to the rearview mirror, where flashing blue lights were closing in. "Oh God, oh God, *oh God!*" With each utterance her voice grew in pitch and timber until the last word was high enough to pierce an eardrum. "Oh God, what do I *do?* I don't have a license!" She gripped the wheel maniacally with both hands, but her eyes were anywhere but on the road. "What do I do, what do I *do?*"

Steve reached forward and took his gun out of the glove box. "Pull over," he said.

She whipped her wild and terrified gaze toward him. "*What?*"

He replied evenly, "Put your blinker on and pull over. Bat your eyelashes, smile pretty, answer his questions." He slipped the gun in between the passenger seat and the console. "And duck when I tell you."

So Tracy pulled over to the emergency lane and sat there with the engine running and traffic roaring by and blue lights spinning behind her, gripping the wheel with both hands while her heart pulsed in her throat and her breath grew dry and choked.

She watched the trooper get out of his car and come slowly toward them. Steve said, "Roll down your window."

She fumbled with the buttons until she found the right one and lowered the driver's side window. A young black man in a Florida state trooper's uniform looked in at her. She smiled woodenly.

"Hi, Officer," she said.

"I need to see your license and registration, please," he said.

Steve leaned forward, his tone amicable and his smile apologetic. "Officer, I'm sorry for what happened back there. My cousin, here, she just got her learner's permit and it's her first time on the freeway. I guess she panicked a little. Scared the hell out of me, I'll tell you that."

The officer's expression relaxed a little with Steve's easy manner. He said, "The expressway can be a dangerous place. You need to make sure you're ready for it. Is this your car?"

Steve answered, "Yes, sir. The paperwork is in the console." He gestured toward it.

"I'll need to see it, please. License, insurance, registration, learner's permit."

"Yes, sir."

Tracy saw Steve's hand move, not toward the console, but toward the space between the seat and the console, and she knew what he was going to do. She slammed the car into gear and punched the gas pedal to the floor. She saw the trooper's eyes as he was flung away from the car and she felt the thud as her back tires plowed over his body; she heard the blare of horns and the screech of tires. But mostly she heard the sound of her own scream, high and wide like a siren in her ears, as she barreled the car down the emergency lane, swinging wildly into the stream of traffic, across lanes, eighty, ninety, a hundred miles an hour. She didn't hear Steve yelling at her. She didn't see the cars she almost sideswiped or the outraged gestures their owners made, and if she had seen them she wouldn't have cared. She just kept pushing the accelerator, harder and harder.

At some point it hit her, and she pulled the car over into the emergency lane, almost clipping a semi in the process. The tires skidded and smoked as she stood on the brake, and gravel from the shoulder clattered across the roof of the car. "I killed him," she whispered. "I killed him, I killed him, I killed him…"

Steve got out of the car, walked behind and jerked open the driver's side door. He dragged

Tracy out of the car by her hair while traffic blew by, rocking them both with the force of the wind. She threw up on his shoes. He pulled her over to the passenger door and shoved her inside, then got behind the wheel and took off. She just sat there with her face buried in her hands, rocking back and forth and moaning softly, not saying a word.

Later Steve would wonder why he'd even bothered putting her back in the car. It was clear to him, and became more clear with every mile that passed, that the fun was over. She was nothing but a liability, as though she'd ever been anything else, and he knew what he had to do. He was going to kill her.

What he did not realize, to his ultimate misfortune, was that Tracy knew that too.

CHAPTER THIRTY-TWO

The emergency dive crew had a small locker room at the marina. Aggie and Flash waited outside the building for Grady to change. Rows of boats swayed in the water, creaking against the pier: masted boats and cabin cruisers, runabouts and catamarans, pleasure boats painted brilliant white and working boats spotted with rust. The air was thick and hot, smelling of diesel fuel and dead fish, and the sparks of sunlight flashing on the brilliant blue water made Aggie's eyes hurt, even behind her dark glasses. Flash lifted his nose to the smell of fried food coming from the Shipshead bar on the other side of the marina, reminding Aggie that neither one of them had had lunch. Her stomach was still too tied in knots to care.

Grady came out of the building and walked up to her without speaking. He stood very close, his expression unreadable, and said quietly, "Don't ever do that again. Please."

She had to tilt her head to look up at him, he was standing so close. But since they were both in uniform and in a public place, it was as close to an embrace as they would get. "Don't worry," she said.

He said, "Good job up there." He stepped back and gestured her toward the parking lot.

Aggie replied heavily, "I don't know about that." As they walked, she told him about what Roger had done to Kayleigh Carnes on the island—or what she had done to him, or what they had done to each other.

"Jesus, that's sick," Grady muttered when she was finished. "He's old enough to be her grandfather."

"You never know what people are hiding inside," Aggie said.

"What's worse," Grady said, "if there is a worse, is that it sounds like the perfect motive for murder. All those twisted up emotions."

"Bishop always says there are only two motives for murder," Aggie agreed. "Money and sex."

He glanced at her. "Let me guess. You don't think Darby did it either."

She gave a halfhearted shrug. "I don't know what to think any more. I guess they're keeping him under psych observation at the hospital?"

"Yeah. JC will want a statement from you, but I doubt they'll let him interview Darby tonight."

"He should get a search warrant. We never did find her phone."

"Right."

They reached her car, and Aggie turned to him. As bad as the day had been so far, the worst part, for her, was not over. She drew a deep, steadying breath.

"How about letting me give you a ride back to the sheriff's office? I need to talk to you...about some family stuff."

They sat in the sheriff's department parking lot with the air-conditioning running while Aggie told him about Lorraine. When she was finished, Grady just sat there for a moment, staring ahead at the row of parked patrol vehicles, and then he said softly, "Damn." He brought his hand to his face, rubbed it over the scruff of his jaw. "You spend all your time worrying about the bad things that can happen, trying to keep the people you love safe from them, and then...cancer. Damn."

Aggie said gently, "Is that what you do, Ryan, worry about the bad things? Is that why you can't sleep?"

He was silent for a moment, still looking straight ahead, and then admitted, "Yeah. It's like...since I went back to work, I keep watching all this dash-cam video. Cops getting shot, kids getting shot. At first it was just for class, right, but then it was like I couldn't stop watching it, couldn't stop thinking about it. You make a mistake, you act too fast, and next thing you know you're putting thirteen bullets in the chest of a school kid. You act too slow and he's doing the same to you."

Aggie said, "You never really talked about the Reichart shooting."

He nodded slowly, not looking at her. "I thought I was okay with it. For a long time I was okay with it. And then…turns out I was wrong. I wasn't okay." Now he looked at her. "I lied to you the other night, when I told you I couldn't remember what the nightmares were about. They're always the same. Traffic stop, the driver gets out of the vehicle and charges me with a gun, I fire, and he goes down, blood everywhere, and then I go over to look at him, and it's you lying there on the ground with your face half shot off, or Pete, or sometimes Bishop."

Aggie reached across the seat and took his hand, holding it hard. He squeezed her fingers back. He said, "I always knew what the job was. But that was before I almost lost you, twice. Now I think…I'm not so willing to roll the dice again."

He was quiet for a moment, and Aggie let him be. He turned their hands, threading his fingers through hers, lining up the gold bands together. He said, "JC thinks I should apply to CID."

Aggie nodded. "Better pay. Great benefits."

"And by the time those guys are called in, the crime's already been done. All they have to do is figure out who did it."

"Not as dangerous," she agreed. "At least in theory."

"I don't know. Maybe it's time I got off the road. I'm not sure how good I am at this anymore."

"If you apply to the state, there's no guarantee you'd get a job anywhere near here," she pointed out. "Who knows where the next opening would be?"

He said, "Yeah. I thought about that."

Aggie leaned her head back against the headrest. "You know, when I came here it was to get away from the things I'd seen on the Chicago PD. I mean, the places we used to go into, Ryan, people living in conditions that were barely fit for rats, mothers feeding their children crack, gang wars, family members shooting each other down in the street and then walking away like nothing happened. After a while I felt it start to seep into my soul, this black stain, and I knew if I stayed there, if I kept on seeing those things, living those things, eventually the stain would eat away at me until I was just as empty, just as hollowed out inside as the people I was supposed to be protecting the city from. I thought here, in Murphy County, I would be safe from all that. I thought that maybe the real world is mostly made up of good people who sometimes make mistakes, and that in a place like this cops really could be the good guys again. But you know something? Here's the place I got shot in the head. Here's the place where a family was slaughtered, and I thought an assassin was my friend. Now a college student is murdered on a deserted island where there shouldn't even have been any people, and one of our neighbors collects child pornography while another bargained favors for sex from a girl he didn't even know. And my best friend has cancer. I think...I don't know, Grady, I think there's no such thing as a safe place. I think that bad things are everywhere, and that if it's your job to fight them then that's what you get to do. Forever. Because if that's your job, well, no matter where you go the bad things are always going to be there."

A faint smile curved his lips and he released a small puff of breath, almost a laugh. "The curse of the superhero, right?"

"Right."

He brought her fingers to his lips and kissed them. "I'll call Pete when I get home, see if he wants us to come over tonight. What do you say we go inside, knock out the paperwork, and put an end to this really shitty day?"

Aggie turned off the engine and opened her door. "You don't have to ask me twice."

Flash followed them inside, thinking about what Aggie had said. He could understand why she and Grady were a little sad, but it all made perfect sense to him. Their job was to stop the bad guys. His job was to stop the bad things, the kinds of things Aggie had been talking about, the kinds of things Grady was afraid of, from hurting the people he loved.

Flash thought he could do anything, as long as he understood what his job was.

CHAPTER THIRTY-THREE

"'The wicked man writhes in pain for all his days,'" JC said mournfully when Aggie finished her statement, "'through all the years that are laid up for the ruthless.' Poor bastard."

Aggie and Flash shared a bag of chips and a three-pack of powdered donuts from the vending machine while Aggie related her recollection of events on the bridge. Grady, watching her, felt much better about his own dietary choices. Bishop stopped by in time to hear the last part and shook his head sadly.

"Just goes to show," he said, "you never know a man's heart." He looked at JC. "Do you need support for the warrant?"

"A couple of deputies would be nice," he replied, stuffing his notepad into his canvas bag. "But I don't think we're going to find anything. If he had the phone, he would have tossed it overboard long before now."

Bishop said, "So are we going to make an arrest?"

"Actually, no," replied JC. Grady lifted an eyebrow at Aggie, but her only response was to placidly offer another chip to Flash. "We need DNA, we need a weapon, we need testimony. Until then, we've got nada. And frankly, I don't think this poor son of a bitch had the balls. But that's just me. I'll be back to do the interview in the morning. But here's the thing. If Darby did it, it would have been a crime of passion. And a crime of passion is what, Chief Malone?"

Aggie looked up from offering Flash a second chip. "It's personal," she said.

He grinned. "Give the lady another bag of chips. Personal is strangulation, stabbing, gunshot wounds to the face or genitals. This was a crime of convenience. A blow to the head, just like the one Darby received. Impersonal. My money is on Door Number Three."

Grady frowned. "Door Number Three? What the hell is that?"

JC replied blithely, "That would be the one we haven't opened yet."

Aggie said, "What about the bracelet we found in the backpack? Did you get my text about the Brunelli emeralds?"

Grady looked at her curiously, and she said, "I'll explain later."

JC answered, "I did speak to the parents, and some of her friends, and none of them knew anything about the bracelet. But I doubt she was killed for it. For one thing, of course, the killer didn't take it. For another, it was fake."

Aggie drew a surprised breath and he explained, "Oh, it was a nice fake, a step above dime-store costume jewelry for sure. But the stones were cheap beryls and the setting was silver plate, not platinum. Platinum doesn't tarnish. Definitely not the Brunelli bracelet, but a pretty nice knock-off."

Grady gave him a mildly skeptical look. "How do you know?"

"The ways of the FDLE are many and wondrous," he declared. "Also, while you were busy talking the ranger off the bridge, I took the bracelet to a couple of local jewelers. They all said the same thing."

He stood and slung his bag over his shoulder. "Been fun, hate to rush, but I need to get home and feed the mutt before he pisses my rug out of spite. Chief Malone, it's been a pleasure." He extended his hand and Aggie, wiping her greasy fingers on a paper napkin, rose to shake it. JC bent to ruffle Flash's ears, adding, "Mr. Flash, good to meet you." Flash grinned up at him and JC turned to Bishop. "Sheriff, I appreciate the cooperation of your department and the loan of Captain Grady here. If you'd be good enough to hold whatever the deputies are able to collect from the dumpster in your evidence room, I'll take custody of it tomorrow."

"We're logging it in now," Bishop told him.

"Then, ladies and gents, I bid you a fond adieu." JC gave them a two-fingered salute at the door. "Keep the faith, good soldiers, for the Lord Almighty fights on the side of the righteous."

Aggie couldn't help smiling when he was gone. "I like him," she said. "We should have him to dinner."

Grady said, "He has a crush on you."

"Then we're definitely having him to dinner." Aggie's phone buzzed and she took it out to read the text.

Bishop said to Grady, "The drama on the bridge didn't do us any favors as far as traffic is concerned. It's backed up over a mile on 44. I'm going to need a couple of extra men on the road to unsnarl it. And you're not going to believe this. Those kids, the ones the press is calling Bonnie and Clyde, made a hit on I-10 West outside of Lake City, dragged a state trooper who stopped them for a broken taillight."

Grady's muscles tightened. "Did he make it?"

Bishop shook his head. "DOA. That makes three murders in as many days for these kids. Anyway, they were still headed west when last seen, so every law enforcement agency from here to Galveston is on standby to join the manhunt. Chances are pretty slim that this is ever going to become our problem, but all shifts are on alert just in case. So if you can pull in an extra man for patrol tonight, I'm going to call it covered. Then you might as well head on home."

Grady glanced at his watch. "Thanks, Sheriff. I could use the time. I've got some family stuff I need to deal with."

Bishop read his expression. "Everything okay?"

Grady gave a brief shake of his head. "No. I'll tell you about it later."

Aggie put her phone away, her expression grim. "The searchers think they may have found something that could be wreckage at the far end of the beach. I need to go check it out before rumors get started or somebody calls the McElroy boys' father." She kissed Grady quickly on the cheek. Flash was already at the door. "I'll see you at home."

"I won't be far behind you," Grady said.

"Let us know." Bishop's frown looked worried. As she reached the door, he added, "Chief."

She looked at him.

"Thanks for your help on the bridge today."

She smiled a brief acknowledgement, and left, her thoughts already on the island, and what new tragedy might be waiting her there.

CHAPTER THIRTY-FOUR

According to the information the search party had phoned into the office, the debris had washed up on the south end of the beach, far from recreational areas, residential development, or beach walkovers. Aggie parked her vehicle on the side of the road, stuffed some evidence bags, bottles of water and Flash's collapsible bowl into a lightweight nylon backpack, and began to push her way through the thicket of thorny vegetation that covered the dune. Flash plowed through with his typical agility and was waiting for her on the beach as she picked her way down to the sand, trying to avoid grabbing the sharp saw palmetto leaves when she slipped. She was already breathing hard and wet with sweat when she reached the beach, and she still had a quarter-mile hike across the sand to the small knot of people waiting there. Flash ran ahead, stopping every twenty or thirty feet to check on her, but she waved him on. There were two boys and two girls waiting for her, all of them fit and tan, wearing swim trunks and red Dogleg Island Lifeguard Corps tee shirts. When she reached them, Flash had already finished examining the collection of debris that they had laid out on the sand and had wandered off, exploring the tide line.

Aggie regarded the display thoughtfully, sipping from her water bottle. One of the lifeguard searchers said, "We found the first life jacket about ten feet up the beach. Cindy spotted the driftwood, only it looks like it might not be ordinary driftwood."

Aggie looked at him. "What do you mean?"

"It could be part of a hull." Another of the boys spoke up. "The *Seabird*—that's Mark and Brian's boat—had a wooden hull, not fiberglass, one of those sweet custom jobs you don't see all that often. And it was blue, they'd just painted it this summer. This wood hasn't been in the ocean very long. I hope I'm wrong, but we thought we'd better pick it up just in case…well, just in case it was important."

"We found the other life jacket down the beach another twenty yards," one of the girls said. "And look—both of the jackets have writing inside."

Aggie squatted down and looked at the initials written in black marker on the underside of the neck support of each jacket: SB. "*Seabird*," she murmured.

"That's what we thought too," someone said unhappily.

Aggie stood up, recapping her water bottle. Two torn and smudged life jackets. Broken planks, painted blue. She took out her phone and snapped a couple of pictures, being sure to include close-ups of the writing on the life jackets. She said to the kids, "So how far did you walk?"

"We parked back at Old Lighthouse Road," one of the boys said. It was a popular spot for surfers. "I'd say we searched maybe four miles of beach?" He looked at the others for conformation. "The volunteers split up into groups, and each of us took a different section of beach."

Aggie said, "Were you together the whole time?" They agreed they had been.

Aggie noticed a backpack at one of the boys' feet and asked if she could look inside. There was nothing but the usual hiking supplies—water bottles, some of them empty, snack bars, a first aid kit with inflatable splints and a couple of compact Mylar emergency blankets. There was no way either the life jackets or the wooden planks could have fit inside.

She said, "Tell me about Brian and Mark's boat. You said it was custom?"

"Well," admitted one of the boys, "more custom than what we're used to seeing around here. Fourteen feet, kick-ass onboard engine, and a console that looks like something off the Starship *Enterprise*. Brian spent a lot of time this year updating the nav system, installing software to track current speeds and depths, that kind of thing. Wooden hull, like I said, but light, and fast enough to race the big boys if they wanted to."

"Centerboard keel," pointed out the other, "great for sail camping."

Aggie looked confused, and he explained, "That just means you can retract the keel when you want to drag it up on the beach, and it makes it easier to launch with a regular trailer. Of course…" He glanced at his friend. "That also makes it more unstable in the water. Easier to capsize."

The other boy nodded, albeit with some reluctance. "That was the first thing I thought of when I heard they were, you know, overdue. I mean, a fourteen-footer is risky in choppy water anyway, but with that flimsy keel…" He lifted a shoulder uncomfortably.

Aggie said, "So did they take you out on the boat much?"

A look went around the group that was difficult to interpret. One of the girls spoke up. "They used to. I mean, we were all pretty tight during the summer, or at least we used to be. Some of us have been together since junior lifeguard training. But this year…I don't know, they seemed different. Like they'd outgrown us or something."

Aggie said, "I don't suppose any of you have an idea of what heading they might have taken yesterday. Did they talk about a favorite dive spot or something?"

Thoughtfully, they all shook their heads. One of the girls said, "Did they dive? No one mentioned it to me."

Down the beach about twenty yards, Aggie could see Flash pawing at something in the sand. She said, "Thanks, everybody. You know, most of the emergency services on Dogleg Island couldn't run without volunteers, and you guys are the best. I mean that."

The kids look gratified, but shrugged it off, as teenagers are wont to do. "So what do you think, Chief?" one of the girls asked anxiously.

Aggie said, "It's not my call. I'll notify the Coast Guard of what you've found, but until they make a decision about whether or not to call off the search, I'd appreciate it if you'd keep this to yourselves. I mean, this could all be unrelated, and think about how your parents would feel if it was one of you. We owe Mr. McElroy the respect of hope, don't you agree? And it shouldn't be spoiled by a lot of gossip and speculation."

They looked at each other and nodded soberly.

Aggie said, "Do you need a ride back to your car?"

"No, ma'am," said one of the girls, and the others agreed. "This isn't even half my morning workout."

Aggie watched them start back up the beach, feeling a brief pang for the time that a four-mile hike had been only half her morning workout, too. Then she turned and walked quickly down the beach to Flash.

He had almost completely uncovered the object he'd been digging in the wet sand for when Aggie reached him, and Aggie uncovered the rest. Just to be sure it was as she remembered, she dipped it into the surf to wash off the sand and grime. It was a white baseball cap with a blue anchor.

Aggie spent a solemn moment studying it, and then she took out her phone and scrolled through her pictures folder. The photograph she had taken of Flash on the lifeguard stand was the same one she'd seen at Walter McElroy's house, only she had cropped out Brian for the photo she had framed for herself. The original was still on her phone, though, and she brought it up just to make sure her memory was accurate. There was Flash sitting atop the red lifeguard stand, looking out over the sea. And on the sand below him was Brian, grinning at the camera, wearing his white baseball cap with the blue anchor—the same one he always wore on duty, the one anyone who saw it would be sure to immediately identify with him.

"*That*'s what was wrong with the picture," Aggie said softly. Because the last time she had seen Brian he hadn't been wearing the cap, and the last time she had seen the cap it had not been on Brian's head. She blew out a long, slow breath. "All right, Flash," she said. "Looks like you just found the answer. The only problem is, I don't know what the question is."

She filled Flash's bowl with water, and while he drank she walked back over to the collection of debris. She placed the baseball cap on the sand beside the other items, snapped a picture, and sent it to Grady with the caption, "Look familiar?"

He texted back almost immediately, "WTF??"

Before she could reply, he called. "What are you thinking, Chief?" He got right to the point.

The reception was staticy this far down the beach, and she turned in slow circles, trying to get a better signal. "I'm starting to think I wish I'd finished law school," she replied, raising her voice a little to be heard over the sound of the surf and the sea breeze. "I could be sitting in a cushy office recovering from my lunchtime martini right now."

He replied, "Told you."

She said, "This is the same debris we found in the trash bag on Wild Horse, right?"

"Looks like it to me. How did it get all the way over on the south end of Dogleg? And why?"

"Did you see the initials on the life vests?"

"SB."

"Mark and Brian's boat was called the *Seabird*. And I have a picture of Brian wearing a white hat with a blue anchor. His father will have no trouble at all identifying the hat. He has the same picture."

"So either somebody has a real fetish for illegally dumping the same bag of trash over and over again..."

"Or whoever stole the bag of trash dumped it out at sea..."

"And what are the chances of all of it washing up in the same place just at the time there's a massive search on for those two boys?"

"There's another possibility," Aggie said. "What if somebody hid those things on Wild Horse until they were needed? And what if what they were needed for is to make the Coast Guard think the *Seabird* had broken up, so they would call off the search?"

"Are you thinking kidnapping?"

"Or piracy. Apparently their boat was pretty state-of-the-art. It might be worth stealing."

"Damn," he said. He was silent for a moment. "You know, there hasn't been a case of piracy in this part of the Gulf since the seventies. But with the craziness that goes on every day off the coast of Mexico…who knows? I hate to think it, but it's not impossible."

"The kids I talked to said the boys had spent a lot of time souping up the engine, adding fancy electronics and software to track current depths and speeds. Think about it. It would be tricky, dumping the evidence so it would all wash up onshore right where it was supposed to, but with the kind of equipment they had onboard…maybe not. And," she remembered, "it had a retractable keel, so it could be pulled up on a beach pretty much anywhere and hidden until no one was searching anymore."

Grady said, "Still, it's a fourteen-foot sailboat. It may have been tricked out, but stealing a boat on the high seas is a lot harder than it looks, and I'm not sure it was worth it. Most boats are commandeered for their cargo."

"Maybe there was cargo," Aggie offered reluctantly.

"You think they were running drugs?"

"No, I don't think that," Aggie said defensively. "That's the last thing I think." And then she admitted unhappily, "I don't know *what* to think. But I've got to call the Coast Guard, and then…" She sighed. "I've got to call their dad. Are you on your way home?"

"Give me twenty minutes."

"You should stop by Pete's. Who knows what time I'll be able to get away?"

"Yeah, okay. I'll call you when I cross the bridge. Love you."

"Me too."

Aggie disconnected and put the phone in her pocket. She blotted her forehead with her shirt sleeve and released a deep, weary sigh. Flash came to her, and she knelt to drape her arm around his neck. "I don't know, Flash," she said. "Maybe I *did* go back to work too soon." Then she looked sharply at him. "Don't you dare tell Grady I said that."

Flash wouldn't dream of it.

CHAPTER THIRTY-FIVE

What Flash loved most about his job, aside from finding things, was helping Aggie figure things out. Of course there were some things he already knew, like where the hat with the anchor had been between the time they'd last seen it and the time he'd dug it out of the sand, and things that Aggie knew and he didn't, like why a man who smelled so strongly of fear would climb over the bridge railing to look down at the water when even Flash would have had trouble keeping his balance on that narrow ledge. But the things that interested him most were those he and Aggie figured out together.

They spent a long time waiting for the Coast Guard and talking on the phone. When at last they got back in the car, the sun was low and his stomach was rumbling, but otherwise he felt fine: invigorated by a swim in the ocean and a nap on the beach while his fur dried in the sun. Aggie looked tired and wilted, though, and her brow was furrowed as she drove them back toward town. "This is what I don't get, Flash," she said. "If this was a kidnapping, and if the life jackets and stuff were planted to make it look like the boat had broken up, whoever did it had to have planned it for days. They had to know the boys at least well enough to realize the hat would be recognized, and they had to be close enough to them to steal it, and if they could get that close, why wait until they were on the water to kidnap them? But here's the real question: why did the perp hide the stuff on Wild Horse Island? Why not in his own house or truck or boat? Why a deserted island? I mean, it's not exactly convenient, is it? It doesn't make sense."

Flash wondered if she had forgotten about the pirates. Pirates, as he was sure she knew, were neither good guys nor bad guys, but in-between guys, and those were the most dangerous kind. They looked and talked and acted like good guys on the outside, they made you laugh, but on the inside they were bad guys. They didn't have to make sense. They were unpredictable.

She placed both hands on top of the steering wheel while she drove, her frown deepening a little as she added in a slightly disgruntled tone, "The Coast Guard didn't think much of my piracy theory. But nobody has any proof the boys were still in American waters, or anywhere close. They were gone twelve hours before they were even reported missing, and with the storm…" Then she shrugged, blowing out a breath. "Maybe the Coast Guard is right. Forget the pirates."

Flash swiveled his head to look at her, lifting his ears. No pirates? That was disappointing.

"No," she said with a shake of her head. "The connection is Wild Horse. Whoever hid the trash, and then planted it to make it look like the *Seabird* had gone down, had some reason to be on Wild Horse Island, some connection to it."

Flash thought about the park ranger who smelled like fear, and Aggie said, "Roger Darby? Then who hit him on the head?"

Flash could have told her the answer to that, because he had smelled it quite clearly on the bloody stick he found. But it must not have been important, because Aggie went on, "And if Roger knew what happened to the boys, why would he confess to everything else and stay quiet about that? Jack Saunders knew the boys, might have gotten the trash bag to the island. But he's been in jail for two days. I don't see how he could have been involved in the kidnapping. If there was one." She shook her head thoughtfully. "No. This all goes back to Kayleigh Carnes, being where she wasn't supposed to be, doing things she wasn't supposed to do...She was murdered, two boys are missing, and the only thing that connects them is a bag of trash." She blew out a breath. "What am I missing, Flash?"

Flash wondered if she had forgotten about the man on the island the day they'd found the trash, and the phone that made the sound that caused Grady to draw his gun. And then he wondered whether if he had chased the man, instead of the scent of horses, things might be different now. That was a big thought, rolling like hungry thunder in the back of his mind, and although Flash usually liked big thoughts, this one made him uneasy because he didn't understand it. And that made him feel bad.

One of Flash's jobs was to learn things, and he knew he should spend some time trying to understand this new big thought. But in fact he was glad when he saw up ahead something that Aggie very much needed to know about. So he put his paws on the dashboard and he barked. He kept on barking until Aggie saw what he saw, and the vehicle slowed down.

Aggie had learned to ignore Flash's barks at her own peril, so the minute he started barking her foot left the gas pedal and she leaned forward, searching the surrounding roadside intently until she saw it: a pink bicycle on its side in the drainage ditch a few hundred feet away from the Island Liquor Store, and beside it, what looked like a pile of rags. Aggie punched on her flasher lights, and, heart in her throat, pulled off the road behind the bicycle.

She called EMS from her radio before she left the car, then stumbled out, plowing through the weeds and thick vines with Flash bounding before her until she reached Billy. She drew a breath for the first time since leaving the car when she saw him move and try to struggle to a sitting position.

"It's okay, Billy," she said, gasping as she sank to her knees beside him. "Don't try to get up, the ambulance is on its way. What happened? Were you hit by a car? Just stay still, okay, help is on its way."

"I ain't drunk, Miss Chief, I swear it," he muttered, although the stench of alcohol on him was strong and his lips were so bruised and swollen that she had trouble understanding the words. His nose was a mass of crusted blood and his left eye was just a purple slit. Nonetheless, he managed to pull himself to a sitting position, and Aggie lent a supporting arm. Flash gave Billy a few quick concerned sniffs, and turned back to check out the bicycle.

"Was it a car?" Aggie repeated. She heard the ambulance siren a mile or so away, and knew there was nothing she could do until it got here except to render what comfort she could and try to find out what had happened. "Do you remember anything?"

He said stuffily, "I felt so bad. You all was so good to me, and bought me new stuff, and a backpack with flowers on it."

Aggie looked around, but didn't see a backpack.

"And then I told you I didn't have no phone, but the phone is what you wanted, and that wasn't true, because I used to have a phone, but I didn't no more. So I thought I'd go get it back for you."

Aggie, who had been searching her pockets for a tissue or a handkerchief or something to clean the blood from his face, sat back on her heels, staring. "Wait. You had her phone? You had Kayleigh's phone?"

"It had a light on it," he said. "I needed a light. At night, you know. You said I needed a light."

Aggie nodded. The siren grew closer. "Where is it, Billy? Where's the phone now?"

"Howie Jacobs, he give me a fifth of Jack Daniels for it. I needed a drink real bad, you know, so I took it, but after you all was so nice to me I felt bad, so I went and I told Howie I wanted my phone back, only he didn't want to give it back, and he hit me real hard, and he laughed, too."

Aggie watched in dismay as a tear trickled from Billy's one good eye. "Then I tried to hit him with my bike only he knocked me down and broke my nose. And it hurt real bad. And while I was lying there he stole my stuff. My new stuff."

Aggie said quietly, "Where did all this happen, Billy?"

"Over there." He jerked his head toward the liquor store. "In back. But..." He swiped his runny eye delicately against his shoulder. "He wasn't so smart after all, because when he went back inside, laughing and all, he left his car open and my phone was inside, so I took it. And then I got on my bike and I pedaled real fast, only I guess I went too fast, because I fell down. But I got the phone for you, Miss Chief."

To Aggie's alarm, he thrust his hand inside the waistband of his pants and, after a moment, came up with a smartphone. "Here it is."

Aggie wished for a pair of gloves as she took the phone, warm and damp from his body. She said, "Thank you, Billy."

The ambulance was upon them, now, siren winding down as it made a wide U-turn to park behind her car. Passersby, pulling over for the emergency vehicles, gawked and gaped and were slow to start moving again. Aggie stood and lifted her arm to the EMTs who were exiting the vehicle. She turned the phone on, holding her breath, and to her relief it wasn't password-protected. The icons loaded on the screen and she pushed the settings button, scrolling for the phone's number. A mixture of surprise and profound disappointment seized her when a local number came up.

Kayleigh Carnes was from North Carolina. Billy had stolen the wrong phone.

She said, "Billy are you sure this is the phone you found in the dumpster with the backpack?"

His rheumy eye shifted away from her. "Didn't say that was where it was."

"Where did you find it then?"

"In my place."

"What place?"

"The red house. My place on the beach. You said not to sleep on the beach, so I don't sleep on the beach. I sleep in the red house and the phone was there, in the sand, under the red house. That's okay, right? You said it was okay."

It took Aggie a moment, but then she said, "The lifeguard stand? That's where you found this?"

He nodded cautiously. "Before the rain. The night before the rain."

"Tuesday night?" she clarified, but he just shrugged. A man who lived on the beach and carried everything he owned in the basket of a bicycle had very little need for a calendar.

The EMT trotted up with his emergency bag over his shoulder. "What've we got, Chief?"

Aggie said, "Assault and battery, broken nose, probably some broken teeth, who knows what else. Keith," she lowered her voice and turned a little away as she added, "can you get the hospital to keep him overnight, make sure he gets a shower and a meal and a good night's sleep?"

He smiled and said, "I'll see what I can do, Chief."

He knelt beside Billy, and Aggie said, "Billy, this is Keith. He's going to take good care of you, stitch up your cuts, and find you a place to sleep tonight where the food is great. Don't worry about your bike. I'm going to take care of it. You can pick it up at the office any time you want." She reached down and grabbed his hand, squeezing his fingers. "Thanks for your help, Billy. Really. You're a brave man."

She thought, even though his swollen lips didn't move, he tried to smile.

Aggie walked back to her car and took out her own phone, dialing Maureen privately because she was not entirely sure that the language she was about to use was fit for the emergency police band. Flash came to sit beside her, looking up at her with interest.

"Mo," Aggie said. "I know you're on your way home, but do you know a guy by the name of Howie Jacobs?"

Maureen replied, "Lives in a single-wide back of his mama's house this side of Island Drive. Back in the day…" That referred to the time she had been part of the Murphy County Sheriff's Department, before she had come to work for Aggie. "We brought him up on larceny and felony assault. He got off. Shiftless no account trash if you ask me. Love to nail his ass."

Aggie said, "You just got your chance. I want you to pick him up on assault and battery and take him directly to detention."

Aggie heard the siren switch on in Maureen's car. "No problem, Chief. It's on my way home."

"And if you see anything worth seizing while you're there, I'll have a warrant before you arrive. In particular, you might keep an eye out for a brand new flowered backpack filled with candy and such."

The silence on the other end of the phone was palpable, and Aggie found herself fiercely blinking back a salty sting in her eyes. "And Mo," she said, her voice going low and hard, "this lowlife shiftless no-account piece of trash just beat up a disabled combat veteran, so if you should find it necessary to use force in the course of this arrest, I want you to know I would never question your judgment."

Maureen replied, "Yes, sir!" Aggie heard the wail of the siren accelerate before she disconnected.

Aggie looked down at Flash. "I know," she said, puffing out a breath that ruffled the bangs of her wig. "Cops aren't supposed to get mad. But you know, Flash, despite what JC says, sometimes the good Lord gets too busy to fight on the side of the righteous. And when that happens, I think it's okay to use your teeth."

Flash was surprised, and a little concerned. He had been taught to believe that it was never okay to use your teeth. But if sometimes it was, if Flash was wrong, how many other things might he be wrong about? How many other things might he not know? It was all very confusing, and disturbing, and he worried about it. He worried about it while the EMTs put Billy on a stretcher and put the stretcher into the ambulance, and while Aggie put the pink bicycle into the back of the SUV, and while they drove up to the liquor store and asked people questions. He worried about it all the way back to the office, and by the time they got there he had decided that the world, and all the rules in it, were a great deal more complicated than he'd ever imagined.

CHAPTER THIRTY-SIX

Traffic started moving again on County Road 44, which was the main artery of Murphy County, at 5:30. At 5:55, Steve and Tracy passed the green highway sign that said, "Welcome to Murphy County." Steve drove carefully, watching the speed limit, watching the traffic. After what had happened on I-10, it was a miracle—a genuine freakin' miracle—they had gotten this far, and he wasn't about to blow it now.

Tracy was hunched up against the window, sleeping, or pretending to sleep. That was fine. He could do without her yammering. It gave him time to think.

All things considered, Steve had decided it was for the best, the way things had gone down. With Crazy Tracy—as he now thought of her—at the wheel they'd put four exits behind them before the first motorist had a chance to dial 911. He'd managed to get the car off the interstate and into a crowded mall parking lot, where he'd surreptitiously switched out the license tag. He noticed the busted taillight then, and he cursed Tracy up one side and down the other, but in the end what was he supposed to do about it? Drive into a Pep Boys and ask them to fix it, then mow down the whole shop when they were done? Picturing that made him laugh a little at his own cleverness, and for a while he wasn't quite as mad at Tracy.

They had to hide out in the mall for almost three hours, keeping an eye on the car to make sure no cops started swarming it. He bought her a frozen yogurt, which she barely touched, and that pissed him off. He didn't even like frozen yogurt.

They got back on the road, and while Crazy Tracy pouted all hunched up against the window, he turned the radio up, keeping tempo to the good songs by drumming on the steering wheel, and tried to decide how best to get rid of her. He'd always known, of course, that she wasn't going to make it to Mexico, he just hadn't wanted to admit it. For one thing, the guys would kill him, literally, if he tried to bring a whiny brat into the mix after all the trouble they'd gone to, with all that was at stake. For another, she was, well, crazy. He'd always known he couldn't take her all the way, but it had been fun while it lasted.

He considered just putting a bullet through her head and dumping her beside the road, but what if something went wrong, somebody called the cops or something, and he had to waste more time hiding out and missed the rendezvous. With only hours to spare now, it was too risky. As they started meandering down those long, boring, coastline roads, oftentimes with water on either side, he thought about making some excuse to get out of the car and then pushing her off the embankment and into the ocean. The problem was, this was flat Florida country, the embankment wasn't very steep, and she might be able to swim. He finally decided the best thing to do was to wait until dark, until it was almost time to meet up with his crew, and then drag her behind a building somewhere and pop her one right in the base of the skull. He'd read somewhere that a bullet in the base of the skull didn't cause as much blowback, and he didn't want to get any more grody than he already was, not with another two days on the open seas to go before he hit the big time.

He was mulling this over, feeling pretty satisfied with the plan, when he saw, four or five car lengths ahead, a brown and tan sheriff's department cruiser pulled over on the side of the road, monitoring traffic. Steve felt his bowels go weak. He looked frantically left and right but saw no escape. No place to turn, no place to hide. And there was no way in God's green earth that the cruiser would not see him when he went past, would not catch the taillight, would not run the tag. This close. Jesus Christ, this close.

But then, like a miracle, the cruiser pulled into a break in the traffic, still three cars ahead of him, and continued going east. Two blocks farther, the deputy sheriff made a left turn onto a side street, and was gone. That was when Steve started to breathe again.

It was a sign, he decided on a rush of exhilaration. Fortune was on his side. He couldn't lose now. He had made it. This thing was *going down.*

On the other hand, it didn't pay to push his luck, so he pulled into the next commercial driveway he saw, just to get off the road. It happened to be a Taco Bell, and he was hungry, so he got in the drive-through lane.

Tracy lifted her head wearily and looked around. "Fast food again?" she complained.

"Last time, baby," Steve said, and he smiled because it was true. So true. He reached across the seat and squeezed her thigh. "Last time, I promise."

CHAPTER THIRTY-SEVEN

B y the time Grady finished his report on the incident at the bridge and rewrote the duty roster, he was within an hour of finishing his regular shift, so Bishop's generosity hadn't amounted to much at all. Still, an hour was better than nothing, and he was just shutting down his computer when Sam Brown knocked tentatively on the frame of his open door. Grady glanced up and gestured him in.

"Excuse me sir." He rushed forward with a folder in his hands. "I was told to leave a copy of this with you. It's an inventory of the items we logged as evidence from the dumpster."

Grady glanced through the list. Tent, sleeping bag, battery operated lantern, cookstove, a variety of package wrappers and foodstuffs that may or may not have been related to Kayleigh Carnes. No phone, no tablet, no notebooks. Grady decided a more thorough examination of the list could wait until morning. He put the folder on his desk. "Thanks, Brown. Good job."

Brown ducked his head and turned to go. "Yes, sir."

"As a matter of fact," Grady added, remembering what Aggie had said about being nice, "how'd you like to drive me back to the marina to pick up my car? Your shift ends at seven, right? You could get off…" He glanced at his watch. "Maybe half an hour early?"

Brown looked surprised, and pleased. "Yes, sir. Happy to, sir!"

As they eased into rush hour traffic, Grady took out his phone, checking his messages. The marina was five miles from the sheriff's office, but in a town like Ocean City, even in rush hour traffic, the drive wouldn't take more than ten minutes. He started typing a text to Aggie.

Brown, sitting straight shouldered and alert in the driver's seat, cleared his throat. "Um, sir. Captain. Do you mind if I ask you something?"

Grady steeled himself with resignation and put away his phone. He'd known this was coming. He deserved it. And now he had to deal with it. He said, "Look, Brown. I know I've been tough on you. I've been tough on everybody. Maybe you think I've singled you out. Maybe I did. But it's not because I don't think you can do the job. The fact is, I think you're exactly the kind of man we want on the Murphy County Sheriff's Department."

Brown shot a surprised glance at him.

"The thing is," Grady went on, "you come to work in a place like this, and it's real easy to let your guard down. You put on your uniform in the morning and you know your day is going to be filled with traffic stops and coffee breaks, helping people get their keys out of their locked cars, taking complaints and serving eviction notices. Week before last we logged two hours tracking down a missing pork roast that a woman swore her neighbor stole from her car. You know who the thief turned out to be? Her own Labrador retriever. What I'm saying is you're exactly the kind of man we want going into those situations. Nice. Easy going, mild tempered, expecting everything to turn out okay." He remembered what Aggie said about Brown reminding her of herself when she was younger, and he added, "My wife is like that. When she worked with the department, she knew the name of everybody on her beat. People liked her. She kept the peace, and she was nice about it."

He was quiet for a moment, remembering that nice young girl in the deputy sheriff's uniform, the one that everybody liked, lying on the floor with a pool of blood spreading around her head. He had to clear his throat before he could go on. "Look, Brown," he said, "most of the time, what you deal with around here is going to be just routine, and everything's going to turn out okay. But for that one time in maybe ten thousand that it's not routine…I just want to make sure you're prepared, that's all. I just want you to be safe. So if I've been a little rough, that's why. Okay?"

Brown, with his eyes on the road, said, "Yes, sir." He paused a moment. "Actually, sir, what I wanted to ask was—are you related to the guy they named the bridge after?"

Grady had to grin. "Yeah." He turned back to his phone. "He was my grandfather. Used to run the ferry before they built the bridge."

Brown said, "Oh."

Grady sent the message, *On my way. Need anything?*

He thought how much he liked doing that; having someone to tell that he was on his way home, having someone to whom he could bring things. And he thought that, as hokey as it sounded, this was really what it was all about, why he did this job, why they all did it. Family. Brown would understand that someday. And in the meantime Grady thought that maybe the best thing he could do for any of them was to help them understand just how precious that was.

Aggie sent back, *Can't face lasagna. Bring food, not healthy.*

He typed, *On it.*

Grady hesitated, looking around. "Hey, Brown," he said. "Do me a favor, will you? Pull in to that Taco Bell over there."

Aggie said tiredly, "Do you know what the best part about being married is, Flash?" Flash looked at her with interest, and she informed him, "Grady."

They had stopped by the office and managed to wheel Billy's bicycle into the narrow space between Maureen's desk and the wall. That left almost no room for Mo to sit, but Aggie had a feeling that would not be an inconvenience for long. As obsessed as Billy was with his bicycle, he would probably be waiting outside the door for Sally Ann to arrive in the morning. Aggie only hoped he got someone to give him a ride across the bridge, instead of trying to walk back to the beach.

Aggie was about to lock up when Maureen called to report that she had Howie Jacobs in custody, along with a certain flowered backpack and all its contents.

"Did he give you any trouble?" Aggie sat down at the desk because she was suddenly too tired to keep standing.

"Nah." She sounded disappointed. "He was too drunk to give anybody any trouble. I'm turning him over to booking now. What do you want to do about the backpack?"

Aggie rubbed her forehead. "We're going to log that as 'recovered stolen property.' We've got enough on Jacobs with the assault and battery charge. Bring it in with you tomorrow, will you, Mo, and make sure Billy gets it? His bicycle is here, too. You can't miss it."

Maureen sounded concerned. "You're not still at the office, honey, are you? Why don't you go on home and get something to eat?"

Aggie said, "Food is on the way, and so am I. I just have a couple of things to do."

When she disconnected, she dialed Walter McElroy again and again got voice mail. Either he was screening calls, or still at the Coast Guard station demanding that the search for his children be continued, or he had succumbed to exhaustion and grief and simply wasn't answering the phone. Either way, Aggie knew she wouldn't talk to him tonight.

She looked down at Flash, who sat by her desk, waiting patiently. "I know you're hungry. Me too. I've got some lasagna at home for you, how does that sound?"

Flash thought that sounded fine, and swished his tail against the floor appropriately.

Aggie felt a little guilty for offering Flash the dinner she wouldn't eat, so she added, "And some chicken leftover from the picnic. I'll buy groceries this weekend, Flash, I promise."

Flash went over to his water bowl and helped himself to a long drink, looking forward to the lasagna and chicken, two of his favorites.

Aggie took out the phone that Billy had given her and started to lock it in her desk, then, out of curiosity, brought up the phone number again and dialed it from her own phone. It rang four times and went to voice mail.

She sat up straight when she heard the familiar voice, and Flash, hearing it too, came back over to her, his ears tilted with curiosity.

"Hey, dudes and dudettes," the voice said, "you've got Mark. Do it."

That's when things started to get interesting.

Grady noticed the broken taillight on the car in the drive-through lane just as he was about to direct

Brown to a parking space so that he could run inside and place his order. He had already decided that if Brown didn't mention it, he wouldn't either, but he should have known better. He'd never met a rookie in his life whose main ambition wasn't to impress his superior.

Brown said, "Captain, should we…?"

Grady repressed a sigh. "Yeah, go ahead and pull around front, though, wait for him to drive through. No need in holding up everybody else's dinner. I'll run the tag. And remember, this is a warning, not a citation. The poor guy isn't even on public streets. We're just doing him a favor."

"Yes, sir."

Grady saw the quick spark of excitement in the young man's eyes, and he realized that this would be Brown's first official independent traffic stop. He managed not to groan out loud, but he thought, *God help us all.* Then he thought about Aggie and he said, "Just routine, Brown. And be nice."

Aggie knew she couldn't get into Mark's voice mail, but it didn't matter. She and Grady sometimes sent each other ten or twenty texts a day; it was their way of being together even when they weren't together. Maybe it was the same with the twins. And even if there wasn't anything from Brian, there might be something from someone that would give her a hint about what their intentions were, and where they had gone…even though it might already be too late to make a difference. She started scrolling through the texts.

The latest ones were yesterday, after Mark had presumably lost his phone. There were six or seven from his father, all after 9:00 p.m.: *Call me. What's wrong? Where are you? You OK?* Aggie scrolled through another dozen or so texts earlier in the day from people at work and friends she didn't recognize. *Where R U? Answer, dick-head! You coming in today?* Then, on Tuesday, she started tracking texts from Brian. She was so tired that at first they made no sense at all, and then she realized she was reading them in backwards chronological order. She found a pen and notepad and began to copy down the texts in the order they were sent.

12:22 from Brian: *Be still. I'll get rid of them.*
12:42: *Good. Get the bag and go. Don't drop anything.*
12:44: *No, the stash is safer where it is. Just get out of there.*
1:14: *Are you crazy? Is he dead? Did you kill him too you stupid A-Hole?*

Aggie sat back in her chair, staring at the words on the screen, trying to make sense of them, unable to make herself believe the sense they made. Twelve twenty-two, Grady had heard the sound of a text message chime. *I'll get rid of them.* By reporting a phony shark attack, perhaps? So that Mark could retrieve the bag of manufactured shipwreck evidence? But why? And what stash was he talking about that was still safe? Roger Darby had logged his arrival on the island a little before 1:00. *Is he dead? Did you kill him too?*

Too?

She scrolled up the screen.

2:45 *Check the news!!*

There was a link. Aggie clicked on it, but it was nothing but a brief clip about that girl who had been kidnapped in Maine. She continued scanning the texts but found nothing more from Brian until 4:00 p.m.

Get here. He just called.
4:03: *No, it's on. Too late to change. No choice. Stick with the plan.*
4:05: *No choice! Meet me at the lifeguard stand. Need to talk.*

And that, presumably, was when Mark had lost his phone.

There were more texts, and Aggie read them all, following the trail that led, like footprints in the sand, backwards through the last week of Mark's life. Sometimes the trail was clear, sometimes murky, sometimes footprints were missing altogether. But the story that was told was indisputable.

She exited the program thoughtfully, and opened Mark's pictures file. There it was, only a few swiped screens down, the inevitable selfie of Mark on the beach, tanned and shirtless and ripped, with his arm around a beautiful, and tragically familiar, girl in a bikini.

"Oh Flash," Aggie said, sitting back in her chair. "This is bad. Really bad."

Sadly, Flash could have told her that.

Steve saw the cop car pull around the restaurant and for a minute he allowed himself the hope that his luck was holding, that it would cruise on out into the stream of traffic like the last one had done. So he kept calm as he paid for the food, passed the spicy-smelling bag of burritos across the seat to Tracy, and drove toward the exit. Even then, there was nothing he could do, no place he could run, when the cop car eased up behind him, turned on its lights, and bleeped the siren. The street in front of him was blocked by cars stopped at a traffic light. The lane next to him led nowhere except back into the drive-through lane. So with his heart pounding and sweat forming on his upper lip, he told Tracy, "Do what I tell you, you hear?"

Tracy, big-eyed, nodded her head stiffly, clutching the bag of burritos with both hands. Steve focused his gaze on the rearview mirror, waiting for the cop to get out. He did not even notice when

Tracy's hand left the paper sack and slipped between the passenger seat and the console, where Steve had hidden the gun.

The tag came back registered to a white Nova in Pinellas County. The car they had stopped was a blue Dodge Dart. "Crap," Grady muttered as the prospect of a quick warning about a broken taillight melted away. "Could be stolen. Could be somebody switched license plates on him without him knowing. Could be he has more than one car and put the wrong tag on, it happens. Get his license and registration and we'll run them through. I'll double check the tag number."

"Yes, sir." Brown was already exiting the vehicle, filled with self-importance as he approached the stopped car.

The western sun shone through the open windows of the stopped car, low in the sky but bright enough to give Grady a clear view of the two people inside, a male driver and a female passenger. He started to punch in a recheck on the tag number when something about the scenario struck him. A man and a woman. A blue Dodge Dart. A broken taillight. He'd glanced at the BOLO once, in the middle of a hectic day with a half-dozen real crises on his mind and no expectation of ever needing the information, so it took a minute to register. And then he saw the passenger, the female, pick up something and hold it in both hands at shoulder height, turning toward Brown as he approached the driver's window. It was a gun.

The scene played out as it had a dozen times in Grady's dreams. Brown leaned down toward the driver's window to speak to the man behind the wheel. He saw the gun, reached for his own weapon, but too late. Grady heard the thunder of the discharge before he saw the impact, before he saw the young deputy's face explode in blood, before he staggered back, almost as though no more than mildly startled, and then crumpled to the pavement. Screams from the parking lot. Static on the radio. Grady, drawing his gun, pushing out from the car, shouting, "Drop your weapon!" Another shot was fired, the one he didn't hear but felt, like a brick in the chest. His legs gave out beneath him and he went down hard, and he'd always thought his last thoughts would be of Aggie, but in fact all he felt was simple surprise.

It all took less than a second, and it all played out in Grady's mind. In the time between recognizing the car and seeing the gun, Grady had picked up the radio mike and now he spoke urgently into it, "Deputy Brown, fall back. Subject is armed and dangerous. I have eyes on a weapon from the passenger side. Fall back. Fall back." He switched to the emergency band and said, "Unit 13 requesting back up at the intersection of Highway 44 and Fourth Street,

Taco Bell parking lot. We have two suspects inside a blue Dodge Dart Florida license Oscar Tango Able Niner Able. One of them is armed."

Grady saw Brown drop to a half crouch just before he reached the back bumper of the car, his hand flying to his service weapon. Grady wanted to scream, *Stay down! Get back here! Stay down!* But he didn't say it, he didn't have time. He switched to the PA and spoke into the mike. "Female passenger." The words echoed throughout the parking lot. People turned and stared. A mother grabbed her children and pressed them up against the side of the building while inside customers came to the windows, raising their hands to shield their eyes from the sun, looking out. He repeated, "Female passenger, put down your weapon."

Brown had moved behind the car, staying low. His gun was out, ready to fire. And that was when Grady realized the girl inside the car had never been pointing the weapon at the deputy. She had been pointing it at the driver.

Grady said forcefully, "Drop the gun outside the window. Drop it now!"

The next seconds went by like hours. He could hear sirens, four of them at least, coming from different directions. He waited for the sound of gunfire. And then he saw the gun appear outside the passenger window, dangling between two fingers, barrel pointed down. She released it and the weapon clattered to the asphalt.

He breathed again.

Two units swarmed into the parking lot, lights blazing and sirens screaming, followed by another and, twenty seconds later, seconds, two more. Within ten minutes both suspects had been safely extracted from the vehicle, cuffed, and removed from the scene. Not a single shot was fired.

CHAPTER THIRTY-EIGHT

When her own cell phone rang, Aggie startled so badly that she spilled coffee all over the note cards she'd arranged over her desk. She started mopping up the mess as she answered impatiently, "Malone."

"'Blessed be those who hunger and thirst after righteousness,'" replied the cheerful voice on the other end, "'for they shall be filled.'"

Aggie tossed the sodden wad of tissues into the trash can and said, "JC?"

"My dearest Chief Malone," he replied, "you've been so generous sharing information with me that I thought I'd return the favor. I have news."

"Kayleigh's killer?"

"Well, no," he admitted. "But that fingerprint on the club that had Roger Darby's blood on it? We ran it through the criminal database with no match. Next step is the military, then the civil service and other bonded government employees. Guess what? Volunteer emergency personnel, including life-guards, are fingerprinted. And the match is…"

"Mark McElroy," Aggie said.

There was a pause. He said, "You're a witch, right?"

Aggie brushed a last drop of coffee off her desk. "JC, I not only know who killed Kayleigh Carnes, but I think I know why."

His tone was abruptly serious. "Talk to me."

Aggie leaned back in her chair, way back, with her eyes focused on the popcorn textured ceiling. She tugged at her bangs to adjust the wig on her sweaty scalp, and Flash, sensing her weariness, put his paws in her lap. She threaded her fingers through the curly hair around his ears. "You know that saying about when you hear hoofbeats, think horses? Well," she said, "sometimes it really is zebras."

There were more sheriff's department vehicles in the Taco Bell parking lot than there were civilian ones; more uniformed deputies than diners. Grady observed with a certain bemused sense of detachment that he hadn't even realized the sheriff's department *had* that many vehicles before.

Bishop came up to him, his eyes squinted in the sun, his face otherwise impassive. "Two more weeks," he said. "You couldn't keep your name out of the newspaper two more weeks."

Grady said, "I'm sorry, Sheriff. But just for the record, this is Brown's collar. He made the stop. And as far as I'm concerned, it's going to be his name in the paper."

Bishop nodded, his gaze shifting to the young deputy who was leaning against his cruiser a few dozen feet away, looking as though he might lose his lunch at any minute. Every cop who passed clapped him on the shoulder, shook his hand, paused to grin and congratulate him. Brown looked stunned by it all.

"Make sure he knows how to fill out a report then," Bishop said. "The justice department will be looking at this one real close."

Grady nodded. "Any idea what would bring them down here? Jesus. Murphy County, of all places."

Bishop shook his head. "Not yet. The boy has clammed up, but I think the girl is ready to write her damn memoir. Our instructions are not to take any statements until the FBI gets here. Suits me."

Grady was quiet for a moment. "I keep thinking how easily this could have all gone sideways. You know, like it did the other time. I mean, you respond to an accidentally tripped burglar alarm and end up in a bloodbath. You face down two armed killers in a parking lot and everybody walks away. It could have gone so wrong."

"But it didn't," Bishop said. "Maybe you need to remember that. This time it didn't."

Grady drew in a breath that was still a little unsteady. "Yeah. Maybe I do."

Bishop said, "The FBI will take custody as soon as they get here. Get your paperwork done, and then get on home. You can come in at noon tomorrow."

"Tomorrow's my day off," Grady reminded him.

DONNA BALL

"Like I said," responded Bishop, "come in at noon." He started to turn away, then added, "Starting Monday, you're back on a regular caseload."

"Yes, sir." Grady managed not to smile. "Does that mean I'm off training duty?"

Replied Bishop, "Not a chance."

Sam Brown straightened up when Grady approached. He still looked shaken, clammy and pale-faced in the sun, the way Grady felt.

Grady said, "So, your first traffic stop and you end up taking down the FBI's Most Wanted. That's a story you'll be telling the rest of your career. How does it feel?"

Brown glanced at him uncertainly. "Not like I thought it would. I didn't do anything except stay down and save my ass." He added quickly, "Excuse the language, sir."

Grady's lips twitched. "You did exactly what you were supposed to do, including the saving your ass part. You listened to your partner, you reacted quickly, you prevented a gunfight in the middle of a public space where innocent bystanders, including children, would almost certainly have been injured." *And,* he thought but did not say, *you avoided the kind of nightmares that could haunt you the rest of your life.* "It might not look much like what you see on TV," Grady went on, "but the perfect takedown isn't about who fires the most shots. It's about remembering your training, working the radio, waiting for backup. Teamwork. Not very glamorous, but there you go."

Brown looked uncomfortable. "I don't mind telling you, sir, I was pretty scared."

"I'm glad to hear it," Grady said, "because so was I." He gave the other man an encouraging clap on the shoulder. "You've got a long career ahead of you, Brown. Let's hope this was your one in ten thousand. But just in case it wasn't, I want you to remember to do it just like this the next time. I'm proud of you."

"Thank you, sir." Brown smiled. "I had a good teacher."

Grady smiled back, and then his phone buzzed. The smile softened as he glanced at the ID. "My wife," he explained to Brown, and thought there probably had never been two more beautiful words in all the history of human language. He turned away to answer it. "Baby," he said, "it's good to hear your voice."

"Where are you?" She sounded worried. "You should have been here half an hour ago. Are you okay?"

"Yeah," he said, surprising himself with the truth of that. "I am." He looked around and he added, "You know something? For the first time in a long time, I think I really am."

She was silent for a moment, curious, letting the meaning behind the words sink in. And before she could question, he added, "I'm sorry I worried you, honey. We took in a couple of bad guys, I have to wait for the FBI to take custody. I'll tell you about it when I get home."

Aggie said cautiously, "FBI?" She took a slightly unsteady breath. "Ryan, maybe you'd better tell me about it now. Better yet, tell me on your way across the bridge. I think I'm going to need some assistance here."

CHAPTER THIRTY-NINE

Flash walked with Aggie up the driveway to the house, and the first thing he noticed was that a pirate flag flew from the crow's nest now instead of the faded stars and stripes that had been there earlier. It made a striking sight, the white skull and crossbones on a black background, snapping against the brilliant pink hue of a dusky sky. Aggie noticed it too, and lifted an eyebrow. "Interesting choice," she said to Flash. He thought so too.

The house looked empty, with the windows reflecting sheets of pinkish gold from the setting sun, but no movement inside. Flash knew it wasn't empty, of course. The garage door was closed, but a quick sniff told him there was a car inside whose engine was still warm. While Aggie rang the doorbell, he veered to the left to secure the perimeter. That was his job.

It took over three minutes for Walter McElroy to answer the doorbell, but Aggie was persistent, and patient. She could afford to be.

When at last he came to the door, McElroy looked tense and distracted, which was hardly surprising under the circumstances. He was clean shaven, though, and his eyes did not look nearly as weary and beaten as they had that morning. He said, "Chief." His eyes darted beyond her, as though looking for something else. "I didn't expect you."

"I called several times. May I come in?"

He said, "This really isn't a good time."

He actually moved the door a few inches to close it, but Aggie ignored both the words and the gesture, and stepped inside. No lights were on, and the big room was illuminated only by the light from the sliding glass doors which led to the pool and framed a beautiful view of the canal and the leftover colors from the setting sun.

"What a nice view," Aggie commented as she looked around. "I love this time of day, don't you?"

He didn't respond, and she added, "I'm surprised to find you alone. Usually people around here rally in time of crisis. You know, bring pies and cakes and make nuisances out of themselves." She smiled to gentle the words.

He said, "People have been coming by. Lorraine and Pete, some of the boys' friends...I asked them to leave. It's too hard. I need to be alone, plan what to do next."

Aggie nodded her understanding. "I guess the Coast Guard officially called off the search, what—a couple of hours ago?"

"That's what they tell me."

"Which is when you raised the pirate flag, I guess. To signal the debris had been found, and the Coast Guard called off the search."

He stared at her. She went on, "I never really thought about it before, but your house is right across from the lagoon. I'll bet you have a great view of the inlet from up there. And of course anyone sailing into the lagoon would have a pretty good view of your crow's nest, too. Especially with binoculars."

He said abruptly, "Chief, I'm really not in the mood for company."

"I understand." She nodded sympathetically. "I just came by to tell you we found Mark's phone."

He looked surprised. "His phone?"

She nodded. "He lost it at the lifeguard stand." She took out the phone.

McElroy said quickly, "Is that it?"

He reached for it, but Aggie held up a hand. "I'm sorry, but I'm going to have to hold on to it. It's part of an ongoing investigation. I really just brought it by to ask you about something."

An uneasy glance toward the sliding door betrayed him. "Chief, I'm sorry, I don't mean to be rude, but I really can't talk to you right now."

"Yes, I know," Aggie said pleasantly, scrolling through the texts, "you're expecting someone. Don't worry, this will only take a minute. "

"Expecting someone? I don't know what you're talking about. I told you, I don't want any company. "

"Well, that's good," Aggie said, "because I know of at least one person who will not be coming tonight. I'll tell you one thing." She glanced up with a wry expression. "I'm glad I'm not the only one who's too lazy to delete my texts. Mark's text folder told the whole story, once I figured out how to put it together. The group texts, especially, the ones Brian sent to you and Mark and that other fellow. Like this one."

She enlarged the picture on the screen and held it up for him to see. It was a photograph of a blue towel spread out on the sand. Stretched out atop it was a diamond chain supporting an enormous emerald pendant, a pair of dangling emerald earrings, and an emerald ring surrounded by diamonds.

"Even I recognized the Brunelli emeralds," she said, and then admitted, "Well, I wouldn't have if I hadn't seen that picture of them in the museum a couple of days ago. I'm guessing the boys found these in the stateroom of the sunken *Sweethaven*? I looked it up, and the insurance claim on the jewelry was more than on the yacht. Seriously. The investigation alone took eighteen months. At the time, of course, the boat was inaccessible. But, as Brian explained to me, the hurricane shifted a lot of things. Brought things to the surface that might have otherwise been buried forever."

She scrolled down a couple of texts. "So here's the one where you copy both boys, telling them to put the jewelry back in the safe and bury it on Wild

Horse. That makes sense. You certainly couldn't afford to be caught with it, and is there any place safer than a deserted island accessible only by boat? There's probably stuff still there that pirates buried three hundred years ago.

"And then..." She scrolled down some more. McElroy just stood there stiffly, watching her, little more than a shadow in the growing dusk. "There are all these back and forths to the boys from a guy named Rider. It took me forever to figure out who he was. I even tried calling the number he texted from, but all I got was an automated message. So I had a friend of mine from the Florida Department of Law Enforcement look it up." She looked up, squinting in the dimness. "Could we have some light?"

He said nothing.

Aggie looked around until she found the light switch, and a bank of overhead globes illuminated the room. "That's better," she said. She walked over to the bookshelves and picked up the black-and-white photo of the boys on the deck of a ship with crew gathered around. "That's him, isn't it?" She pointed to the bearded man in the back. "Steve Rider. I used to have such a good memory for details, but this morning, when I saw the photo, all I could think was that something about it looked familiar. The boys worked on that salvage boat with him, then he went to prison for a couple of years, then they got back in touch on Facebook, and when the boys needed someone to fence something for them, they knew who to call. Or text."

She put the photograph down and turned to look at McElroy. "So I can understand why the boys would latch on to something like this and refuse to let go. They're kids, they think they're indestructible. But you're a grown man, a lawyer. You watch the news. You had to know that with half the law enforcement agencies in the country looking for him this past week, Rider was never going to make it to Florida. You had to know the plan didn't have a chance."

He said coldly, "I think you'd better go, Chief."

She glanced at her watch. "Actually, we have a few minutes. The rendezvous wasn't until 8:30." She held up the phone to him again with a mildly apologetic shrug and explained. "Group text. Time, date, Google-map directions. It was a good idea, though. Yours is the only house on the canal, so no one would see them come or go. And this time of day it's still light enough to navigate, but by the time they got into open waters it would be too dark for them to be spotted. Unfortunately, of course, Rider isn't coming. Right about now he's being transferred into the custody of the FBI from the Murphy County Detention Center."

She turned off the light and opened the sliding glass door. "It's such a nice night," she said. "Let's go wait by the pool, shall we?"

He didn't move.

Aggie's voice went a degree or so cooler. "Mr. McElroy, I need you to come outside. Please."

He followed her outside, his demeanor radiating carefully controlled anger. And anger, as any astute analyst of the human condition could tell you, is often the same thing as fear. He said, "Chief Malone, I can't imagine what you think you know, and frankly I don't care. This is completely inappropriate."

Aggie sat down in one of the pool chairs in the shadow of the eaves. She saw Flash lying beneath a curtain of bougainvillea a few feet away, watching the dock. If McElroy noticed he didn't mention it, or care.

Aggie stretched out her legs before her and said, "I'll tell you what I know." In fact, it wasn't a particularly nice night; it was thick and muggy and hot and even the easterly breeze from the water did little to part the humidity. Aggie took a breath before continuing.

"Earlier this summer the boys went diving and discovered the wreck of the *Sweethaven*. You told them about the safe in the stateroom and the thirty-five-million-dollar set of wedding emeralds that was in it. You're the one who handled the insurance claim, you had all the details, and after the way Brunelli treated you afterwards, you probably felt you were entitled. The boys were experienced salvage divers. They found the safe and brought it up and yes, the jewelry was still inside. The problem was finding a way to turn the jewelry into cash. And that's where the boys' old buddy Steve from the salvage boat in Maine came in. He'd gone to prison for fencing stolen jewelry, and had made some very interesting contacts on the inside. So they set up a plan to take the jewels across the Gulf of Mexico to sell them to some broker Steve knew. Of course, trying to take a fourteen-foot sailboat to Mexico was risky, but they're better than average sailors. They might even have made it."

As she spoke, Aggie could see Walter McElroy's face grow tighter, his muscles tenser. Now he said coolly, "That is the most ridiculous theory I've ever heard."

Aggie nodded. "I didn't think you were behind that part of it. You must have had another plan. What happened?"

His nostrils flared, and she could hear his breaths, slow and hard. He said, "There are no charges to be made here. The wreck of the *Sweethaven* was in international waters, the Florida laws of marine salvage don't apply. The jewelry belongs to the insurance company that paid for it, and I was negotiating a fair bounty. They were at eighteen percent, I thought I could get it to twenty. They would have spent more than that on attorney's fees if we let the courts assign the bounty. They would have agreed."

It took Aggie a moment to do the math in her head. "Wow," she said. "Twenty percent is seven million dollars. Not bad. But," she pointed out, "not as good as thirty-five million. So what happened to the plan?"

He said nothing for a moment. Then, tightly, "Both of the boys are over twenty-one. If they decide to sail out of the country without telling anyone they're leaving, it's their choice. And if you're implying this was a fraudulent report to the Coast Guard of a missing vessel—which it wasn't—I'd advise any client of mine who found himself facing that accusation to simply pay the fine and get on with his life. I don't know why you're here."

Flash stood up from beneath the bougainvillea bush and began to move quietly toward the dock. Walter did not appear to notice.

Aggie said, growing weary, "The sad thing is, you probably don't. I'm here because of Kayleigh Carnes."

He looked genuinely puzzled. "Kayleigh...? I don't know who that is."

Aggie said, "There are some pretty sexy pictures of her on Mark's phone. From what I could tell from the texts, they hooked up earlier this summer while she was down on vacation. He's the one who showed her Wild Horse Island. She got the idea to spend the summer there doing research, only I'm not sure how excited Mark was about that. What I do know is that she somehow ended up with an emerald bracelet—whether Mark gave it to her, maybe as a bribe for keeping quiet, or whether she stole it I'm not sure. But now she's dead, and from what I've been able to piece together from the texts, both boys buried her on the island, which means both of them are facing murder charges. They didn't have time to wait for your plan. They had to take a chance on their own. So they came up with this wild scheme to disappear overnight and then plant debris to make it look like their boat had broken up so the Coast Guard would call off the search. They'd be declared dead and could sail out of the country with the jewels. Of course you didn't know that part of the plan until it was already in motion. You were genuinely upset when you thought they were missing, and I saw your texts to Mark last night on his phone. I'm guessing they must have gotten in touch with you shortly after I left and told you how much trouble they were in. You let them know where to plant the debris so the lifeguards would find it. After all, I'd just told you where they were searching. But were you really going to let them sail off to Mexico with a killer?"

"No," he said hoarsely. "No, I wasn't going to do that."

"Did they tell you they had killed someone? That that was why they had to run?"

He said, "They weren't going to run. I was going to make them turn themselves in."

"Maybe," Aggie said. "Of course that would be more believable if you'd called the police the minute you heard from them. On the other hand, maybe you figured that as long as you had the jewelry you could work something out, sell it legally or illegally and you all could disappear. But the worst part is, the truly senseless, horrible part, is that it was all for nothing. The emeralds aren't real. The jewelry is paste."

Walter McElroy stood just outside the sliding glass door, and as the evening shadows increased, all that was really visible of him was his face. His eyes were still and dark, and his skin had grown whiter and tighter with every word she spoke until now it was almost translucent. He said hoarsely, "What?"

"I know. It's hard to tell from a photograph. Even the bracelet we found was pretty convincing."

He sounded stunned now, his voice growing weak and confused. "But...there was no bracelet in the photograph. What are you talking about?"

Aggie nodded. "Mark had probably already given it to Kayleigh when that picture was taken. But trust me when I tell you the jewelry was fake. The thing is, the real emeralds were set in platinum, and platinum doesn't tarnish. These settings are black with tarnish. Silver."

She pushed herself to her feet. "Apparently, really wealthy people who own really expensive jewelry always have replicas made. It seems kind of stupid to me, but they never—or hardly ever—wear the real thing. What went down with that ship was the replica set. The real ones were probably broken up and sold years ago, or maybe Brunelli still has them locked away some place, who knows? It's insurance fraud, of course, but not my case, thank goodness."

McElroy said, "Paste?" His voice sounded dull, flat. "All this time...they were paste?"

Aggie pushed opened the screen door of the pool enclosure and stepped out onto the lawn. "Right on time," she said.

Flash watched from the shadows as the blue boat, powered by the gentle thrum of a trolling engine, bumped against the dock. There was Brian, who always took time to rub Flash's ears, and Mark, who used to throw the flying disc for him on the beach and sometimes shared chips left over from his lunch while they sat together on the lifeguard stand and watched the water. But it was Mark who'd been hiding in the bushes when his phone made the sound that caused Grady to draw his gun, and Mark who'd thrown the bloody stick into the weeds by the marsh. It made no sense to Flash that regular people like Mark and Brian could be both bad guys and good guys; it didn't seem right. Or at least it hadn't made sense, until he saw the pirate flag flying from the top of the house. Then he understood everything.

Mark got out first, wearing a dark tee shirt and a navy baseball cap that made him hard to see at twilight, and quickly tied off the boat. Brian sprang lightly onto the dock and looked all around in a darting, suspicious way. He wasn't wearing any cap at all.

Aggie started walking down the dock toward the boys, and Flash, whose job it was to watch her back, jumped lightly up onto the dock and followed. At first neither of the boys saw them, because the dock was long and the shadows were deep, and they started walking toward the house. But suddenly Brian, who was walking a little in front of Mark as he almost always did, stopped and flung out his arm to stop his brother. He spun back toward the boat and Flash tensed all his muscles, ready to run, but Aggie called, "Stop where you are, boys! Turn around and put your hands behind your heads."

Brian hesitated. Flash could hear him say something to Mark about playing along, which caused Flash some concern because Brian clearly did not realize this wasn't a game. Brian turned slowly, an ineffable grin spreading across his face. "Hey, Chief!" he called. "It's me! It's us!"

She said sharply, "Hands!"

Brian carefully laced his hands behind his head and, after a moment, so did Mark. "Whoa, what's up?" he said. "Some welcome home."

Aggie said, "It's over, guys. Let's not make this any harder than it has to be, okay?"

They were over the water now, with the black green waves of the canal slapping gently against the pilings and the last few sparks of sunset glinting off the mast of the boat a few feet away. Mark shuffled his feet a half step backward toward the boat and Flash eased around Aggie toward him, just in case she hadn't seen him. But of course she had. "Don't think about trying to make a break for the boat," she said. "There'll be an FDLE boat waiting at the inlet before you get there, and they will shoot you if you try to escape." She removed a pair of handcuffs from her belt. "Mark and Brian, get down on your knees, please. I'm here to arrest you for the murder of Kayleigh Carnes."

It was at that moment that the screen door to the pool enclosure slammed and Walter McElroy started charging toward them. "You idiots!" he screamed. "You stupid idiots!"

And then it all happened at once. Mark spun around and stumbled toward the boat. Aggie ran toward him, and so did Flash. Brian flung out his arm and struck Aggie hard across the chest just as Flash came abreast of Mark. One more leap and Mark would be in the boat.

Flash remembered what Aggie had said about sometimes using your teeth, and he knew he could stop Mark. That was when he saw Brian strike Aggie. She staggered, flailed for balance, and fell backwards into the water.

Time slowed down, as it sometimes did, and Flash thought about choices: the choice he'd made to chase the horses and not the man, the choice good people made to do bad things, the choice to bring down the bad guys or let them go. Someday, he knew, he might have to use his teeth, but not today. Today the choice was easy. He jumped in the water after Aggie.

When she had first joined the Murphy County Sheriff's Department, Aggie had taken a requisite course on water safety. She remembered the instructor saying that most drownings occur due to disorientation. The victim, unable to tell where the surface lies, doesn't know which way to swim. Grady had said the same thing about scuba diving. It was essential always to keep the light in view.

But there was no light. The water was pitch-black, she had fallen backwards, she had no idea where the pier was. Her shoes and her utility belt dragged her down, even as she flailed desperately with her arms, trying to break surface, trying to find air. The entire Atlantic Ocean seemed to be pressing into her eyes when she opened them, battering against her lungs. She wanted to scream. Her chest burned, her throat burned, her arms and legs were on fire. Panic spun inside her head. She couldn't see. She had to breathe. She had to open her mouth and...

Then she saw, inches before her eyes, a blur of white. She flung out her hand and felt a paw, and another one. Desperately she turned herself in the direction Flash swam, clawing at water, throwing herself forward, until she felt the wooden piling of the dock. She pulled herself up, drawing in a single fiery gasp of air when her head broke the surface. Then strong hands grabbed her arms, pulling her up, and she collapsed on the dock, wheezing and coughing while Grady rubbed her back and said, "That's it, deep breaths, you're okay, you're okay." And Flash, shaking off his fur, showered the dock with water.

To Aggie's blurry, stinging eyes the dock seemed to be covered with deputies. Two of them had Mark on his face with his hands cuffed behind his back, another one was jerking Brian, also cuffed, to his feet. Another had his hand on Walter McElroy's arm, talking to him earnestly. But the only one who mattered extended his hand to help her to her feet, his eyes still shadowed with the remnants of terror, his smile strong and encouraging. "You okay now, Chief?"

She nodded, coughing, and gripped his forearm, letting him pull her up. Her wig was gone, her shoes were sodden, and her utility belt sagged on her hips. Droplets of water splashed on the already-wet dock and drained from her cuffs as she stood. "Thanks," she said with her first clear breath, "for the backup."

Grady lifted a shoulder, pretending nonchalance. "Hey, these guys were just standing around a parking lot, looking for something to do."

Aggie dropped to one knee and extended her arm to Flash, hugging him hard when he came to her. She didn't say anything, but she didn't have to. They understood each other that way, he and Aggie.

Aggie stood up and walked over to Brian. He looked at her with a mixture of anger, outrage and contempt in his eyes. Aggie said to the deputy who was holding him, "Did you read him his rights?"

"Sure did, Chief."

"Both of them," added the deputy who was hauling Mark to his feet.

Aggie wiped a drop of canal water from her nose with the back of her hand. "I'm sorry I missed it."

"You can't hold me," Brian said angrily. "This is crazy! I have a right to found plunder in international waters. You've got no right to hold me! You're crazy!"

Aggie said, "You're facing murder charges. You were willing to risk your life taking that boat across the Gulf of Mexico with an ex-con, trusting him to negotiate a deal with some Mexican drug lord for bogus emeralds, and you call *me* crazy?"

Brian stared at her, fixating on the only part of the accusation that seemed to register with him. "What do you mean, bogus? What are you talking about?"

Aggie just shook her head. "You're the smart one, Brian. You had to know how risky this was. The chances of it working were maybe one in a million. You could have come up with a better plan."

His jaw tightened. He looked at his brother, whose chest was heaving, his eyes terrified. Aggie said softly, "But you didn't have time, did you? After Kayleigh died you couldn't wait for a better time, a better plan. You had to take a chance. You had to try to save Mark. And once we found the body, you had no choice."

Mark said hoarsely, "It was an accident, okay? We had a fight. She ran away, tripped, hit her head. I tried to help her! I tried to..." His voice broke. "But there was so much blood, and she was having convulsions, and then she wasn't any more, and I couldn't find a pulse. I didn't kill her! I didn't!"

Aggie said, "So you buried her. Both of you."

Brian swallowed hard and nodded. "That's right. That's what happened. It was an accident. We didn't know what else to do. There was..." He swallowed again. "There was too much at stake."

Aggie said simply, "She was alive when you buried her."

She watched as denial, then understanding, then horror rose in Brian's eyes. Mark whispered, "No. No, that's not right. It can't be. That's not right. She was dead, I know she was!"

Aggie couldn't look at him as his gasps turned to sobs. His knees gave way and he sagged between the two deputies who held him.

Aggie said, "Take them to booking." She turned and walked down the dock to Grady and Flash, who were waiting to take her home.

CHAPTER FORTY

The weekend after Labor Day was typically the slowest weekend of the year for Murphy County. The season was over, children were back in school, the tourists had gone, and even shoplifters and drunk drivers seemed to find some reason to just chill out at home. So that was the weekend the Sheriff's Department chose to host its annual beach party welcoming new recruits. They had no trouble getting a permit from the Dogleg Island police chief to cordon off a section of the beach, and the afternoon was filled with volleyball, flying disc competitions, body surfing, and picnicking. Pete's Place, which always catered the event, kept three grills going: one with hamburgers, one with hot dogs, one with barbecue chicken, along with a dizzying array of sides and coolers packed with iced soft drinks. As the sun began to fade, the grills were replaced by bonfires for roasting marshmallows and s'mores, damp towels were spread out to dry, and shirts and cover-ups were pulled on against the cooling breeze that rolled in from the ocean.

Flash had won six games of flying disc, sampled everything on the menu, including two pieces of chicken without the bones, which Aggie said were bad for him, and he now thought Pete's barbecue-chicken-without-the-bones might be his new favorite thing. He'd jumped waves with the children and floated on a raft with Aggie and had fallen off the surfboard with Grady. Now he lay on a beach towel beside Aggie's chair in the flickering shadows cast by the fire, panting happily with almost-delirious exhaustion. The world would be a much better place, he decided, if there were more days like this and fewer days that ended with someone pointing a gun at them or Aggie falling into a canal.

Grady dropped down onto the towel beside Flash, lifted one of his paws a few inches off the towel, and declared, "The winners and still champions, huh, Flash?" Flash grinned his agreement. Grady had been on his team for most of flying disc wins.

Grady rested a hand on Flash's damp fur and with the other caressed Aggie's ankle, looking up at her. "You look so pretty today," he said. "Did I mention that?"

Aggie pulled her foot from the sand and nudged Grady's knee affectionately with her toe. "Once or twice."

She wasn't wearing her wig, and hadn't worn it for weeks. It had something to do, Flash had heard her say, with solidarity with Lorraine, who had also shaved off all her hair. When she was in the sun,

Aggie wore a hat, and when she wasn't working, like today, she wore big earrings that Flash found fascinating to watch, the way they spun and sparkled in the light.

She said, "I forgot to tell you. We decided on a nautical theme for the living room. Blue and white striped slipcovers. They can go in the washing machine when they get dirty, and they're less expensive than reupholstering."

"I like it. When did you decide that?"

"Last week, at Chemo Tuesday."

Chemo Tuesdays were when Aggie drove Lorraine to the hospital, where they spent a few hours in a room, chatting and looking at magazines and fabric samples. Flash didn't much care for the smell of the room, but he liked being with Lorraine, who had said loud words to the nurses until they let him come in with her. Pretty soon other patients were smiling and waving at him, and when he went to visit with them they seemed to enjoy it. After a while the nurses started keeping a box of dog treats at their station and sneaking them to him in their pockets when they came in to check on people, so it all worked out pretty well.

Aggie glanced across the bonfire at Lorraine, who was stretched out in a lounge chair with a beach blanket over her legs, telling a story with big hand gesticulations that had the people who were gathered around her doubled over with laughter. Pete bent down to hand her a drink, and she paused in her story to cup her hand around his neck, pull his head down, and kiss him on the mouth. Watching them made Aggie smile.

"Also," said Aggie, "I picked a date."

"Oh, yeah? For what?"

She gave him an exasperated look, and he said quickly, "Right! The reception. Cool. When is it?"

"December twenty-third," she said. "Lorraine will be finished with the first round by then, and your folks can spend the holidays with us. Pete's going to do heavy hors d'oeuvres and Jason is doing the dessert bar. We're having it at the pavilion at Beachside Park. I e-mailed your mother, and she's already making reservations."

Grady cast her an admiring look, squeezing her ankle. "You've been busy."

"Yeah, well, things have been a little less hectic around the office since the council approved a part-time deputy."

"And all you had to do was ask," observed Grady blandly. "Imagine that."

This time when Aggie poked him with her toe it wasn't quite so affectionate, and he rocked back, grinning at her.

Bishop came up, wearing shorts and a flowered shirt, a red plastic cup in his hand and a satisfied look on his face. "It's good to see everybody having a good time," he said. "They deserve it." He gave a pleased nod of his head and added, "We've got a good team."

The capture of the notorious Bonnie and Clyde had not only shone a very favorable national spotlight on the fragile sheriff's department, but had boosted morale higher than it had been in years. The bizarre nature of the crime that had brought the couple to Florida was still tossed about on late-night talk shows, and there was even talk about a movie. In perhaps the most unusual twist of all, Tracy was now being hailed as a folk hero for engineering Steve Rider's surrender, despite the fact that testimony and video footage from three different sources implicated her as a cop-killer who was at least as dangerous as the man she claimed had kidnapped her.

Grady's class of recruits were now full-time road deputies, although still under the supervision of a field training officer. Sam Brown was handling his notoriety well, although his camera shyness was painful to watch. A pleasant side effect of his sudden fame, however, was a corresponding increase in popularity, and he had brought a pretty dental assistant from Ocean City as his date to the party.

Grady hadn't had a nightmare in weeks.

The Brunelli emeralds—or at least the replicas— had been found in a concealed compartment inside the navigation console of the *Seabird* and turned over to the Florida Department of Law Enforcement, who eventually released them to the FBI. That part of the story had been somewhat downplayed in the press, as had the McElroys' involvement with Steve Rider. Both boys were being held without bond in the Murphy County Detention Center and were represented by a team of lawyers from Tallahassee which appeared to be led by their father. Walter

McElroy remained under investigation but so far had not been charged.

Bishop glanced at Aggie. "What's the word on Darby?"

She shook her head. "Not much. Shirley moved out. I think she has a sister in Texas. Roger turned in his resignation. I don't know how much longer he'll stay here. A small town like this, there's no way to keep a secret, and the story is just so humiliating." Again, she shook her head. "So many lives ruined."

"To say nothing of Kayleigh Carnes," Grady pointed out.

Aggie nodded somberly. "The weirdest part," she said, "or I should say *one* of the weirdest parts—is that we were so frantic to find her phone, and looking for it led us to find so many other things, but in the end everything we really needed to solve the case was on Mark's phone. And we found it without even looking for it."

Mark had admitted to tossing Kayleigh's phone into the ocean, but by the time he and Brian came back to clear out her campsite the next day, Roger Darby had already done so. Mark had torn up the note that Jack Saunders left on the pier when he came back to hide the bag of debris. According to their statements, Mark and Brian had held back the emerald bracelet when they photographed the jewelry for their father, for "security", Brian had said— which probably meant they had never intended to accept the insurance company payment their father had negotiated at all. Mark claimed he'd only intended to let Kayleigh borrow the bracelet, teasing her with the promise of more in exchange for her silence. When he found out about her involvement with the park ranger he'd demanded the bracelet be returned, she refused, they'd argued. He'd grabbed her arm, she'd pulled away, fallen, and hit her head on a rock at the cove. He adamantly maintained that her death had been an accident. Brian claimed absolutely no knowledge of the incident at all. His only involvement had been to help Mark dig the grave beside the marsh.

Both boys seemed genuinely shocked to learn the bracelet had been fake.

"You know," Aggie said, sipping lemonade from her cup, "if you think about it, as messed up as everything seemed at the time, in the end it all kind of worked out for the best, didn't it?" Bishop and Grady looked at her, puzzled, and she explained, "If Roger hadn't tried to jump off the bridge, you wouldn't have driven to the marina. If Lorraine hadn't told me she was sick, I never would have asked you to ride back to the office with me and you wouldn't have left your car. If you hadn't been going back to pick up your car you would have taken an entirely different route home, and Bonnie and Clyde might never have been caught. Maybe JC was right. Maybe God does fight on the side of the righteous."

"Now those," declared JC, coming up behind them, "are words I never get tired of hearing. 'JC was right.' Sheriff." He clapped Bishop on the shoulder and saluted him with his own red plastic cup. "You give a hell of a party. Thanks for the invite."

Bishop conceded mildly, "Anything we can do to promote good relations with the FDLE."

JC dropped cross-legged to the sand at Aggie's feet. "I have news," he announced. "The McElroy boys are pleading to second-degree murder, all other charges dropped, out in ten years, fifteen max."

Aggie looked at Grady, whose face was impassive. "The state doesn't have any real evidence of intent on Mark's part," she pointed out to him. "Maybe it was an accident. Maybe they didn't know she was dead."

"They're lifeguards," Grady said briefly. He took Aggie's cup and drank from it. "You're telling me they can't assess life signs?"

"Which is why it's a good deal for them," JC pointed out. "A jury might reach the same conclusion, as we pointed out on numerous occasions. Frankly…" He crunched on ice from his cup. "I tend to believe the kid. He found out she was boinking the ranger, lost his temper, big fight, she fell—or maybe he even pushed her, who knows?—resulting in neurological damage that mimicked death, or at least it might seem that way to a panicked kid all hyped up on adrenaline and guilt. He called his big brother for help, and they decided to just bury her and get the hell out of Dodge. After all, they had bigger fish to fry with a freakin' fortune in emeralds buried in the woods. Oh, and here's something you won't believe." He paused for effect. "They were real."

Aggie sat up straight in her chair, and both Grady and Bishop demanded, "What?"

"But you said the bracelet was a copy," Aggie insisted. "You said platinum doesn't tarnish!"

"The bracelet," JC assured her, "was a copy. Apparently Mrs. Brunelli was wearing the real one the night the boat went down, and put the fake bracelet in the safe with the rest of the set. But the necklace, the earrings, the ring...they were the real McCoy. Total value about twenty-nine million."

"Oh my God," Aggie said, sinking back into her chair. "*That's* why Mr. McElroy seemed so confused when I told him about the bracelet. He'd handled the insurance claim and he knew the bracelet hadn't gone down with everything else on the boat. And out of thirty-five million dollars worth of jewelry, the kids picked the one piece that wasn't real to hold out for themselves."

"In their defense," Bishop pointed out, "it did *look* like the most valuable piece, and it would've been the easiest to break down and sell for the stones."

Aggie grinned, shaking her head. "Boy, talk about just desserts."

But Grady was unamused. "Wait a minute," he said to JC. "You're telling me those kids stole twenty-nine million dollars' worth of jewelry, murdering a girl in the process, and the best you can do is ten years?"

JC held up a cautionary finger. "Ah, but here's the rub. Were they stolen or were they salvaged?

And if they were salvaged, can they be considered bounty? McElroy wasn't lying about negotiating with the insurance company. Of course, they hadn't signed any legal documents yet so there's room for doubt about what his real intentions were, but even if they were honest the question of ownership could tie up the courts for years. That, of course would blow a hole as big as Texas in any case we tried to make for murder during the commission of a felony. If it makes you feel any better though…" He tapped more ice from his cup into his mouth. "We're still investigating McElroy the elder, trying to find out what he knew and when he knew it, and if any of it is provable in a court of law. I'll tell you what, though, he has got one brass set on him, negotiating a plea bargain for his sons while he's still under suspicion of collusion. 'For the Lord is a God of justice, blessed are those who wait for him.' Isaiah 30:18." He shrugged. "If you ask me, though, it's not looking good for the blessed."

Grady made a sour face and tugged gently at one of Flash's ears. "Maybe you can explain that one to me, Flash," he said. "Sometimes I don't even know what the point of this job is supposed to be."

Flash could have explained that to him, of course. Their job was to catch the bad guys, even when they sometimes looked like friends, and to do it whenever they could without using their teeth. But he thought, by the way Aggie tapped Grady lightly on the head with her cup, he already knew that.

"Oh, and hey." JC dug into the pocket of his cargo shorts and brought out his phone. "I thought you might like to see this. It's video Kayleigh sent her professor the day before she died. This is what she was all excited about finding, apparently."

He passed the phone to Aggie, and Bishop and Grady leaned in to see. A delighted smile spread over Aggie's face; amazement was on Grady's. Aggie looked at Grady. "We have got to take Flash," she said.

And that was how, two weeks later, Flash ended up crouched in the tall grass of the inland prairie on Wild Horse Island, the wind ruffling his fur, his eyes on three long-legged, wild-maned horses who munched at the grass a few hundred yards away. The whole world was filled with their scent. Aggie and Grady stood a few feet behind him, very still. Aggie, in hiking boots and a big hat, was taking video with her phone while Grady stood with his arm around her waist, shaking his head in silent wonder.

Suddenly, one of the horses snorted and lifted its head. Almost as one, the small herd spun and took off running, flattening the grass and throwing clouds of dust in their wake. Flash couldn't help it. He took off at a leap, paws scattering earth, wind slicing through his fur, his ears filled with the thunder of hooves. Behind him he heard Aggie give a cry of delighted laughter, and Grady whooped his encouragement. Flash ran with the horses, all legs and flying grass and wild, hot scent. It was powerful, it was magnificent, it was magic.

It was everything he'd ever dreamed it would be.

About the Author....

Donna Ball is the author of over a hundred novels under several different pseudonyms in a variety of genres that include romance, mystery, suspense, paranormal, western adventure, historical and women's fiction. Recent popular series include the Ladybug Farm series by Berkley Books and the Raine Stockton Dog Mystery series. Donna is an avid dog lover and her dogs have won numerous titles for agility, obedience and canine musical freestyle. She divides her time between the Blue Ridge mountains and the east coast of Florida. You can contact her at www.donnaball.net.

9 780996 561020